The **ROALD DAHL** *Treasury*

The ROALD DAHL Treasury

PUFFIN

PUFFIN BOOKS

Published by the Penguin Group
Penguin Books Ltd, 80 Strand, London WC2R 0RL, England
Penguin Group (USA), Inc., 375 Hudson Street, New York, New York 10014, USA
Penguin Books Australia Ltd, 250 Camberwell Road, Camberwell, Victoria 3124, Australia
Penguin Books Canada Ltd, 10 Alcorn Avenue, Toronto, Ontario, Canada M4V 3B2
Penguin Books India (P) Ltd, 11 Community Centre, Panchsheel Park, New Delhi – 110 017, India
Penguin Group (NZ), cnr Airborne and Rosedale Roads, Albany, Auckland 1310, New Zealand
Penguin Books (South Africa) (Pty) Ltd, 24 Sturdee Avenue, Rosebank 2196, South Africa

Penguin Books Ltd, Registered Offices: 80 Strand, London WC2R 0RL, England

www.penguin.com

First published by Jonathan Cape Ltd 1997
Published in Puffin Books 2003
5 7 9 10 8 6

Roald Dahl's titles published in hardback by Jonathan Cape Ltd:
Danny the Champion of the World; *The Wonderful Story of Henry Sugar*; *The Enormous Crocodile*; *The Twits*; *George's Marvellous Medicine*;
The BFG; *The Witches*; *The Giraffe and the Pelly and Me*; *Going Solo*; *Matilda*; *Rhyme Stew*; *Esio Trot*; *The Minpins*; *My Year*; *Revolting Recipes*.
Titles published in hardback in Puffin Books: *James and the Giant Peach*, *Charlie and the Chocolate Factory*; *Fantastic Mr Fox*.
All paperback editions are published by Puffin Books except *Revolting Recipes* which is published by Red Fox.

Published in this treasury for the first time in 1997:
'Letter from America', p50, 'Letters from Abroad', p53, 'The Owl and the Pussy-cat', p55, 'Hickety, Pickety', p142, 'The Crocodile', p146,
'A Poem in Reply to Schoolchildren', p325, 'Roald Dahl talking', p443 and 'As I grow old', p444 © Roald Dahl Nominee Ltd 1997

'The BFG Stamp' p164 is reproduced by permission of The Post Office
'The Roald Dahl Guide to Railway Safety' pp 305-7 by permission of The British Railways Board
'Roald Dahl, Author' p116 by permission of Puffin Books

Printed in Singapore

British Library Cataloguing in Publication Data
A CIP catalogue record for this book is available from the British Library

ISBN 0-141-31733-7

Contents

PART FOUR

MATTERS OF IMPORTANCE

On publishing Roald Dahl

IF I tell you that there has never been anyone the least bit like Roald Dahl you might think that an exaggeration. And yet it is true. For a start he was extremely tall, and as he held his head slightly to one side and smiled, it was as if he were up in the clouds, looking down upon the world. He lived life to the full and greatly enjoyed the funny side of it, though he could also be exceedingly serious. Something special about Roald was that whatever he felt, he did so more deeply than the rest of us.

But what distinguished Roald most of all is that he was, quite simply, a magician. Those who were lucky enough to get to know him experienced his magic powers directly. And for others, perhaps Roald became a writer so that he could cast his spells by telling them stories. He was able to catch readers young and old in the first sentence of a story and to hold them to the very end. This way he reached hundreds, thousands, even millions of people.

Not content with the status of a magician, Roald also developed the most original imaginative powers. Let me give you just a couple of examples: Who else could have invented the BFG and then gone on to make him blow dreams through the window of little Sophie's bedroom? Or we have the thrilling ending of *The Witches*, where a little boy who has been turned into a mouse, plans his travels accompanied by his grandmother, exterminating his witch enemies all around the world.

I should explain where I come in. It was my good 'fortune to be Roald's publisher. This means that when he finished a manuscript he would send it to me. I would put other work aside and read it right away. Then we would discuss the text and the jacket picture and the illustrations and anything else which was to become a part of the finished book. I was delighted by almost everything Roald wrote but in my opinion, his most wonderful books of all were his novels and I got the feeling that it was in writing these that he most enjoyed himself. I remember him saying to me that he found picture books, for the younger readers, with the fewest words, the hardest to write. Although I was sometimes able to make some useful suggestions about a manuscript, the contribution of which I am proudest is to have introduced Roald to Quentin Blake who became his principal illustrator and his good friend.

The Treasury contains selections from fiction and non-fiction, prose and poetry taken from Roald Dahl's best-loved children's books. We have also included some letters and poems which have never before been published. Quentin Blake has produced a very large number of new illustrations especially for this book and in addition we have invited a few other artists to take part, each working in their own and highly varied style. The artists are: Patrick Benson, Raymond Briggs, Babette Cole, Bert Kitchen, Lane Smith, Posy Simmonds, Ralph Steadman, Fritz Wegner and Christopher Wormell.

May *The Roald Dahl Treasury* delight everyone already familiar with Roald's writings and may it excite equally those for whom some of the books included are new. We all know that Roald's gifts made him a storyteller whose work delighted a colossal number of readers but even beyond its appeal, his writing has extraordinary qualities and through these qualities it enriches us. This is called literature.

I would like to take this opportunity of expressing my thanks to Roald's widow, Liccy, for the confidence she has shown in entrusting to us the task of putting together this book. 'Us' applies especially to my colleagues, Delia Huddy, Paul Welti and of course, to Quentin Blake, who in addition to producing his marvellous illustrations has contributed so much to many aspects of this book. Speaking for all of us who have worked on the publication of *The Roald Dahl Treasury*, I would like to say that we see this book as a celebration of Roald Dahl's genius. We hope that it will have a similar meaning for you also.

TOM MASCHLER

About my father

BEFORE you read this book, think for a moment about what it might be like to have Roald Dahl as a father. Let me give you a taste of it.

My father bought (for twenty pounds) an old car, called a Morris 1000. As you will read in the pages ahead, Dad had many adventures on motorbikes or in cars. His nose was almost sliced off when his ancient half-sister crashed their first car. At boarding school, he rode his forbidden motorcycle 'in a state of absolute bliss through the highways and byways of Derbyshire'. He also writes about a journey in a Ford Prefect from Dar es Salaam to Nairobi. So it probably won't surprise you to learn that he passed on to me a fascination with cars and the marvellous sense of independence they can give you. He never thought of them as vehicles taking you from A to B. Instead, he was always open to the possibility of adventure. Even when he drove us to the school bus in the morning (in his nightshirt, dressing gown and slippers – horrors!) we would take a detour to follow a fire engine with sirens wailing. So when he bought the Morris, he thought it would be a good idea to teach us how to drive. I was ten years old at the time. We had an orchard with long avenues between rows of apple trees which made ideal roads. Before we set off the first time around the orchard, he told me a bit about how the engine ran, how the clutch and gears worked.

"As you slowly lift your foot off the clutch, push the accelerator gently."

I stalled the engine a couple of times and luckily, just before he got fed up (he didn't have much patience), I got the hang of it. Dad went back to his work hut to write while I drove round and round for hours. A few months later, feeling restless in the orchard, I started driving on the road. I would wait until Dad went for his afternoon

sleep, then I'd jump into the family car, gingerly start the engine and drive away. I felt like Danny, The Champion of the World!

Occasionally there were complications. One day I drove to the village and stopped to buy some sweets. When I tried to start the engine again, nothing happened. I began to sweat. I waited until I knew that Dad would be back in his work hut and I called him from a pay phone. I wasn't looking forward to the conversation. When he was writing he didn't like to be disturbed.

"Dad," I said, "I'm in the village."

"Yes," he answered.

"I've got the car and it won't start."

"You are an ass," was all he said.

He drove down to the village and fiddled around with the spark plugs for a minute. The car started straightaway and we drove home in tandem. He never said another word about it. He was much more irritated that I had disturbed him in the middle of writing than anything else. I felt as though he wanted to say: "Look, if you are going to take the car out you must at least know how to do simple repairs."

I think Dad knew that he had instilled a spirit of adventure in me. He, after all, had taught me how to drive. And I'm sure he never thought for a moment that I would stay within the confines of the orchard for long.

At other times, he would make the adventure up himself. We had fifty different coloured glass balls hanging from our bedroom ceiling known in our house as witch balls. Dad told us that if any witches tried to enter our bedroom, they would be so horrified by the ugliness of their reflection in the balls that they would never return. If I woke during the night and heard the wind howling through the trees, I was convinced that a witch had just left our bedroom and was wailing in fury after seeing itself. I'm sure you realise that the stories he told us were rarely cosy or sweet; they always had a spooky edge. He told us about disgusting people who wanted to capture humans, about creatures who could only survive on the supple bones of small children and about strange old men who lurked in the undergrowth. To this day I am uneasy about walking by myself in the lovely beech woods above our house: I am always on the lookout for Vermicious Knids and Grunchers.

Every evening after my sister Lucy and I had gone to bed, my father would walk slowly up the stairs, his bones creaking louder than the staircase, to tell us a story. I can see him now, leaning against the wall of our bedroom with his hands in his pockets looking in to the distance, reaching in to his imagination. It was here, in our bedroom, that he began telling many of the stories that later became the books you know. One night in particular, I remember telling him that I was having a rotten time at school. I watched him thinking. He said nothing for a few seconds, then he began telling us about these marvellous powders that are blown in to the bedroom through a long blowpipe. These dream powders work wonders on your brain as you sleep. Of course we pumped him for information: "How does it work? Who blows it through the window?" He was still thinking and didn't answer all of our questions immediately.

"These extraordinary powders will work on anything from maths problems to constipation," he declared. "The powder is absorbed by your brain and will cause you to dream powerful dreams that will change the way you think." With that he said goodnight and disappeared down the stairs. Sometime later, after the lights had been switched out and we were almost asleep, I heard a noise outside the window. I opened my eyes and saw, in the shadows, a long stick push between the curtains and heard the loud whoosh of a blowing sound. Although I did not realise it at the time, it was Dad who, after leaving our bedroom, had fetched a ladder and a yellow bamboo cane from the vegetable garden and climbed up to our window to blow the magic powder over us. This is precisely how the idea for the BFG came about.

As you can see from all this, the most important quality about my father was his ability to make everything seem like an adventure. "A parent must be sparky," he used to say. He taught us early that going for a walk in the woods was really a treasure hunt. He used to find flints that looked like faces or fish heads. He told us that the dells in the woods were made by bombs during the war or by crashing aeroplanes and if we looked carefully we might find pieces of the plane or even the half-buried pilot. He had a great knack for finding treasures in the ground. Several pieces of old pottery, a meteorite, and funny-shaped stones that he found, still lie on a table next to the writing chair where he worked every day for forty years. He loved to collect things. When he was young it was birds' eggs and chocolate wrappers. As an adult he collected wine and paintings. However, he also collected ideas. He had a small exercise book in which he wrote down any germ of an idea. Sometimes he just wrote down words that he liked the sound of. His mind was twitchy, like his fingers, which were always moving as though he wished he could wrap them around a pencil and keep writing.

Ideas jumped about inside his head. Not only ideas for stories, but for inventions too. He once told me that he would like to have been an inventor. He was fascinated by the limitlessness of the imagination. He experimented with almost anything. Once he bought a pair of tennis shoes that were a little tight. He wanted to stretch them so he thought about the problem until he came up with an idea. He filled two plastic bags with water, sealed them tightly, and placed one bag inside each shoe. Then he put them in the freezer, knowing that water expands as it freezes and would therefore stretch them. It was a success. This is how his mind worked. As children, if we told him that we were bored he would immediately start thinking of things to do and make. During one long summer holiday, he invented an elaborate machine using a wooden board, an old tin can filled with melted lead, wire, and a crayon, which drew endless patterns. He also taught us how to make small hot air balloons with tissue paper, wire, and a piece of cotton wool soaked in methylated spirits. When the cotton wool was lit, the balloon filled with hot air and would rise in to the sky. He did this in the evening so that we could see the flame glowing through the tissue paper as the balloon disappeared into the night.

My father often said, "There is no end to what you can invent if you put your mind to it. You can go on for ever." I think that is worth remembering.

OPHELIA DAHL

The Hut

Ralph Steadman visited Gipsy House in Buckinghamshire.
Inside a hut at the top of the garden Roald Dahl wrote his stories.

EACH day Roald Dahl sat in his mother's old armchair next to a low table upon which was arranged small personal objects that formed a landscape through which his thoughts could roam. He would sharpen six pencils and then begin to write on lined foolscap pads of yellow paper. On another table stood a black desk lamp draped with a flannel which kept it at the perfect angle over his home-made green baize writing board. An old eiderdown covered his legs. A shabby suitcase had been nailed to the floor so that he could press against it to ease the pain in his back. The arrangement was not accidental. During

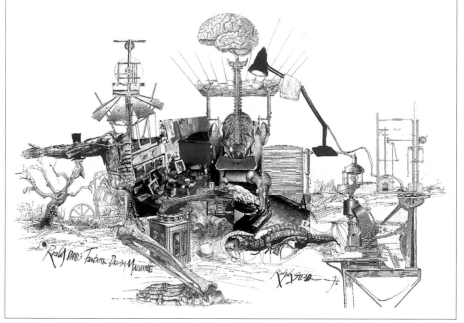

11

the Second World War he used to fly an aeroplane called the Hawker Hurricane in which he crashed and suffered spinal injuries. The room reminded me of an aeroplane cockpit. This was his creative space capsule inside which his imagination blossomed with wild, mischievous ideas.

Behind a small brown cushion at the base of the chair back I discovered a roughly cut hole which one day in desperation he had made to alleviate the pressure of abscesses which formed on his spine.

In my mind I went down that dark hole to search for clues that might have triggered his thoughts. I imagined his spinal column as a fuel pipe to his brain which was the engine that drove his powers of invention.

Outside in the garden there was a maze. At its entrance a slate paving stone had been laid. Carved into it was a message: "…Watch with glittering eyes the whole world around you because the greatest secrets are always hidden in the most unlikely places.

Those who don't believe in magic will never find it." I have tried to follow his example.

RALPH STEADMAN

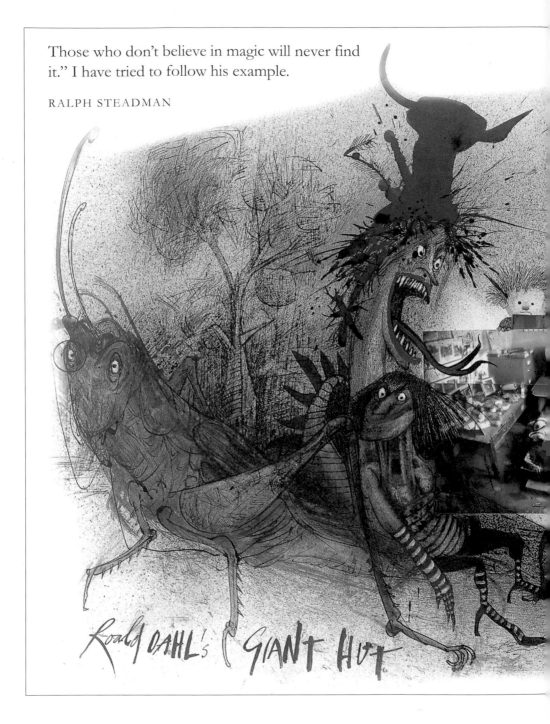

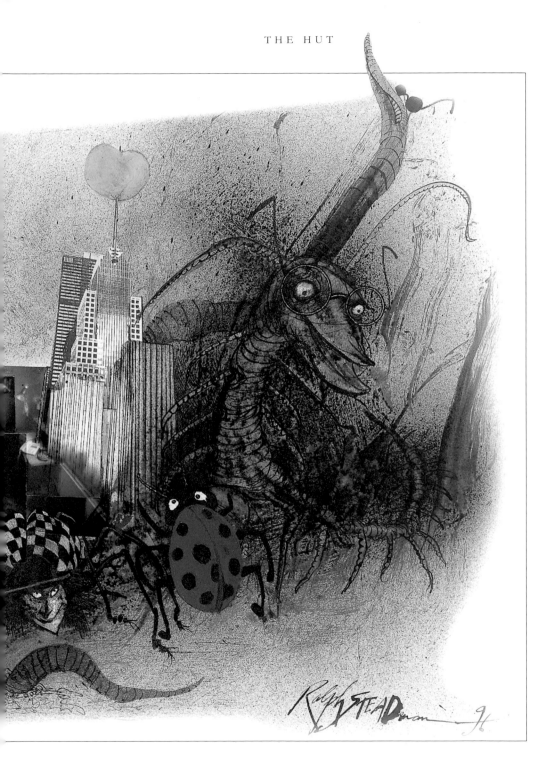

PART ONE

Animals

Be nice to frogs...

Be nice to frogs, by the way.
They are your friends in the garden.
They eat the beastly slugs and never
harm your flowers.

from MY YEAR

The Twits

AN EXTRACT

*Muggle-Wump the monkey has a plan to get his revenge on Mr and
Mrs Twit. With the help of the Roly-Poly Bird and all the other birds on the
roof, the monkeys have painted the ceiling with glue…*

"WHAT now?" they all said, looking at Muggle-Wump.

"Ah-ha!" cried Muggle-Wump. "Now for the fun! Now for
the greatest upside down trick of all time! Are you ready?"

"We're ready," said the monkeys. "We're ready," said the birds.

"Pull out the carpet!" shouted Muggle-Wump. "Pull this huge
carpet out from under the furniture and stick it on to the ceiling!"

"On to the *ceiling!*" cried one of the small monkeys. "But that's
impossible, Dad!"

"I'll stick *you* on to the ceiling if you don't shut up!" snapped
Muggle-Wump.

"He's dotty!" they cried.

"He's barmy!"

"He's batty!"

"He's nutty!"

"He's screwy!"

"He's wacky!" cried the Roly-Poly Bird. "Poor old Muggles has
gone off his wump at last!"

"Oh, do stop shouting such rubbish and give me a hand," said
Muggle-Wump, catching hold of one corner of the carpet. "Pull,
you nitwits, pull!"

The carpet was enormous. It covered the entire floor from wall to wall. It had a red and gold pattern on it. It is not easy to pull an enormous carpet off the floor when the room is full of tables and chairs. "Pull!" yelled Muggle-Wump. "Pull, pull, pull!" He was like a demon hopping round the room and telling everyone what to do. But you couldn't blame him. After months and months of standing on his head with his family, he couldn't wait for the time when the terrible Twits would be doing the same thing. At least that's what he hoped.

With the monkeys and the birds all pulling and puffing, the carpet was dragged off the floor and finally hoisted up on to the ceiling. And there it stuck.

All at once, the whole ceiling of the living-room was carpeted in red and gold.

"Now the table, the big table!" shouted Muggle-Wump. "Turn the table upside down and put a dollop of sticky glue on to the bottom of each leg. Then we shall stick that on to the ceiling as well!"

Hoisting the huge table upside down on to the ceiling was not an easy job, but they managed it in the end.

"Will it stay there?" they cried. "Is the glue strong enough to hold it up?"

"It's the strongest glue in the world!" Muggle-Wump replied. "It's the special bird-catching bird-killing glue for smearing on trees!"

"Please," said the Roly-Poly Bird. "I have asked you before not to mention that subject. How would *you* like it if it was Monkey Pie they made every Wednesday and all your friends had been boiled up and I went on talking about it?"

"I do beg your pardon," said Muggle-Wump. "I'm so excited I hardly know what I'm saying. Now the chairs! Do the same with the chairs! All the chairs must be stuck upside down to the ceiling! And in their right places! Oh, do hurry up, everybody! Any moment now, those two filthy freaks are going to come rushing in with their guns!"

The monkeys, with the birds helping them, put glue on the bottom of each chair leg and hoisted them up to the ceiling.

"Now the smaller tables!" shouted Muggle-Wump. "And the big sofa! And the sideboard! And the lamps! And all the tiny little things! The ashtrays! The ornaments! And that beastly plastic gnome on the sideboard! Everything, absolutely everything must be stuck to the ceiling!"

It was terribly hard work. It was especially difficult to stick everything on to the ceiling in exactly its right place. But they got it done in the end.

"What now?" asked the Roly-Poly Bird. He was out of breath and so tired he could hardly flap his wings.

"Now the pictures!" cried Muggle-Wump. "Turn all the pictures upside down! And will one of you birds please fly out on to the road and watch to see when those frumptious freaks are coming back."

"I'll go," said the Roly-Poly Bird. "I'll sit on the telephone wires and keep guard. It'll give me a rest."

They had only just finished the job when the Roly-Poly Bird came swooping in, screaming, "They're coming back! They're coming back!"

Quickly, the birds flew back on to the roof of the house. The monkeys rushed into their cage and stood upside down one on top of the other. A moment later, Mr and Mrs Twit came marching into the garden, each carrying a fearsome-looking gun.

"I'm glad to see those monkeys are still upside down," said Mr Twit.

"They're too stupid to do anything else," said Mrs Twit. "Hey, look at all those cheeky birds still up there on the roof! Let's go inside and load our lovely new guns and then it'll be *bang bang bang* and Bird Pie for supper."

Just as Mr and Mrs Twit were about to enter the house, two black ravens swooped low over their heads. Each bird carried a paint-brush in its claw and each paint-brush was smeared with sticky glue. As the ravens whizzed over, they brushed a streak of sticky glue on to the tops of Mr and Mrs Twit's heads. They did it with the lightest touch but even so the Twits both felt it.

"What was *that?*" cried Mrs Twit. "Some beastly bird has dropped his dirty droppings on my head!"

"On mine too!" shouted Mr Twit. "I felt it! I felt it!"

"Don't touch it!" cried Mrs Twit. "You'll get it all over your hands! Come inside and we'll wash it off at the sink!"

"The filthy dirty brutes," yelled Mr Twit. "I'll bet they did it on purpose! Just wait till I've loaded up my gun!"

Mrs Twit got the key from under the doormat (where Muggle-Wump had carefully replaced it) and into the house they went.

"*What's this?*" gasped Mr Twit as they entered the living-room.

"*What's happened?*" screamed Mrs Twit.

They stood in the middle of the room, looking up.

All the furniture, the big table, the chairs, the sofa, the lamps, the little side tables, the cabinet with bottles of beer in it, the ornaments, the electric fire, the carpet, everything was stuck upside down to the ceiling. The pictures were upside down on the walls. And the floor they were standing on was absolutely bare. What's more, it had been painted white to look like the ceiling.

"*Look!*" screamed Mrs Twit. "*That's the floor! The floor's up there! This is the ceiling! We are standing on the ceiling!*"

"We're UPSIDE DOWN!" gasped Mr Twit. "We *must* be upside down. We are standing on the ceiling looking down at the floor!"

"Oh help!" screamed Mrs Twit. "Help help help! I'm beginning to feel giddy!"

"So am I! So am I!" cried Mr Twit. "I don't like this one little bit!"

"We're upside down and all the blood's going to my head!" screamed Mrs Twit. "If we don't do something quickly, I shall die, I know I will!"

"I've got it!" cried Mr Twit. "I know what we'll do! *We'll stand on our heads, then anyway we'll be the right way up!*"

So they stood on their heads, and of course, the moment the tops of their heads touched the floor, the sticky glue that the ravens had brushed on a few moments before did its job. They were stuck. They were pinned down, cemented, glued, fixed to the floorboards.

Through a crack in the door the monkeys watched. They'd jumped right out of their cage the moment the Twits had gone inside. And the Roly-Poly Bird watched. And all the other birds flew in and out to catch a glimpse of this extraordinary sight.

The Enormous Crocodile

I̶N the biggest brownest muddiest river in Africa, two crocodiles lay with their heads just above the water. One of the crocodiles was enormous. The other was not so big.

"Do you know what I would like for my lunch today?" the Enormous Crocodile asked.

"No," the Notsobig One said. "What?"

The Enormous Crocodile grinned, showing hundreds of sharp white teeth. "For my lunch today," he said, "I would like a nice juicy little child."

"I never eat children," the Notsobig One said. "Only fish."

"Ho, ho, ho!" cried the Enormous Crocodile. "I'll bet if you saw a fat juicy little child paddling in the water over there at this very moment, you'd gulp him up in one gollop!"

"No, I wouldn't," the Notsobig One said. "Children are too tough and chewy. They are tough and chewy and nasty and bitter."

"*Tough* and *chewy!*" cried the Enormous Crocodile. "*Nasty* and *bitter!* What awful tommy-rot you talk! They are juicy and yummy!"

"They taste so bitter," the Notsobig One said, "you have to cover them with sugar before you can eat them."

"Children are bigger than fish," said the Enormous Crocodile. "You get bigger helpings."

"You are greedy," the Notsobig One said. "You're the greediest croc in the whole river."

"I'm the bravest croc in the whole river," said the Enormous Crocodile. "I'm the only one who dares to leave the water and go through the jungle to the town to look for little children to eat."

"You've only done that once," snorted the Notsobig One. "And what happened then? They all saw you coming and ran away."

"Ah, but today when I go, they won't see me at all," said the Enormous Crocodile.

"Of course they'll see you," the Notsobig One said. "You're so enormous and ugly, they'll see you from miles away."

The Enormous Crocodile grinned again, and his terrible sharp teeth sparkled like knives in the sun. "Nobody will see me," he said, "because this time I've thought up secret plans and clever tricks."

"*Clever tricks?*" cried the Notsobig One. "You've never done anything clever in your life! You're the stupidest croc on the whole river!"

"I'm the cleverest croc on the whole river," the Enormous Crocodile answered. "For my lunch today I shall feast upon a fat juicy little child while you lie here in the river feeling hungry. Goodbye."

The Enormous Crocodile swam to the side of the river, and crawled out of the water.

A gigantic creature was standing in the slimy oozy mud on the river-bank. It was Humpy-Rumpy, the Hippopotamus.

"Hello, hello," said Humpy-Rumpy. "Where on earth are you off to at this time of day?"

"I have secret plans and clever tricks," said the Crocodile.

"Oh dear," said Humpy-Rumpy. "I'll bet you're going to do something horrid."

The Enormous Crocodile grinned at Humpy-Rumpy and said:

> *"I'm going to fill my hungry empty tummy*
> *With something yummy yummy yummy yummy!"*

"What's so yummy?" asked Humpy-Rumpy.

"Try to guess," said the Crocodile. "It's something that walks on two legs."

"You don't mean…" said Humpy-Rumpy. "You don't *really* mean you're going to eat a little child?"

"Of course I am," said the Crocodile.

"Oh, you horrid greedy grumptious brute!" cried Humpy-Rumpy. "I hope you get caught and cooked and turned into crocodile soup!"

The Enormous Crocodile laughed out loud at Humpy-Rumpy. Then he waddled off into the jungle.

Inside the jungle, he met Trunky, the Elephant. Trunky was nibbling leaves from the top of a tall tree, and he didn't notice the Crocodile at first. So the Crocodile bit him on the leg.

"Ow!" said Trunky in his big deep voice. "Who did that? Oh, it's you, is it, you beastly Crocodile. Why don't you go back to the big brown muddy river where you belong?"

"I have secret plans and clever tricks," said the Crocodile.

"You mean you've *nasty* plans and *nasty* tricks," said Trunky. "You've never done a nice thing in your life."

The Enormous Crocodile grinned up at Trunky and said:

> *"I'm off to find a yummy child for lunch.*
> *Keep listening and you'll hear the bones go crunch!"*

"Oh, you wicked beastly beast!" cried Trunky. "Oh, you foul and filthy fiend! I hope you get squashed and squished and squizzled and boiled up into crocodile stew!"

The Enormous Crocodile laughed out loud and disappeared into the thick jungle.

A bit further on, he met Muggle-Wump, the Monkey. Muggle-Wump was sitting in a tree, eating nuts.

"Hello, Crocky," said Muggle-Wump. "What are you up to now?"

"I have secret plans and clever tricks," said the Crocodile.

"Would you like some nuts?" asked Muggle-Wump.

"I have better things to eat than nuts," sniffed the Crocodile.

"I didn't think there *was* anything better than nuts," said Muggle-Wump.

"Ah-ha," said the Enormous Crocodile,

> *"The sort of things that I'm going to eat*
> *Have fingers, toe-nails, arms and legs and feet!"*

Muggle-Wump went pale and began to shake all over. "You aren't really going to gobble up a little child, are you?" he said.

"Of course I am," said the Crocodile. "Clothes and all. They taste better with the clothes on."

"Oh, you horrid hoggish croc!" cried Muggle-Wump. "You slimy creature! I hope the buttons and buckles all stick in your throat and choke you to death!"

The Crocodile grinned up at Muggle-Wump and said, "I eat monkeys, too." And quick as a flash, with one bite of his huge jaws, he bit

through the tree that Muggle-Wump was sitting in, and down it came.
But just in time, Muggle-Wump jumped into the next tree and swung
away through the branches.

A bit further on, the Enormous Crocodile met the Roly-Poly Bird.
The Roly-Poly Bird was building a nest in an orange tree.

"Hello there, Enormous Crocodile!" sang the Roly-Poly Bird. "We
don't often see you up here in the jungle."

"Ah," said the Crocodile. "I have secret plans and clever tricks."

"I hope it's not something nasty," sang the Roly-Poly Bird.

"*Nasty!*" cried the Crocodile. "Of course it's not nasty! It's delicious!

> *"It's luscious, it's super,*
> *It's mushious, it's duper,*
> *It's better than rotten old fish.*
> *You mash it and munch it,*
> *You chew it and crunch it!*
> *It's lovely to hear it go squish!"*

"It must be berries," sang the Roly-Poly Bird. "Berries are my
favourite food in the world. Is it raspberries, perhaps? Or could it be
strawberries?"

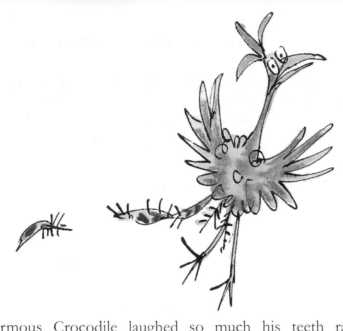

The Enormous Crocodile laughed so much his teeth rattled
together like pennies in a moneybox. "Crocodiles don't eat berries,"
he said. "We eat little boys and girls. And sometimes we eat Roly-Poly
Birds, as well." Very quickly, the Crocodile reached up and snapped
his jaws at the Roly-Poly Bird. He just missed the Bird, but he
managed to catch hold of the long beautiful feathers in its tail. The
Roly-Poly Bird gave a shriek of terror and shot straight
up into the air, leaving its tail feathers behind in the
Enormous Crocodile's mouth.

At last, the Enormous Crocodile came out of the other side of the jungle into the sunshine. He could see the town not far away.

"Ho-ho!" he said, talking aloud to himself. "Ha-ha! That walk through the jungle has made me hungrier than ever. One child isn't going to be nearly enough for me today. I won't be full up until I've eaten at least three juicy little children."

He started to creep forward towards the town.

The Enormous Crocodile crept over to a place where there were a lot of coconut trees.

He knew that children from the town often came here looking for coconuts. The trees were too tall for them to climb, but there were always some coconuts on the ground that had fallen down.

The Enormous Crocodile quickly collected all the coconuts that were lying on the ground. He also gathered together several fallen branches.

"Now for Clever Trick Number One!" he whispered to himself. "It won't be long before I am eating the first part of my lunch!"

He took all the coconut branches and held them between his teeth.

He grasped the coconuts in his front paws. Then he stood straight up in the air, balancing himself on his tail.

He arranged the branches and the coconuts so cleverly that he now looked exactly like a small coconut tree standing among the big coconut trees.

Soon, two children came along. They were brother and sister. The boy was called Toto. His sister was called Mary. They walked around looking for fallen coconuts, but they couldn't find any because the Enormous Crocodile had gathered them all up.

"Oh look!" cried Toto. "That tree over there is much smaller than the others! And it's full of coconuts! I think I could climb that one quite easily if you help me up the first bit."

Toto and Mary ran towards what they thought was the small coconut tree.

The Enormous Crocodile peered through the branches, watching them as they came closer and closer. He licked his lips. He began to dribble with excitement.

Suddenly there was a tremendous whooshing noise. It was Humpy-Rumpy, the Hippopotamus. He came crashing and snorting out of the jungle. His head was down low and he was galloping at a terrific speed.

"Look out, Toto!" shouted Humpy-Rumpy. "Look out, Mary! That's not a coconut tree! It's the Enormous Crocodile and he wants to eat you up!"

Humpy-Rumpy charged straight at the Enormous Crocodile. He caught him with his giant head and sent him tumbling and skidding over the ground.

"Ow-eeee!" cried the Crocodile. "Help! Stop! Where am I?"

Toto and Mary ran back to the town as fast as they could.

But crocodiles are tough. It is difficult for even a hippopotamus to hurt them.

The Enormous Crocodile picked himself up and crept towards the place where the children's playground was.

"Now for Clever Trick Number Two!" he said to himself. "This one is certain to work!"

There were no children in the playground at that moment. They were all in school.

The Enormous Crocodile found a large piece of wood and placed it in the middle of the playground. Then he lay across the piece of wood and tucked in his feet so that he looked almost exactly like a see-saw.

When school was over, the children all came running on to the playground.

"Oh look!" they cried. "We've got a new see-saw!"

They all crowded round, shouting with excitement.

"Bags I have the first go!"

working the roundabout jumped off it and ran away as fast as he could.

The Enormous Crocodile cursed the Roly-Poly Bird and waddled back into the bushes to hide.

"I'm so hungry now," he said to himself, "I could eat six children before I am full up!"

Just outside the town, there was a pretty little field with trees and bushes all round it. This was called The Picnic Place. There were several wooden tables and long benches, and people were allowed to go there and have a picnic at any time.

The Enormous Crocodile crept over to The Picnic Place. There was no one in sight.

"Now for Clever Trick Number Four!" he whispered to himself.

He picked a lovely bunch of flowers and arranged it on one of the tables.

From the same table, he took away one of the benches and hid it in the bushes.

Then he put himself in the place where the bench had been.

By tucking his head under his chest, and by twisting his tail out of sight, he made himself look very much like a long wooden bench with four legs.

Soon two boys and two girls came along carrying baskets of food. They were all from one family, and their mother had said they could go out and have a picnic together.

"Which table shall we sit at?" said one.

"Let's take the table with the lovely flowers on it," said another.

The Enormous Crocodile kept as quiet as a mouse. "I shall eat them all," he said to himself. "They will come and sit on my back and I will swizzle my head around quickly, and after that it'll be *squish crunch gollop.*"

Suddenly a big deep voice from the jungle shouted, "Stand back, children! Stand back! Stand back!"

The children stopped and stared at the place where the voice was coming from.

Then, with a crashing of branches, Trunky the Elephant came rushing out of the jungle.

"That's not a bench you were going to sit on!" he bellowed. "It's the Enormous Crocodile, and he wants to eat you all up!"

Trunky trotted over to the spot where the Enormous Crocodile was standing, and quick as a flash he wrapped his trunk around the Crocodile's tail and hoisted him up into the air.

"Hey! Let me go!" yelled the Enormous Crocodile, who was now dangling upside down. "Let me go! Let me go!"

"No," Trunky said. "I will not let you go. We've all had quite enough of your clever tricks."

Trunky began to swing the Crocodile round and round in the air. At first he swung him slowly.

Then he swung him faster...
And FASTER...
And FASTER...
And FASTER STILL...

   Soon the Enormous Crocodile was just a blurry circle going round
and round Trunky's head.
   Suddenly, Trunky let go of the Crocodile's tail, and the Crocodile
went shooting high up into the sky like a huge green rocket.
   Up and up he went…
   Higher and higher…
   Faster and faster…

He was going so fast and so high that soon the earth was just a tiny dot miles below.

He whizzed on and on.

He whizzed far into space.

He whizzed past the moon.

He whizzed past stars and planets.

Until at last...

With the most tremendous BANG the Enormous Crocodile crashed headfirst into the hot hot sun.

And he was sizzled up like a sausage!

The
Enormous Crocodile

from REVOLTING RECIPES

TO MAKE ONE CENTREPIECE
(TO NIBBLE AT) YOU WILL NEED:

wire coat hanger with the hook cut off (optional)
cocktail sticks [toothpicks]
a long tray or board
palette knife [metal spatula]

THE CROCODILE:

1 large baguette (body)
4 oz / 100 g [³/4 cup] whole blanched almonds (teeth)
14 oz / 400 g frozen chopped spinach (skin)
2 globe artichokes (scales)
1 slice ham or tongue (tongue)
store-bought white fondant icing [decorating icing]
1 egg, hard-boiled (eyeballs)
1 black olive, cut in half (pupils)
2 cooked sausages (legs)
12 cocktail gherkins (toes)

Steps 1 to 7 should be done the day before serving.

1. Slice one end of the baguette horizontally in half along one third of its length to make the mouth.

2. Now slice the other end horizontally to make the body, leaving ½ to ¾ inch / 1 to 2 cm unsliced (this is the neck). Carefully lift off the top of the body section.

3. Hollow out the top and bottom of his body. Then hollow out the lower jaw, leaving a wide border for the lower lip.

4. Insert his "almond teeth" into the border.

5. Fold the coat hanger in half and carefully place it inside his mouth to prop open the jaws.

6. Defrost, drain, and cook the spinach. Set aside.

7. Boil the artichokes for 30 to 40 minutes, drain, and set aside. When cold, pluck off the leaves, discarding the hairy choke and keeping hearts (a treat for adults later).

EGG FILLING:

(quantities depend on the size of the baguette)
6 to 8 eggs, hard-boiled
salt and pepper
3 to 4 tablespoons mayonnaise
1 carton cress or 1 small bunch watercress, leaves chopped

8. EGG FILLING: Finely chop the hard-boiled eggs, and season with salt and pepper. Mix in the mayonnaise and cress.

9. BODY AND TONGUE: Stuff the crocodile's body with the egg filling. Put in his tongue.

10. Secure any loose teeth with white icing.

11. SKIN AND SCALES: Spread the cooked spinach over the body and head with a small palette knife. Mould the mixture to look like scaly skin. Position artichoke leaves to look like scales.

12. EYES: Cut the hard-boiled egg in half and turn the egg yolks around so that they protrude. Add the pupils (olive halves). Secure with cocktail sticks.

13. LEGS: Slice the sausages in half lengthways and position. Hold in place with cocktail sticks.

14. TOES: Add the cocktail gherkins.

NOTE: IMPORTANT

This recipe is designed to create a centrepiece for a party or other special occasion. If you wish to eat the croc, simply follow the recipe but do not insert the coat hanger. His jaws will be closed, but he'll still be delicious!

Warn children that there are sharp cocktail sticks in the crocodile's eyes and legs.

The Pig

from DIRTY BEASTS

IN England once there lived a big
And wonderfully clever pig.
To everybody it was plain
That Piggy had a massive brain.
He worked out sums inside his head,
There was no book he hadn't read,
He knew what made an airplane fly,
He knew how engines worked and why.
He knew all this, but in the end
One question drove him round the bend:
He simply couldn't puzzle out
What LIFE was really all about.
What was the reason for his birth?
Why was he placed upon this earth?

His giant brain went round and round.
Alas, no answer could be found,
Till suddenly one wondrous night,
All in a flash, he saw the light.
He jumped up like a ballet dancer
And yelled, "By gum, I've got the answer!
They want my bacon slice by slice
To sell at a tremendous price!
They want my tender juicy chops
To put in all the butchers' shops!
They want my pork to make a roast
And that's the part'll cost the most!
They want my sausages in strings!
They even want my chitterlings!
The butcher's shop! The carving knife!
That is the reason for my life!"
Such thoughts as these are not designed
To give a pig great peace of mind.
Next morning, in comes Farmer Bland,

A pail of pigswill in his hand,
And Piggy with a mighty roar,
Bashes the farmer to the floor . . .
Now comes the rather grizzly bit
So let's not make too much of it,
Except that you *must* understand
That Piggy *did eat* Farmer Bland,
He ate him up from head to toe,
Chewing the pieces nice and slow.
It took an hour to reach the feet,
Because there was so much to eat,
And when he'd finished, Pig, of course,
Felt absolutely no remorse.
Slowly he scratched his brainy head
And with a little smile, he said,
"I had a fairly powerful hunch
That he might have me for his lunch.
And so, because I feared the worst,
I thought I'd better eat *him* first."

Dear Mr. Roald Dahl:

I believe that I am the biggest fan of yours~~bo~~ in the world. You've probably gotten letters like this one saying the exact same thing, but I write this very sincerely.

I have read "Charlie and the Chocolate Factory", "Charlie and the Great ~~Gtt~~ Glass Elevator", "James and the Giant Peach", "Matilda", "The Witches", "The BFG", "Fantastic Mr. Fox", "Boy", "Danny, the Champion of the World", "The Magic Finger", and my favorite, "The Wonderful Story of Henry Sugar and Six More". I also read "My Uncle Oswald". While I read it, my mother saw me giggling and read the page.

I was heavily punished, but was allowed to finish the book.

Mr. Dahl, I believe that you ~~art~~ are the greatest writer who ever lived.

Your books are thoughtful, creative, and especially funny. After reading your books, I have decided to <u>try</u> to become a writer. I've never been very good at writing, but you've given me inspiration.

In 1987, I thought that you were dead, but then out came "Boy" and "Matilda".

My name is Robin (masculine form) Chan. I live in Florida & in the city of Cape Coral, a gigantic sub-- urban expanse of houses. If you were to ~~tot~~ look on a map, you probably would find it since its so small, but it is directly west of Miami on the Gulf coas I am fourteen years old ~~am~~ and am a student at Fort Myers High School. I shall send you my picture.

I realize that you must have a lot of requests for this, but could you please write back to me?

If you would write to me, I would
be most grateful. I would treat
your letter as a prized posession,
worthy of passing from generation
to generation. I ought to warn
you, I am extremely persistent.
This won't be the last letter you
get from me.
    If you do decide to write
to me, my address is :

            Robin Chan
        Cape Coral, FL
            U. S. A.

    I again beg : You're my idol !
Please write back.
                Your enthusiastic fan,
                Robin Chan
P.S. Please excuse the untidiness of
this letter. I am ~~them~~ trembling with
excitement!

Letters from Abroad

When children wrote to Roald Dahl they often received a poem in reply.

DEAR children, far across the sea,
How good of you to write to me.
I love to read the things you say
When you are miles and miles away.
Young people, and I think I'm right,
Are nicer when they're out of sight.

The Owl and the Pussy-cat

THE Owl and the Pussy-cat went away
In a beautiful pea-green car.
At a nearby inn they had some gin
And a pound of caviar.
The Owl looked up to the stars above
And sang to a small guitar,
"Oh lovely Pussy! Oh Pussy my love!
What a beautiful Pussy you are,
You are,
What a beautiful Pussy you are!"

Pussy said to the Owl,
"Oh, you dirty old fowl!
You frequenter of taverns and bars!
You won't make me sin just by giving me gin
And by lifting your voice to the stars.

If I ever decide to turn into a bride
I will not want to live in a tree.
The fates will pick out without any doubt
A beautiful Tom-cat for me! For me!
A beautiful Tom-cat for me!"

The Owl said, "I – would soon teach you to fly,
And catch mice on the wing all night long.
I would love you forever, forsaking you never.
You couldn't say that of a Tom."

56

The Puss said, "Yes quite, but it wouldn't be right,
And I couldn't stay out in all weathers.
I couldn't make love with a beak up above,
And I wouldn't want kittens with feathers!
Oh no!
I wouldn't want kittens with feathers."

Fantastic Mr Fox

AN EXTRACT

ON a hill above the valley there was a wood.
In the wood there was a huge tree.
Under the tree there was a hole.
In the hole lived Mr Fox and Mrs Fox and their four Small Foxes.
Every evening as soon as it got dark, Mr Fox would say to Mrs Fox, "Well, my darling, what shall it be this time? A plump chicken from Boggis? A duck or a goose from Bunce? Or a nice turkey from Bean?" And when Mrs Fox had told him what she wanted, Mr Fox would creep down into the valley in the darkness of the night and help himself.

Boggis and Bunce and Bean knew very well what was going on, and it made them wild with rage. They were not men who liked to give anything away. Less still did they like anything to be stolen from them. So every night each of them would take his shotgun and hide in a dark place somewhere on his own farm, hoping to catch the robber.

But Mr Fox was too clever for them. He always approached a farm with the wind blowing in his face, and this meant that if any man were lurking in the shadows ahead, the wind would carry the smell of that man to Mr Fox's nose from far away. Thus, if Mr Boggis was hiding behind his Chicken House Number One, Mr Fox would smell him out from fifty yards off and quickly change direction, heading for Chicken House Number Four at the other end of the farm.

"Dang and blast that lousy beast!" cried Boggis.

"I'd like to rip his guts out!" said Bunce.

"He must be killed!" cried Bean.

"But how?" said Boggis. "How on earth can we catch the blighter?"

Bean picked his nose delicately with a long finger. "I have a plan," he said.

"You've never had a decent plan yet," said Bunce.

"Shut up and listen," said Bean. "Tomorrow night we will all hide just outside the hole where the fox lives. We will wait there until he comes out. Then… *Bang! Bang-bang-bang.*"

"Very clever," said Bunce. "But first we shall have to find the hole."

"My dear Bunce, I've already found it," said the crafty Bean. "It's up in the wood on the hill. It's under a huge tree…"

Creating Characters

MOST of the stories I write all begin with a small germ of an idea for a story. I then take that idea and begin working with it. All the finer points to the story are worked out as I sit in my chair and write. Books do grow in other ways. One book I wrote, *The Giraffe and the Pelly and Me*, began with no plot in my head at all but instead with three characters.

Now for me, writing the text of a short first-rate illustrated book for young children is the most difficult task of all, more difficult than a novel, short story, or a full length children's book. If you find this hard to believe, I suggest you give it a try yourself.

I believe I managed to achieve this once with *The Enormous Crocodile* with the help of Quentin Blake's marvellous illustrations. And, each year since then, I've put everything else aside and given a week or two to try to get started on another short book for the very young. On each occasion I have given up in despair. The plot was never right and what I wrote was neither funny nor exciting.

Finally, I was determined to see it through to the end however long it took. So with no plot at all in my head I picked out three animals as the main characters and I tested them on Quentin.

"What about a Giraffe?" I asked him.

"I've never done a Giraffe," he said. "I'd like that."

"And a Pelican?"

"That ought to be fun too," he said, "with its huge beak."

"And I want to keep the Monkey," I said, "because you drew it so wonderfully in *The Enormous Crocodile*. So if I give you a Giraffe and a Pelican and a Monkey will you be happy?"

"Super," Quentin said. "Have you got a story yet?"

"No."

So I started trying to build a story round these three creatures. It was very difficult. For seven months I wrote and discarded and I rewrote, and you must believe me when I tell you that I have a file of discards and rewrites which contains exactly three hundred and fourteen handwritten and typewritten pages. The finished story runs to thirty-four and a half typewritten pages. That's how difficult I found it. But, throughout all those months it was fascinating to watch one little cog after another falling into place as the story began to take on some sort of shape.

The Giraffe
and the Pelly and Me

Nᴏᴛ far from where I live there is a queer old empty wooden house standing all by itself on the side of the road. I long to explore inside it but the door is always locked, and when I peer through a window all I can see is darkness and dust. I know the ground floor used once to be a shop because I can still read the faded lettering across the front which says THE GRUBBER. My mother has told me that in our part of the country in the olden days a grubber was another name for a sweet-shop, and now every time I look at it I think to myself what a lovely old sweet-shop it must have been.

On the shop-window itself somebody has painted in white the words FOR SAIL.

One morning, I noticed that FOR SAIL had been scraped off the shop-window and in its place somebody had painted SOLED. I stood there staring at the new writing and wishing like mad that it had been me who had bought it because then I would have been able to make it into a grubber all over again. I have always longed and longed to own a sweet-shop. The sweet-shop of my dreams would be loaded from top to bottom with Sherbet Suckers and Caramel Fudge and Russian Toffee and Sugar Snorters and Butter Gumballs and thousands and thousands of other glorious things like that. Oh boy, what I couldn't have done with that old Grubber shop if it had been mine!

On my next visit to The Grubber, I was standing across the road gazing at the wonderful old building when suddenly an enormous bathtub came sailing out through one of the second-floor windows and crashed right on to the middle of the road!

A few moments later, a white porcelain lavatory pan with the wooden seat still on it came flying out of the same window and landed with a wonderful splintering crash just beside the bathtub. This

was followed by a kitchen sink and an empty
canary-cage and a four-poster bed and two
hot-water bottles and a rocking horse
and a sewing-machine and goodness
knows what else besides.

It looked as though some
madman was ripping out the
whole of the inside of the
house, because now pieces of
staircase and bits of the ban-
isters and a whole lot of old
floorboards came whistling
through the windows.

Then there was silence.
I waited and waited but
not another sound
came from within the
building. I crossed the
road and stood right
under the windows
and called out, "Is
anybody at home?"
There was no answer.

THE GRU

SOLED

In the end it began to get dark so I had to turn away and start walking home. But you can bet your life nothing was going to stop me from hurrying back there again tomorrow morning to see what the next surprise was going to be.

When I got back to the Grubber house the next morning, the first thing I noticed was the new door. The dirty old brown door had been taken out and in its place someone had fitted a brand-new red one. The new door was fantastic. It was twice as high as the other one had been and it looked ridiculous. I couldn't begin to imagine who would want a tremendous tall door like that in his house unless it was a giant.

As well as this, somebody had scraped away the SOLED notice on the shop-window and now there was a whole lot of different writing all over the glass. I stood there reading it and reading it and trying to figure out what on earth it all meant.

I tried to catch some sign or sound of movement inside the house but there was none... until all of a sudden... out of the corner of my eye... I noticed that one of the windows on the top floor was slowly beginning to open outwards...

Then a HEAD appeared at the open window.

I stared at the head. The head stared back at me with big round dark eyes.

Suddenly, a second window was flung wide open and of all the crazy things a gigantic white bird hopped out and perched on the window-sill. I knew what this one was because of its amazing beak which was shaped like a huge orange-coloured basin. The Pelican looked down at me and sang out:

> *"Oh, how I wish*
> *For a big fat fish!*
> *I'm as hungry as ever could be!*
> *A dish of fish is my only wish!*
> *How far are we from the sea?"*

"We are a long way from the sea," I called back to him, "but there is a fishmonger in the village not far away."

"A fish *what?*"

"A fish*monger.*"

"Now what on earth would that be?" asked the Pelican. "I have heard of a fish-*pie* and a fish-*cake* and a fish-*finger*, but I have never heard of a fish-*monger*. Are these mongers good to eat?"

This question baffled me a bit, so I said, "Who is your friend in the next window?"

"She is the Giraffe!" the Pelican answered. "Is she not wonderful? Her legs are on the ground floor and her head is looking out of the top window!"

As if all this wasn't enough, the window on the *first floor* was now flung wide open and out popped a Monkey!

The Monkey stood on the window-sill and did a jiggly little dance. He was so skinny he seemed to be made only out of furry bits of wire, but he danced wonderfully well, and I clapped and cheered and did a little dance myself in return.

"We are the Window-Cleaners!" sang out the Monkey.

"We will polish your glass
Till it's shining like brass
And it sparkles like sun on the sea!
We are quick and polite,
We will come day or night,
The Giraffe and the Pelly and me!

We're a fabulous crew,
We know just what to do,
And we never stop work to drink tea.
All your windows will glow
When we give them a go,
The Giraffe and the Pelly and me!

We use water and soap
Plus some kindness and hope,
But we never use ladders, not we.
Who needs ladders at all
When you're thirty feet tall?
Not Giraffe, and not Pelly! Not me!"

I stood there enthralled. Then I heard the Giraffe saying to the Pelican in the next window, "Pelly, my dear, be so good as to fly down and bring that small person up here to talk to us."

At once the Pelican spread his huge white wings and flew down on to the road beside me. "Hop in," he said, opening his enormous beak.

I stared at the great orange beak and backed away.

"Go ON!" the Monkey shouted from up in his window. "The Pelly isn't going to *swallow* you! Climb IN!"

I said to the Pelican, "I'll only get in if you promise not to shut your beak once I'm inside."

"You have nothing to fear!" cried the Pelican,

"And let me tell you why.
I have a very special beak!
A special beak have I!
You'll never see a beak so fine,
I don't care where you go.
There's magic in this beak of mine!
Hop in and don't say NO!"

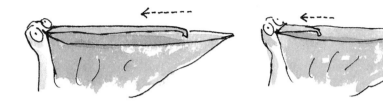

"I will *not* hop in," I said, "unless you swear on your honour you won't shut it once I'm inside. I don't like small dark places."

"When I have done what I am just about to do," said the Pelican, "I won't be *able* to shut it. You don't seem to understand how my beak works."

"Show me," I said.

"Watch this!" cried the Pelican.

I watched in amazement as the top half of the Pelican's beak began to slide smoothly backwards into his head until the whole thing was almost out of sight.

"It bends and goes down inside the back of my neck!" cried the Pelican. "Is that not sensible? Is it not magical?"

"It's unbelievable," I said. "It's exactly like one of those metal tape-measures my father's got at home. When it's out, it's straight. When you slide it back in, it bends and disappears."

"Precisely," said the Pelican. "You see, the top half is of no use to me unless I am chewing fish. The bottom half is what counts, my lad! The bottom half of this glorious beak of mine is the bucket in which we carry our window-cleaning water! So if I didn't slide the top half away I'd be standing around all day long holding it open!

"So I slide it away
For the rest of the day!
Even so, I'm still able to speak!
And wherever I've flown
It has always been known
As the Pelican's Patented Beak!

If I want to eat fish
(That's my favourite dish)
All I do is I give it a tweak!
In the blink of an eye
Out it pops! And they cry,
'It's the Pelican's Patented Beak!'"

"Stop showing off down there!" shouted the Monkey from the upstairs window. "Hurry up and bring that small person up to us! The Giraffe is waiting!"

I climbed into the big orange beak, and with a swoosh of wings the Pelican carried me back to his perch on the window-sill.

The Giraffe looked out of her window at me and said, "How do you do? What is your name?"

"Billy," I told her.

"Well, Billy," she said, "we need your help and we need it fast. We *must have* some windows to clean. We've spent every penny we had on buying this house and we've got to earn some more money quickly. The Pelly is starving, the Monkey is famished and I am perishing with hunger. The Pelly needs fish. The Monkey needs nuts and I am even more difficult to feed. I am a Geraneous Giraffe and a Geraneous Giraffe cannot eat anything except the pink and purple flowers of the tinkle-tinkle tree. But these, as I am sure you know, are hard to find and expensive to buy."

The Pelican cried out, "Right now I am so hungry I could eat a stale sardine!

"Has anyone seen a stale sardine
Or a bucket of rotten cod?
I'd eat the lot upon the spot,
I'm such a hungry bod!"

Every time the Pelican spoke, the beak I was standing in jiggled madly up and down, and the more excited he got, the more it jiggled.

The Monkey said, "What Pelly's *really* crazy about is salmon!"

"Yes, yes!" cried the Pelican. "Salmon! Oh, glorious salmon! I dream about it all day long but I never get any!"

"And *I* dream about walnuts!" shouted the Monkey. "A walnut fresh from the tree is so scrumptious-galumptious, so flavory-savory, so sweet to eat that it makes me all wobbly just thinking about it!"

At exactly that moment, a huge white Rolls-Royce pulled up right below us, and a chauffeur in a blue and gold uniform got out. He was carrying an envelope in one gloved hand.

"Good heavens!" I whispered. "That's the Duke of Hampshire's car!"

"Who's he?" asked the Giraffe.

"He's the richest man in England!" I said.

The chauffeur knocked on the door of The Grubber.

"We're up here!" the Giraffe called down to him.

He looked up and saw us. He saw the Giraffe, the Pelly, the Monkey and me all staring down at him from above, but not a muscle moved in his face, not an eyebrow was raised. The chauffeurs of very rich men are never surprised by anything they see. The chauffeur said, "His Grace The Duke of Hampshire has instructed me to deliver this envelope to The Ladderless Window-Cleaning Company."

"That's us!" cried the Monkey.

The Giraffe said, "Be so good as to open the envelope and read us the letter."

The chauffeur unfolded the letter and began to read, " 'Dear Sirs, I saw your notice as I drove by this morning. I have been looking for a decent window-cleaner for the last fifty years but I have not found one yet. My house has six hundred and seventy-seven windows in it (not counting the greenhouses) and all of them are filthy. Kindly come and see me as soon as possible. Yours truly, Hampshire.' That," added the chauffeur in a voice filled with awe and respect, "was written by His Grace The Duke of Hampshire in his own hand."

The Giraffe said to the chauffeur, "Please tell His Grace The Duke that we will be with him as soon as possible."

The chauffeur touched his cap and got back into the Rolls-Royce.

"Whoopee!" shouted the Monkey.

"Fantastic!" cried the Pelican. "That must be the best window-cleaning job in the world!"

"Billy," said the Giraffe, "what is the house called and how do we get there?"

"It is called Hampshire House," I said. "It's just over the hill. I'll show you the way."

"We're off!" cried the Monkey. "We're off to see the Duke!"

The Giraffe stooped low and went out through the tall door. The Monkey jumped off the window-sill on to the Giraffe's back. The

Pelican, with me in his beak hanging on for dear life, flew across and
perched on the very top of the Giraffe's head. And away we went.

It wasn't long before we came to the gates of Hampshire House,
and as the Giraffe moved slowly up the great wide driveway, we all
began to feel just a little bit nervous.

"What's he like, this Duke?" the Giraffe asked me.

"I don't know," I said. "But he's very very famous and very rich.
People say he has twenty-five gardeners just to look after his
flower-beds."

Soon the huge house itself came into view, and what a house it was!
It was like a palace! It was bigger than a palace!

"Just look at those windows!" cried the Monkey. "They'll keep us
going for ever!"

Then suddenly we heard a man's voice a short distance away to the right. "I want those big black ones at the top of the tree!" the man was shouting. "Get me those great big black ones!"

We peered round the bushes and saw an oldish man with an immense white moustache standing under a tall cherry tree and pointing his walking-stick in the air. There was a ladder against the tree and another man, who was probably a gardener, was up the ladder.

"Get me those great big black juicy ones right at the very top!" the old man was shouting.

"I can't reach them, Your Grace," the gardener called back. "The ladder isn't long enough!"

"Damnation!" shouted the Duke. "I *was* so looking forward to eating those big ones!"

"Here we go!" the Pelican whispered to me, and with a swish and a swoop he carried me up to the very top of the cherry tree and there he perched. "Pick them, Billy!" he whispered. "Pick them quickly and put them in my beak!"

The gardener got such a shock he fell off the ladder. Down below us, the Duke was shouting, "My gun! Get me my gun! Some damnable monster of a bird is stealing my best cherries! Be off with you, sir! Go away! Those are *my* cherries, not yours! I'll have you shot for this, sir! Where *is* my gun?"

"Hurry, Billy!" whispered the Pelican. "Hurry, hurry, hurry!"

"My gun!" the Duke was shouting to the gardener. "Get me my gun, you idiot! I'll have that thieving bird for breakfast, you see if I don't."

"I've picked them all," I whispered to the Pelican.

At once the Pelly flew down and landed right beside the furious figure of the Duke of Hampshire, who was prancing about and waving his stick in the air!

"Your cherries, Your Grace!" I said as I leaned over the edge of the Pelican's beak and offered a handful to the Duke.

The Duke was staggered. He reeled back and his eyes popped nearly out of their sockets. "Great Scott!" he gasped. "Good Lord!

What's this? Who are *you?*"

And now the Giraffe, with the Monkey dancing about on her back, emerged suddenly from the bushes. The Duke stared at them. He looked as though he was about to have a fit.

"*Who are these creatures?*" he bellowed. "Has the whole world gone completely dotty?"

"We are the Window-Cleaners!" sang out the Monkey.

> *"We will polish your glass*
> *Till it's shining like brass*
> *And it sparkles like sun on the sea!*
> *We will work for Your Grace*
> *Till we're blue in the face,*
> *The Giraffe and the Pelly and me!"*

"You *asked* us to come and see you," the Giraffe said.

The truth was at last beginning to dawn on the Duke. He put a cherry into his mouth and chewed it slowly. Then he spat out the stone. "I like the way you picked these cherries for me," he said. "Could you also pick my apples in the autumn?"

"We could! We could! Of course we could!" we all shouted.

"And who are *you?*" the Duke said, pointing his stick at me.

"He is our Business Manager," the Giraffe said. "His name is Billy. We go nowhere without him."

"Very well, very well," the Duke muttered. "Come along with me and let's see if you're any good at cleaning windows."

I climbed out of the Pelican's beak and the kindly old Duke took me by the hand as we all walked towards the house.

When we got there, the Duke said, "What happens next?"

"It is all very simple, Your Grace," the Giraffe replied. "I am the ladder, the Pelly is the bucket and the Monkey is the cleaner. Watch us go!"

With that, the famous window-cleaning gang sprang into action. The Monkey jumped down from the Giraffe's back and turned on the garden tap. The Pelican held his great beak under the tap until it was full of water. Then, with a wonderful springy leap the Monkey leaped up once again on to the Giraffe's back. From there he scrambled, as easily as if he were climbing a tree, up the long long neck of the Giraffe until he stood balancing on the very top of her head. The Pelican remained standing on the ground beside us, looking up at the Giraffe.

"We'll do the top floor first!" the Giraffe shouted down. "Bring the water up, please."

The Duke called out, "Don't worry about the two top floors. You can't reach them anyway."

"Who says we can't reach them?" the Giraffe called back.

"I do," the Duke said firmly, "and I'm not having any of you risking your silly necks around here."

If you wish to be friends with a Giraffe, never say anything bad about its neck. Its neck is its proudest possession.

"What's wrong with my neck?" snapped the Giraffe.

"Don't argue with me, you foolish creature!" cried the Duke. "If you can't reach it, you can't reach it and that's the end of it! Now get on with your work!"

"Your Grace," the Giraffe said, giving the Duke a small superior smile, "there are no windows in the world I cannot reach with this magical neck of mine."

The Monkey, who was dancing about most dangerously on top of the Giraffe's head, cried out, "Show him, Giraffey! Go on and show him what you can do with your magical neck!"

The next moment, the Giraffe's neck, which heaven knows was long enough already, began to grow longer... and LONGER... and LONGER... and LONGER... and HIGHER... and HIGHER...

and HIGHER... until at last the Giraffe's head with the Monkey on top of it was level with the windows of the top floor.

The Giraffe looked down from her great height and said to the Duke, "How's that?"

The Duke was speechless. So was I. It was the most magical thing I had ever seen, more magical even than the Pelican's Patented Beak.

Up above us, the Giraffe was beginning to sing a little song, but she sang so softly I could hardly catch the words. I think it went something like this:

> *"My neck can stretch terribly high,*
> *Much higher than eagles can fly.*
> *If I ventured to show*
> *Just how high it would go*
> *You'd lose sight of my head in the sky!"*

The Pelican, with his huge beak full of water, flew up and perched on one of the top-floor window-sills near the Monkey, and now the great window-cleaning business really began.

The speed with which the team worked was astonishing. As soon as one window was done, the Giraffe moved the Monkey over to the next one and the Pelican followed. When all the fourth-floor windows on that side of the house were finished, the Giraffe simply drew in her magical neck until the Monkey was level with the third-floor windows and off they went again.

"Amazing!" cried the Duke. "Astonishing! Remarkable! Incredible! I haven't seen out of any of my windows for forty years! Now I shall be able to sit indoors and enjoy the view!"

Suddenly I saw all three of the Window-Cleaners stop dead in their tracks. They seemed to freeze against the wall of the house. None of them moved.

"What's happened to them?" the Duke asked me. "What's gone wrong?"

"I don't know," I answered.

Then the Giraffe, with the Monkey on her head, tiptoed very gingerly away from the house and came towards us. The Pelican flew with them. The Giraffe came up very close to the Duke and whispered, "Your Grace, there is a man in one of the bedrooms on the third floor. He is opening all the drawers and taking things out. He's got a pistol!"

The Duke jumped about a foot in the air. "Which room?" he snapped. "Show me at once!"

"It's the one on the third floor where the window is wide open," the Giraffe whispered.

"By Gad!" cried the Duke. "That's the Duchess's bedroom! He's after her jewels! Call the police! Summon the army! Bring up the cannon! Charge with the Light Brigade!" But even as he spoke the Pelican was flying up into the air. As he flew, he turned himself upside down and tipped the window-cleaning water out of his beak. Then I

saw the top half of that marvellous patented beak sliding out of his head, ready for action.

"What's that crazy bird up to?" cried the Duke.

"Wait and see," shouted the Monkey. "Hold your breath, old man! Hold your nose! Hold your horses and watch the Pelly go!"

Like a bullet the Pelican flew in through the open window, and five seconds later out he came again with his great orange beak firmly closed. He landed on the lawn beside the Duke.

A tremendous banging noise was coming from inside the Pelican's beak. It sounded as though someone was using a sledgehammer against it from the inside.

"He's got him!" cried the Monkey. "Pelly's got the burglar in his beak!"

"Well done, sir!" shouted the Duke, hopping about with excitement. Suddenly he pulled the handle of his walking-stick upwards, and out of the hollow inside of the stick itself he drew a long thin sharp shining sword. "I'll run him through!" he shouted, flourishing the sword like a fencer. "Open up, Pelican! Let me get at him! I'll run the bounder through before he knows what's happened to him! I'll spike him like a pat of butter! I'll feed his gizzards to my foxhounds!"

But the Pelican did not open his beak. He kept it firmly closed and shook his head at the Duke.

The Giraffe shouted, "The burglar is armed with a pistol, Your Grace! If Pelly lets him out now he'll shoot us all!"

"He can be armed with a *machine-gun* for all I care!" bellowed the Duke, his massive moustaches bristling like brushwood. "I'll handle the blighter! Open up, sir! Open up!"

Suddenly there was an ear-splitting BANG and the Pelican leaped twenty feet into the air. So did the Duke.

"Watch out!" the Duke shouted, taking ten rapid paces backwards. "He's trying to shoot his way out!" And pointing his sword at the Pelican, he bellowed, "Keep that beak closed, sir! Don't you dare let him out! He'll murder us all!"

"Shake him up, Pelly!" cried the Giraffe. "Rattle his bones! Teach him not to do it again!" The Pelican shook his head so fast from side to side that the beak became a blur and the man inside must have felt he was being scrambled like eggs. "Well done, Pelly!" cried the Giraffe. "You're doing a great job! Keep on shaking him so he doesn't fire that pistol again!"

At this point, a lady with an enormous chest and flaming orange hair came flying out of the house screaming, "My jewels! Somebody's stolen my jewels! My diamond tiara! My diamond necklace! My diamond bracelets! My diamond earrings! My diamond rings! They've had the lot! My rooms have been ransacked!"

And then this massive female, who fifty-five years ago had been a world-famous opera-singer, suddenly burst into song.

"My diamonds are over the ocean,
My diamonds are over the sea,
My diamonds were pinched from my bedroom,
Oh, bring back my diamonds to me."

We were so bowled over by the power of the lady's lungs that all of us, excepting the Pelican, who had to keep his beak closed, joined in the chorus.

"Bring back, bring back,
Oh, bring back my diamonds to me, to me.
Bring back, bring back,
Oh, bring back my diamonds to me!"

"Calm yourself, Henrietta," said the Duke. He pointed to the Pelican and said, "This clever bird, this brilliant burglar-catching creature has saved the day! The bounder's in his beak!"

The Duchess stared at the Pelican. The Pelican stared back at the Duchess and gave her a wink.

"If he's in there," cried the Duchess, "why don't you let him out! Then you can run him through with that famous sword of yours! I want my diamonds! Open your beak, bird!"

"No, no!" shouted the Duke. "He's got a pistol! He'll murder us all!" Someone must have called the police because suddenly no less than four squad cars came racing towards us with their sirens screaming.

Within seconds we were surrounded by six policemen, and the Duke was shouting to them, "The villain you are after is inside the beak of that bird! Stand by to collar him!" And to the Pelican he said, "Get ready to open up! Are you ready... steady... *go!* Open her up!"

The Pelican opened his gigantic beak and immediately the policemen pounced upon the burglar who was crouching inside. They snatched his pistol away from him and dragged him out and put handcuffs on his wrists.

"Great Scott!" shouted the Chief of Police. "It's the Cobra himself!"

"The who? The what?" everyone asked. "Who's the Cobra?"

"The Cobra is the cleverest and most dangerous cat-burglar in the world!" said the Chief of Police. "He must have climbed up the drainpipe. The Cobra can climb up anything!"

"My diamonds!" screamed the Duchess. "I want my diamonds! Where are my diamonds?"

"Here they are!" cried the Chief of Police, fishing great handfuls of jewellery from the burglar's pocket.

The Duchess was so overcome with relief that she fell to the ground in a faint.

When the police had taken away the fearsome burglar known as the Cobra, and the fainting Duchess had been carried into the house by her servants, the old Duke stood on the lawn with the Giraffe, the Pelican, the Monkey and me.

"Look!" cried the Monkey. "That rotten burglar's bullet has made a hole in poor Pelly's beak!"

"That's done it," said the Pelican. "Now it won't be any use for holding water when we clean the windows."

"Don't you worry about that, my dear Pelly," said the Duke, patting him on the beak. "My chauffeur will soon put a patch over it the same way he mends the tyres on the Rolls. Right now we have far more important things to talk about than a little hole in a beak."

We stood there waiting to see what the Duke was going to say next.

"Now listen to me, all of you," he said. "Those diamonds were worth millions! Millions and millions! And *you* have saved them!"

The Monkey nodded. The Giraffe smiled. The Pelican blushed.

"No reward is too great for you," the Duke went on. "I am therefore going to make you an offer which I hope will give you pleasure. I hereby invite the Giraffe and the Pelican and the Monkey to live on my estate for the rest of their lives.

"I shall give you my best and largest hay-barn as your private house. Central heating, showers, a kitchen and anything else you desire for your comfort will be installed.

"In return, you will keep my windows clean, and pick my cherries and my apples. If the Pelican is willing, perhaps he will also give me a ride in his beak now and again."

"A pleasure, Your Grace!" cried the Pelican. "Would you like a ride now?"

"Later," said the Duke. "I'll have one after tea."

At this point, the Giraffe gave a nervous little cough and looked up at the sky.

"Is there a problem?" asked the Duke. "If there is, do please let me hear it."

"I don't like to sound ungrateful or pushy," murmured the Giraffe, "but we do have one very pressing problem. We are all absolutely famished. We haven't eaten for days."

"My *dear* Giraffey!" cried the Duke. "How very thoughtless of me. Food is no problem around here."

"I'm afraid it is not quite as easy as all that," said the Giraffe. "You see, I myself happen to be . . ."

"Don't tell me!" cried the Duke. "I know it already! I am an expert on the animals of Africa. The moment I saw you I knew you were no ordinary giraffe. You are of the Geraneous variety, are you not?"

"You are absolutely right, Your Grace," said the Giraffe. "But the trouble with us is that we only eat . . ."

"You don't have to tell me that either!" cried the Duke. "I know perfectly well a Geraneous Giraffe can eat only one kind of food. Am I not right in thinking that the pink and purple flowers of the tinkle-tinkle tree are your only diet?"

"Yes," sighed the Giraffe, "and that's been my problem ever since I arrived on these shores."

"That is no problem at all here at Hampshire House," said the Duke. "Look over there, my dear Giraffey, and you will see the only planta-tion of tinkle-tinkle trees in the entire country!"

The Giraffe looked. She gave a gasp of aston-ishment, and at first she was so overwhelmed she couldn't even speak. Great tears of joy began running down her cheeks.

"Help yourself," said the Duke. "Eat all you want."

"Oh, my sainted soul!" gasped the Giraffe. "Oh, my naked neck! I cannot *believe* what I am seeing!"

The next moment she was galloping full speed across the lawns and whinnying with excitement and the last we saw of her, she was burying her head in the beautiful pink and purple flowers that blossomed on the tops of the trees all around her.

"As for the Monkey," the Duke went on, "I think he also will be pleased with what I have to offer. All over my estate there are thousands of giant nut trees…"

"Nuts?" cried the Monkey. "What kind of nuts?"

"Walnuts, of course," said the Duke.

"**Walnuts!**" screamed the Monkey. "Not *walnuts?* You don't really mean *walnuts?* You're pulling my leg! You're joking! You can't be serious! I must have heard wrong!"

"There's a walnut tree right over there," the Duke said, pointing.

The Monkey took off like an arrow, and a few seconds later he was high up in the branches of the walnut tree, cracking the nuts and guzzling what was inside.

"That leaves only the Pelly," said the Duke.

"Yes," said the Pelican nervously, "but I'm afraid that what I eat does not grow on trees. I only eat fish. Would it be too much trouble, I wonder, if I were to ask you for a reasonably fresh piece of haddock or cod every day?"

"Haddock or cod!" shouted the Duke, spitting out the words as though they made a bad taste in his mouth. "Cast your eyes, my dear Pelly, over there to the south."

The Pelican looked across the vast rolling estate and in the distance he saw a great river.

"That is the River Hamp!" cried the Duke. "The finest salmon river in the whole of Europe!"

"*Salmon!*" screeched the Pelican. "Not *salmon?* You don't really mean *salmon?*"

"It's full of salmon," the Duke said, "and I own it. You can help yourself."

Before he had finished speaking the Pelican was in the air. The Duke and I watched him as he flew full speed towards the river. We saw him circle over the water, then he dived and disappeared. A few moments later, he was in the air again, and he had a gigantic salmon in his beak.

I stood alone with the Duke on the lawn beside his great house. "Well, Billy," he said, "I'm glad they are all happy. But what about you, my lad? I am wondering if you happen to have just one extra special little wish all for yourself. If you do, I'd love you to tell me about it."

There was a sudden tingling in my toes. It felt as though something tremendous might be going to happen to me any moment.

"Yes," I murmured nervously. "I do have one extra special little wish."

"And what might that be?" said the Duke in a kindly voice.

"There is an old wooden house near where I live," I said. "It's called The Grubber and long ago it used to be a sweet-shop. I have wished and wished that one day somebody might come along and make it into a marvellous new sweet-shop all over again."

"Somebody?" cried the Duke. "What do you mean, *somebody?* You and I will do that! We'll do it together! We'll make it into the most wonderful sweet-shop in the world! And *you*, my boy, will own it!"

Whenever the old Duke got excited, his enormous moustaches started to bristle and jump about. Right now they were jumping up and down so much it looked as though he had a squirrel on his face. "By Gad, sir!" he cried, waving his stick. "I shall buy the place today! Then we'll all get to work and have the whole thing ready in no time! You just wait and see what sort of a sweet-shop we are going to make out of this Grubber place of yours!"

It was amazing how quickly things began to happen after that. There was no problem about buying the house because it was owned by the Giraffe and the Pelly and the Monkey, and they insisted upon giving it to the Duke for nothing.

Then builders and carpenters moved in and rebuilt the whole of the inside so that once again it had three floors. On all these floors they put together rows and rows of tall shelves, and there were ladders to climb up to the highest shelves and baskets to carry what you bought.

Then the sweets and chocs and toffees and fudges and nougats began pouring in to fill the shelves. They came by aeroplane from every country in the world, the most wild and wondrous things you could ever imagine.

There were Gumtwizzlers and Fizzwinkles from China, Froth-blowers and Spitsizzlers from Africa, Tummyticklers and Gobwangles from the Fiji Islands and Liplickers and Plushnuggets from the Land of the Midnight Sun.

For two whole weeks the flood of boxes and sacks continued to arrive. I could no longer keep track of all the countries they came from, but you can bet your life that as I unpacked each new batch I sampled it carefully. I can remember especially the Giant Wangdoodles from Australia, every one with a huge ripe red strawberry hidden inside its crispy chocolate crust... and the Electric Fizzcocklers that made every hair on your head stand straight up on

end as soon as you popped one into your mouth…
and there were Nishnobblers and Gumglotters and
Blue Bubblers and Sherbet Slurpers and Tongue Rakers, and as well as
all this, there was a whole lot of splendid stuff from the great Wonka
factory itself, for example the famous Willy Wonka Rainbow Drops –
suck them and you can spit in seven different colours. And his
Stickjaw for talkative parents. And his Mint Jujubes that will give the
boy next door green teeth for a month.

On the Grand Opening Day, I decided to allow all my customers to
help themselves for free, and the place was so crowded with children
you could hardly move. The television cameras and the newspaper
reporters were all there, and the old Duke himself stood outside in
the road with my friends the Giraffe and the Pelly and the Monkey
watching the marvellous scene. I came out of the shop to join them
for a few moments and I brought each of them a bag of extra special
sweets as a present.

To the Duke, because the weather was a little chilly, I gave some
Scarlet Scorchdroppers that had been sent to me from Iceland. The
label said that they were guaranteed to make the person who sucked
them as warm as toast even if he were standing stark naked at the
North Pole in mid-winter. The moment the Duke popped one into
his mouth, thick smoke came gushing out of the old boy's nostrils in
such quantities that I thought his moustaches were going up in

flames. "Terrific!" he cried, hopping about. "Tremendous stuff! I'll take a case of them home with me!"

To the Giraffe I gave a bag of Glumptious Globgobblers. The Globgobbler is an especially delicious sweet that is made somewhere near Mecca, and the moment you bite into it, all the perfumed juices of Arabia go squirting down your gullet one after the other. "It's wonderful!" cried the Giraffe as a cascade of lovely liquid flavours poured all the way down her long long throat. "It's even better than my favourite pink and purple flowers!"

To the Pelican I gave a big bag of Pishlets. Pishlets, as you probably know, are bought by children who are unable to whistle a tune as they walk along the street but long to do so. They had a splendid effect upon the Pelican, for after he had put one of them into his beak and chewed it for a while, he suddenly started singing like a nightingale. This made him wildly excited because Pelicans are not song-birds. No Pelican had ever been known to whistle a tune before.

To the Monkey I gave a bag of Devil's Drenchers, those small fiery black sweets that one is not allowed to sell to children under four years old. When you have sucked a Devil's Drencher for a minute or so, you can set your breath alight and blow a huge column of fire twenty feet into the air. The Duke put a match to the Monkey's breath and shouted, "Blow, Monkey, blow!" A sheet of orange flame shot up as high as the roof of the Grubber house and it was wonderful.

"I've got to leave you now," I said. "I must go and look after my customers in the shop."

"We must go, too," said the Giraffe. "We have one hundred windows to clean before dark."

I said goodbye to the Duke, and then one by one I said goodbye to the three best friends I had ever had. Suddenly, we all became very quiet and melancholy, and the Monkey looked as though he was about to cry as he sang me a little song of farewell:

"We have tears in our eyes
As we wave our goodbyes
We so loved being with you, we three.
So do please now and then
Come and see us again,
The Giraffe and the Pelly and me.

All you do is to look
At a page in this book
Because that's where we always will be.
No book ever ends
When it's full of your friends
The Giraffe and the Pelly and me."

The Boy Who
Talked with Animals

from THE WONDERFUL STORY OF HENRY SUGAR

Fishermen have landed a turtle on a beach in Jamaica. Visitors want his shell; the hotel manager wants him for turtle meat. But a small boy, David, is hysterical at his capture and to the amazement of everyone flings his arms round the turtle's neck and talks to him gently. David's father persuades the fishermen to let the turtle return to the sea...

THE crowd moved a few yards up the beach. The tug of war men let go the rope and moved back with the others.

Willy got down on his hands and knees and crept very cautiously up to one side of the turtle. Then he began untying the knot in the rope. He kept well out of the range of the big flippers as he did this.

When the knot was untied, Willy crawled back. Then the four other fishermen stepped forward with their poles. The poles were about seven feet long and immensely thick. They wedged them underneath the shell of the turtle and began to rock the great creature from side to side on its shell. The shell had a high dome and was well shaped for rocking.

"Up and down!" sang the fishermen as they rocked away. "Up and

down! Up and down! Up and down!" The old turtle became thoroughly upset, and who could blame it? The big flippers lashed the air frantically, and the head kept shooting in and out of the shell.

"Roll him over!" sang the fishermen. "Up and over! Roll him over! One more time and over he goes!"

The turtle tilted high up on to its side and crashed down in the sand the right way up.

But it didn't walk away at once. The huge brown head came out and peered cautiously around.

"Go, turtle, go!" the small boy called out. "Go back to the sea!"

The two hooded black eyes of the turtle peered up at the boy. The eyes were bright and lively, full of the wisdom of great age. The boy looked back at the turtle, and this time when he spoke, his voice was soft and intimate. "Goodbye, old man," he said. "Go far away this time." The black eyes remained resting on the boy for a few seconds  more. Nobody moved. Then, with  great dignity, the massive beast turned away and began waddling toward the edge of the ocean. He didn't hurry. He moved sedately over the sandy beach, the big shell rocking gently from side to side as he went.

The crowd watched in silence.

He entered the water.

He kept going.

Soon he was swimming. He was in his element now. He swam gracefully and very fast, with the head held high. The sea was calm, and he made little waves that fanned out behind him on both sides, like the waves of a boat. It was several minutes before we lost sight of him, and by then he was half-way to the horizon.

The guests began wandering back toward the hotel. They were

curiously subdued. There was no joking or bantering now, no laughing. Something had happened. Something strange had come fluttering across the beach.

I walked back to my small balcony and sat down with a cigarette. I had an uneasy feeling that this was not the end of the affair.

The next morning at eight o'clock, the Jamaican girl, the one who had told me about Mr Wasserman and the coconut, brought a glass of orange juice to my room.

"Big *big* fuss in the hotel this morning," she said as she placed the glass on the table and drew back the curtains. "Everyone flying about all over the place like they was crazy."

"Why? What's happened?"

"That little boy in number twelve, he's vanished. He disappeared in the night."

"You mean the turtle boy?"

"That's him," she said. "His parents is raising the roof and the manager's going mad."

"How long's he been missing?"

"About two hours ago his father found his bed empty. But he could've gone any time in the night I reckon."

"Yes," I said. "He could."

"Everybody in the hotel searching high and low," she said. "And a police car just arrived."

"Maybe he just got up early and went for a climb on the rocks," I said.

Her large dark haunted-looking eyes rested a moment on my face, then travelled away. "I do not think so," she said, and out she went.

I slipped on some clothes and hurried down to the beach. On the beach itself, two native policemen in khaki uniforms were standing with Mr Edwards, the manager. Mr Edwards was doing the talking. The policemen were listening patiently. In the distance, at both ends of the beach, I could see small groups of people, hotel servants as well as hotel guests, spreading out and heading for the rocks. The morning was beautiful. The sky was smoke blue, faintly glazed with yellow. The sun was up and making diamonds all over the smooth sea. And Mr Edwards was talking loudly to the two native policemen, and waving his arms.

I wanted to help. What should I do? Which way should I go? It would be pointless simply to follow the others. So I just kept walking toward Mr Edwards.

About then, I saw the fishing-boat. The long wooden canoe with a single mast and a flapping brown sail was still some way out to sea,

but it was heading for the beach. The two natives aboard, one at either end, were paddling hard. They were paddling very hard. The paddles rose and fell at such a terrific speed they might have been in a race. I stopped and watched them. Why the great rush to reach the shore? Quite obviously they had something to tell. I kept my eyes on the boat. Over to my left, I could hear Mr Edwards saying to the two policemen, "It is perfectly ridiculous. I can't have people disappearing just like that from the hotel. You'd better find him fast, you under-stand me? He's either wandered off somewhere and got lost or he's been kidnapped. Either way, it's the responsibility of the police . . ."

The fishing-boat skimmed over the sea and came gliding up on to the sand at the water's edge. Both men dropped their paddles and jumped out. They started running up the beach. I recognized the one in front as Willy. When he caught sight of the manager and the two policemen, he made straight for them.

"Hey, Mr Edwards!" Willy called out. "We just seen a crazy thing!"

The manager stiffened and jerked back his neck. The two policemen remained impassive. They were used to excitable people. They met them every day.

Willy stopped in front of the group, his chest heaving in and out with heavy breathing. The other fisherman was close behind him. They were both naked except for a tiny loincloth, their black skins shining with sweat.

"We been paddling full speed for a long way," Willy said, excusing his out-of-breathness. "We thought we ought to come back and tell it as quick as we can."

"Tell what?" the manager said. "What did you see?"

"It was crazy, man! Absolutely crazy!"

"Get on with it, Willy, for heaven's sake."

"You won't believe it," Willy said. "There ain't nobody going to believe it. Isn't that right, Tom?"

"That's right," the other fisherman said, nodding vigorously. "If Willy here hadn't been with me to prove it, I wouldn't have believed it myself!"

"Believed what?" Mr Edwards said. "Just tell us what you saw."

"We'd gone off early," Willy said, "about four o'clock this morning, and we must've been a couple of miles out before it got light enough to see anything properly. Suddenly, as the sun comes up, we see right ahead of us, not more'n fifty yards away, we see something we couldn't believe not even with our own eyes . . ."

"What?" snapped Mr Edwards. "For heaven's sake get on!"

"We sees that old monster turtle swimming away out there, the one on the beach yesterday, and we sees the boy sitting high up on the turtle's back and riding him over the sea like a horse!"

"You gotta believe it!" the other fisherman cried. "I sees it too, so you gotta believe it!"

Mr Edwards looked at the two policemen. The two policemen looked at the fishermen. "You wouldn't be having us on, would you?" one of the policemen said.

"I swear it!" cried Willy. "It's the gospel truth! There's this little boy riding high up on the old turtle's back and his feet isn't even touching the water! He's dry as a bone and sitting there comfy and easy as could be! So we go after them. Of course we go after them. At first we try creeping up on them very quietly, like we always do when we're catching a turtle, but the boy sees us. We aren't very far away at this time, you understand. No more than from here to the edge of the water. And when the boy sees us, he sort of leans forward as if he's saying something to that old turtle, and the turtle's head comes up and he starts swimming like the clappers of hell! Man, could that turtle go! Tom and me can paddle pretty quick when we want to, but we've no chance against that monster! No chance at all! He's going at least twice as fast as we are! Easy twice as fast, what you say, Tom?"

"I'd say he's going *three times* as fast," Tom said. "And I'll tell you why. In about ten or fifteen minutes, they're a mile ahead of us."

"Why on earth didn't you call out to the boy?" the manager asked. "Why didn't you speak to him earlier on, when you were closer?"

"We never *stop* calling out, man!" Willy cried. "As soon as the boy sees us and we're not trying to creep up on them any longer, then we start yelling. We yell everything under the sun at that boy to try and get him aboard. 'Hey, boy!' I yell at him. 'You come on back with us! We'll give you a lift home! That ain't no good what you're doing there, boy! Jump off and swim while you got the chance and we'll pick you up! Go on boy, jump! Your mammy must be waiting for you at home,

boy, so why don't you come on in with us?' And once I shouted at him, 'Listen, boy! We're gonna make you a promise! We promise not to catch that old turtle if you come with us!'"

"Did he answer you at all?" the manager asked.

"He never even looks round!" Willy said. "He sits high up on that shell and he's sort of rocking backwards and forwards with his body just like he's urging the old turtle to go faster and faster! You're gonna lose that little boy, Mr Edwards, unless someone gets out there real quick and grabs him away!"

The manager's normally pink face had turned white as paper. "Which way were they heading?" he asked sharply.

"North," Willy answered. "Almost due north."

"Right!" the manager said. "We'll take the speedboat! I want you with us, Willy. And you, Tom."

The manager, the two policemen and the two fishermen ran down to where the boat that was used for water-skiing lay beached on the sand. They pushed the boat out, and even the manager lent a hand, wading up to his knees in his well-pressed white trousers. Then they all climbed in.

I watched them go zooming off.

Two hours later, I watched them coming back. They had seen nothing.

All through that day, speed-boats and yachts from other hotels along the coast searched the ocean. In the afternoon, the boy's father hired a helicopter. He rode in it himself and they were up there three hours. They found no trace of the turtle or the boy.

For a week, the search went on, but with no result.

And now, nearly a year has gone by since it happened. In that time, there has been only one significant bit of news. A party of Americans, out from Nassau in the Bahamas, were deep-sea fishing off a large island called Eleuthera. There are literally thousands of coral reefs and small uninhabited islands in this area, and upon one of these tiny islands, the captain of the yacht saw through his binoculars the figure of a small person. There was a sandy beach on the island, and the small person was walking on the beach. The binoculars were passed around, and everyone who looked through them agreed that it was a child of some sort. There was, of course, a lot of excitement on board and the fishing lines were quickly reeled in. The captain steered the yacht straight for the island. When they were half a mile off, they were able, through the binoculars, to see clearly that the figure on the beach was a boy, and although sunburnt, he was almost certainly white-skinned, not a native. At that point, the watchers on the yacht also spotted what looked like a giant turtle on the sand near the boy. What happened next, happened very quickly. The boy, who had probably caught sight of the approaching yacht, jumped on to the turtle's back and the huge creature entered the water and swam at great speed around the island and out of sight. The yacht searched for two hours, but nothing more was seen either of the boy or the turtle.

There is no reason to disbelieve this report. There were five people on the yacht. Four of them were Americans and the captain was a Bahamian from Nassau. All of them in turn saw the boy and the turtle through the binoculars.

To reach Eleuthera Island from Jamaica by sea, one must first travel north-east for two hundred and fifty miles and pass through the Windward Passage between Cuba and Haiti. Then one must go north-north-west for a further three hundred miles at least. This is a total distance of five hundred and fifty miles, which is a very long journey for a small boy to make on the shell of a giant turtle.

Who knows what to think of all this?

One day, perhaps, he will come back, though I personally doubt it. I have a feeling he's quite happy where he is.

Stealing a Magpie

from MY YEAR

I once stole a young magpie from the nest and tamed it and kept it for a couple of years as a pet. I never put it in a cage. That wasn't necessary. It stayed around all the time in the garden and would sit on my shoulder like a parrot. When I went for walks it would follow me the whole way there and back, circling overhead, and when I woke up in the mornings, it would be sitting on the sill of the open window. Oh yes, you can tame a magpie quite easily if you get it young enough but you mustn't ever trust it completely. It will peck suddenly at shiny objects. I knew a farmer the other side of Aylesbury who had his own tame magpie sitting on his hand and he was trying to teach it to talk. Suddenly the bird caught sight of a glint of light in the man's eye and stabbed at it with its long sharp beak. The farmer, who lived in Grendon Underwood and was called Richard Holt, lost the eye. He also got rid of the magpie.

Little Red Riding Hood and the Wolf

from REVOLTING RHYMES

As soon as Wolf began to feel
That he would like a decent meal,
He went and knocked on Grandma's door.
When Grandma opened it, she saw
The sharp white teeth, the horrid grin,
And Wolfie said, "May I come in?"
Poor Grandmamma was terrified,
"He's going to eat me up!" she cried.
And she was absolutely right.
He ate her up in one big bite.

But Grandmamma was small and tough,
And Wolfie wailed, "That's not enough!
I haven't yet begun to feel
That I have had a decent meal!"
He ran around the kitchen yelping,
"I've *got* to have a second helping!"
Then added with a frightful leer,
"I'm therefore going to wait right here
Till Little Miss Red Riding Hood
Comes home from walking in the wood."
He quickly put on Grandma's clothes
(Of course he hadn't eaten those).
He dressed himself in coat and hat.
He put on shoes and after that
He even brushed and curled his hair,
Then sat himself in Grandma's chair.

In came the little girl in red.
She stopped. She stared. And then she said,

"What great big ears you have, Grandma."
"All the better to hear you with," the Wolf replied.
"What great big eyes you have, Grandma,"
  said Little Red Riding Hood.
"All the better to see you with," the Wolf replied.

He sat there watching her and smiled.
He thought, I'm going to eat this child.
Compared with her old Grandmamma
She's going to taste like caviar.

Then Little Red Riding Hood said, *"But Grandma,*
  what a lovely great big furry coat you have on."

106

"That's wrong!" cried Wolf. "Have you forgot
To tell me what BIG TEETH I've got?
Ah well, no matter what you say,
I'm going to eat you anyway."
The small girl smiles. One eyelid flickers.
She whips a pistol from her knickers.
She aims it at the creature's head

And *bang bang bang*, she shoots him dead.
A few weeks later, in the wood,
I came across Miss Riding Hood.
But what a change! No cloak of red,
No silly hood upon her head.
She said, "Hello, and do please note
My lovely furry WOLFSKIN COAT."

The Three Little Pigs

from REVOLTING RHYMES

THE animal I really dig
 Above all others is the pig.
Pigs are noble. Pigs are clever,
Pigs are courteous. However,
Now and then, to break this rule,
One meets a pig who is a fool.
What, for example, would you say
If strolling through the woods one day,
Right there in front of you you saw
A pig who'd built his house of STRAW?
The Wolf who saw it licked his lips,
And said, "That pig has had his chips."

"Little pig, little pig, let me come in!"
"No, no, by the hairs on my chinny-chin-chin!"
"Then I'll huff and I'll puff and I'll blow your house in!"

The little pig began to pray,
But Wolfie blew his house away.
He shouted, "Bacon, pork and ham!
Oh, what a lucky Wolf I am!"
And though he ate the pig quite fast,
He carefully kept the tail till last.
Wolf wandered on, a trifle bloated.
Surprise, surprise, for soon he noted
Another little house for pigs,
And this one had been built of TWIGS!

"Little pig, little pig, let me come in!"
"No, no, by the hairs on my chinny-chin-chin!"
"Then I'll huff and I'll puff and I'll blow your house in!"

The Wolf said, "Okay, here we go!"
He then began to blow and blow.
The little pig began to squeal.
He cried, "Oh Wolf, you've had *one* meal!
Why can't we talk and make a deal?"
The Wolf replied, "Not on your nelly!"
And soon the pig was in his belly.
"Two juicy little pigs!" Wolf cried,
"But still I am not satisfied!
I know full well my Tummy's bulging,
But oh, how I adore indulging."
So creeping quietly as a mouse,
The wolf approached another house,
A house which also had inside
A little piggy trying to hide.
But this one, Piggy Number Three,
Was bright and brainy as could be.

No straw for him, no twigs or sticks.
This pig had built his house of BRICKS.
"You'll not get *me!*" the Piggy cried.
"I'll blow you down!" the Wolf replied.
"You'll need," Pig said, "a lot of puff,
And I don't think you've got enough."
Wolf huffed and puffed and blew and blew.
The house stayed up as good as new.
"If I can't blow it *down*," Wolf said,
"I'll have to blow it *up* instead.
I'll come back in the dead of night
And blow it up with dynamite!"
Pig cried, "You brute! I might have known!"
Then, picking up the telephone,
He dialled as quickly as he could
The number of Red Riding Hood.

"Hello," she said. "Who's speaking? *Who?*
Oh, hello Piggy, how d'you do?"
Pig cried, "I need your help, Miss Hood!
Oh help me, please! D'you think you could?"
"I'll try, of course," Miss Hood replied.
"What's on your mind?"… "*A Wolf!*" Pig cried.
"I know you've dealt with wolves before,
And now I've got one at my door!"
"My darling Pig," she said, "my sweet,
That's something *really* up my street.
I've just begun to wash my hair.
But when it's dry, I'll be right there."

A short while later, through the wood,
Came striding brave Miss Riding Hood.
The Wolf stood there, his eyes ablaze
And yellowish, like mayonnaise.
His teeth were sharp, his gums were raw,
And spit was dripping from his jaw.
Once more the maiden's eyelid flickers.
She draws the pistol from her knickers.
Once more, she hits the vital spot,
And kills him with a single shot.
Pig, peeping through the window, stood
And yelled, "Well done, Miss Riding Hood!"

Ah, Piglet, you must never trust
Young ladies from the upper crust.
For now, Miss Riding Hood, one notes,
Not only has *two* wolfskin coats,
But when she goes from place to place,
She has a PIGSKIN TRAVELLING CASE.

Moles

from MY YEAR

I love seeing molehills because they tell me that only a few inches below the surface some charming and harmless little fellow is living his own private busy life scurrying up and down his tunnels hunting for food... Do you know anything about moles? They are remarkable animals. They are shy and gentle and their fur coats are softer than velvet. They are so shy that you will seldom see one on the surface. Each mole has his or her own private network of tunnels which are not much more than five or six inches below the surface, and the front paws of the little creature are shaped like huge spades to make digging easy. The molehills that you see are not of course their houses. They are simply piles of loose soil that a mole has pushed up out of the way because, after all, if you are digging an underground tunnel you have to put the excavated soil somewhere.

A mole can dig about three feet of tunnel in an hour and he usually owns about one hundred yards of his own private tunnelling which no other moles go into. All moles prefer to live solitary lives, each one trotting up and down his own network of tunnels day and night, searching for food. His food consists of worms, leatherjackets, centipedes and beetle grubs, and the fantastic thing is that he actually has to eat *one half of his own bodyweight* of these tiny delicacies every single day in order to stay alive! No wonder he is a busy fellow. Just imagine how much food you would have to eat to consume half your own body weight! Fifty hamburgers, one hundred loaves of bread and a bucketful of Mars Bars *and* the rest of it each and every day. It makes one quite ill to think about it.

The mole is not a very attentive husband. When mating time arrives, he simply burrows into the tunnel of a female neighbour, and after he has mated with her, he returns once again to his own territory, leaving his wife to give birth and rear the babies on her own. Mind you, we all know a few human males who behave in more or less the same way but let's not get into that.

Being a gardener myself, I have always regarded the mole as a friend because he eats all the horrid centipedes and leatherjackets and other pests that damage our flowers and vegetables. A lot of country people wage savage war against the poor moles because of the molehills they make, and they kill them in all sorts of cruel ways, using traps or poison or even poisonous gas. But I will tell you a very simple method of persuading a mole to leave your garden or your field. Moles cannot stand noise of any sort. It makes them even more nervous than they already are. So when I see a molehill in the garden, I get an empty wine bottle (plenty of those around our house) and I bury it in the ground close to the molehill, leaving only the neck of the bottle sticking up. Now when the wind blows across the open top of the bottle it makes a soft humming sound. This goes on all day and night because there is almost always some sort of a breeze blowing. The constant noise just above his tunnel drives the mole half crazy and he very soon packs up and goes somewhere else. This is not a joke. It really works. I have done it often.

The Lion

from DIRTY BEASTS

THE lion just adores to eat
A lot of red and tender meat
And if you ask the lion what
Is much the tenderest of the lot,
He will not say a roast of lamb
Or curried beef or devilled ham
Or crispy pork or corned beef hash
Or sausages or mutton mash.
Then could it be a big plump hen?
He answers no. What is it, then?
Oh, lion dear, could I not make
You happy with a lovely steak?
Could I entice you from your lair
With rabbit pie or roasted hare?
The lion smiled and shook his head.
He came up very close and said,
"The meat I am about to chew
Is neither steak nor chops. IT'S YOU."

Autograph _Roald Dahl_

Birthday 13 September, 1916

Colour of eyes Blue-grey

Colour of hair Greyish

Special virtue Never satisfied with what I've done.

Special vice Drinking

Favourite colour Yellow

Favourite food Caviar

Favourite music Beethoven

Favourite personality My wife and children

Favourite sound Piano

Favourite TV programme News

Favourite smell Bacon frying

Favourite book when young "Mr. Midshipman Easy"

If I wasn't an author I'd like to be A Doctor

My most frightening moment In a Hurricane, 1941, RAF

My funniest moment Being born

Motto

My candle burns at both ends
It will not last the night
But ah my foes and oh my friends
It gives a lovely light.

Tortoises

AUTHOR'S NOTE *from* ESIO TROT

SOME years ago, when my own children were small, we usually kept a tortoise or two in the garden. In those days, a pet tortoise was a common sight crawling about on the family lawn or in the back yard. You could buy them quite cheaply in any pet-shop and they were probably the least troublesome of all childhood pets, and quite harmless.

Tortoises used to be brought into England by the thousand, packed in crates, and they came mostly from North Africa. But not many years ago a law was passed that made it illegal to bring any tortoises into the country. This was not done to protect us. The little tortoise was not a danger to anybody. It was done purely out of kindness to the tortoise itself. You see, the traders who brought them in used to cram hundreds of them tightly into the packing-crates without food or water and in such horrible conditions that a great many of them always died on the sea-journey over. So rather than allow this cruelty to go on, the Government stopped the whole business.

The things you are going to read about in this story all happened in the days when anyone could go out and buy a nice little tortoise from a pet-shop.

Esio Trot

Mr Hoppy lived in a small flat high up in a tall concrete building. He lived alone. He had always been a lonely man and now that he was retired from work he was more lonely than ever.

There were two loves in Mr Hoppy's life. One was the flowers he grew on his balcony. They grew in pots and tubs and baskets, and in summer the little balcony became a riot of colour.

Mr Hoppy's second love was a secret he kept entirely to himself.

The balcony immediately below Mr Hoppy's jutted out a good bit further from the building than his own, so Mr Hoppy always had a fine view of what was going on down there. This balcony belonged to an attractive middle-aged lady called Mrs Silver. Mrs Silver was a widow who also lived alone. And although she didn't know it, it was she who was the object of Mr Hoppy's secret love. He had loved her from his balcony for many years, but he was a very shy man and he had never been able to bring himself to give her even the smallest hint of his love.

Every morning, Mr Hoppy and Mrs Silver exchanged polite conversation, the one looking down from above, the other looking up, but that was as far as it ever went. The distance between their balconies might not have been more than a few yards, but to Mr Hoppy it seemed like a million miles. He longed to invite Mrs Silver up for a cup of tea and a biscuit, but every time he was about to form the words on his lips, his courage failed him. As I said, he was a very very shy man.

Oh, if only, he kept telling himself, if only he could do something tremendous like saving her life or rescuing her from a gang of armed thugs, if only he could perform some great feat that would make him a hero in her eyes. If only. . .

The trouble with Mrs Silver was that she gave all her love to somebody else, and that somebody was a small tortoise called Alfie. Every day, when Mr Hoppy looked over his balcony and saw Mrs Silver whispering endearments to Alfie and stroking his shell, he felt absurdly jealous. He wouldn't even have minded becoming a tortoise himself if it meant Mrs Silver stroking his shell each morning and whispering endearments to him.

Alfie had been with Mrs Silver for years and he lived on her balcony summer and winter. Planks had been placed around the sides of the balcony so that Alfie could walk about without toppling over the edge, and in one corner there was a little house into which Alfie would crawl every night to keep warm.

When the colder weather came along in November, Mrs Silver would fill Alfie's house with dry hay, and the tortoise would crawl in there and bury himself deep under the hay and go to sleep for months on end without food or water. This is called hibernating.

In early spring, when Alfie felt the warmer weather through his shell, he would wake up and crawl very slowly out of his house on to the balcony. And Mrs Silver would clap her hands with joy and cry out, "Welcome back, my darling one! Oh, how I have missed you!"

It was at times like these that Mr Hoppy wished more than ever that he could change places with Alfie and become a tortoise.

Now we come to a certain bright morning in May when something happened that changed and indeed electrified Mr Hoppy's life. He was leaning over his balcony-rail watching Mrs Silver serving Alfie his breakfast.

"Here's the heart of the lettuce for you, my lovely," she was saying. "And here's a slice of fresh tomato and a piece of crispy celery."

"Good morning, Mrs Silver," Mr Hoppy said. "Alfie's looking well this morning."

"Isn't he gorgeous!" Mrs Silver said, looking up and beaming at him.

"Absolutely gorgeous," Mr Hoppy said, not meaning it. And now, as he looked down at Mrs Silver's smiling face gazing up into his own, he thought for the thousandth time how pretty she was, how sweet and gentle and full of kindness, and his heart ached with love.

"I do so wish he would *grow* a little faster," Mrs Silver was saying. "Every spring, when he wakes up from his winter sleep, I weigh him on the kitchen scales. And do you know that in all the eleven years I've had him he's not gained more than *three ounces!* That's almost *nothing!*"

"What does he weigh now?" Mr Hoppy asked her.

"Just thirteen ounces," Mrs Silver answered. "About as much as a grapefruit."

"Yes, well, tortoises are very slow growers," Mr Hoppy said solemnly. "But they can live for a hundred years."

"I know that," Mrs Silver said. "But I do so wish he would grow just a little bit bigger. He's such a tiny wee fellow."

"He seems just fine as he is," Mr Hoppy said.

"No, he's *not* just fine!" Mrs Silver cried. "Try to think how miserable it must make him feel to be so titchy! Everyone wants to grow up."

"You really *would* love him to grow bigger, wouldn't you?" Mr Hoppy said, and even as he said it his mind suddenly went *click* and an amazing idea came rushing into his head.

"Of course I would!" Mrs Silver cried. "I'd give *anything* to make it happen! Why, I've seen pictures of giant tortoises that are so huge people can ride on their backs! If Alfie were to see those he'd turn green with envy!"

Mr Hoppy's mind was spinning like a fly-wheel. Here, surely, was his big chance! Grab it, he told himself. Grab it quick!

"Mrs Silver," he said. "I do actually happen to know how to make tortoises grow faster, if that's really what you want."

"You do?" she cried. "Oh, please tell me! Am I feeding him the wrong things?"

"I worked in North Africa once," Mr Hoppy said. "That's where all these tortoises in England come from, and a bedouin tribesman told me the secret."

"Tell me!" cried Mrs Silver. "I beg you to tell me, Mr Hoppy! I'll be your slave for life."

When he heard the words *your slave for life*, a little shiver of excitement swept through Mr Hoppy. "Wait there," he said. "I'll have to go in and write something down for you."

In a couple of minutes Mr Hoppy was back on the balcony with a

sheet of paper in his hand. "I'm going to lower it to you on a bit of string," he said, "or it might blow away. Here it comes."

Mrs Silver caught the paper and held it up in front of her. This is what she read:

ESIO TROT, ESIO TROT,
TEG REGGIB REGGIB!
EMOC NO, ESIO TROT,
WORG PU, FFUP PU, TOOHS PU!
GNIRPS PU, WOLB PU, LLEWS PU!
EGROG! ELZZUG! FFUTS! PLUG!
TUP NO TAF, ESIO TROT, TUP NO TAF!
TEG NO, TEG NO! ELBBOG DOOF!

"What *does* it mean?" she asked. "Is it another language?"

"It's tortoise language," Mr Hoppy said. "Tortoises are very backward creatures. Therefore they can only understand words that are written backwards. That's obvious, isn't it?"

"I suppose so," Mrs Silver said, bewildered.

"Esio trot is simply tortoise spelled backwards," Mr Hoppy said. "Look at it."

"So it is," Mrs Silver said.

"The other words are spelled backwards, too," Mr Hoppy said. "If you turn them round into human language, they simply say:

TORTOISE, TORTOISE,
GET BIGGER BIGGER!
COME ON, TORTOISE,
GROW UP, PUFF UP, SHOOT UP!
SPRING UP, BLOW UP, SWELL UP!
GORGE! GUZZLE! STUFF! GULP!
PUT ON FAT, TORTOISE, PUT ON FAT!
GET ON, GET ON! GOBBLE FOOD!"

Mrs Silver examined the magic words on the paper more closely. "I guess you're right," she said. "How clever. But there's an awful lot of poos in it. Are they something special?"

"Poo is a very strong word in any language," Mr Hoppy said, "especially with tortoises. Now what you have to do, Mrs Silver, is hold Alfie up to your face and whisper these words to him three times a day, morning, noon and night. Let me hear you practise them."

Very slowly and stumbling a little over the strange words, Mrs Silver read the whole message out loud in tortoise language.

"Not bad," Mr Hoppy said. "But try to get a little more expression into it when you say it to Alfie. If you do it properly I'll bet you anything you like that in a few months' time he'll be twice as big as he is now."

"I'll try it," Mrs Silver said. "I'll try anything. Of course I will. But I can't believe it'll work."

"You wait and see," Mr Hoppy said, smiling at her.

Back in his flat, Mr Hoppy was simply quivering all over with excitement. *Your slave for life*, he kept repeating to himself. What bliss!

But there was a lot of work to be done before that happened.

The only furniture in Mr Hoppy's small living-room was a table and two chairs. These he moved into his bedroom. Then he went out and bought a sheet of thick canvas and spread it over the entire living-room floor to protect his carpet.

Next, he got out the telephone-book and wrote down the address of every pet-shop in the city. There were fourteen of them altogether.

It took him two days to visit each pet-shop and choose his tortoises. He wanted a great many, at least one hundred, perhaps more. And he had to choose them very carefully.

To you and me there is not much difference between one tortoise and another. They differ only in their size and in the colour of their shells. Alfie had a darkish shell, so Mr Hoppy chose only the darker-shelled tortoises for his great collection.

Size, of course, was everything. Mr Hoppy chose all sorts of different sizes, some weighing only slightly more than Alfie's thirteen ounces, others a great deal more, but he didn't want any that weighed less.

"Feed them cabbage leaves," the pet-shop owners told him. "That's all they'll need. And a bowl of water."

When he had finished, Mr Hoppy, in his enthusiasm, had bought no less than one hundred and forty tortoises and he carried them home in baskets, ten or fifteen at a time. He had to make a lot of trips and he was quite exhausted at the end of it all, but it was worth it. Boy, was it worth it! And what an amazing sight his living-room was when they were all in there together! The floor was swarming with tortoises of different sizes, some walking slowly about and exploring, some munching cabbage leaves, others drinking water from a big shallow

dish. They made just the faintest rustling sound as they moved over the canvas sheet, but that was all. Mr Hoppy had to pick his way carefully on his toes between this moving sea of brown shells whenever he walked across the room. But enough of that. He must get on with the job.

Before he retired Mr Hoppy had been a mechanic in a bus-garage. And now he went back to his old place of work and asked his mates if he might use his old bench for an hour or two.

What he had to do now was to make something that would reach down from his own balcony to Mrs Silver's balcony and pick up a tortoise. This was not difficult for a mechanic like Mr Hoppy.

First he made two metal claws or fingers, and these he attached to

the end of a long metal tube. He ran two stiff wires down inside the tube and connected them to the metal claws in such a way that when you pulled the wires, the claws closed, and when you pushed them, the claws opened. The wires were joined to a handle at the other end of the tube. It was all very simple.

Mr Hoppy was ready to begin.

Mrs Silver had a part-time job. She worked from noon until five o'clock every weekday afternoon in a shop that sold newspapers and sweets. That made things a lot easier for Mr Hoppy.

So on that first exciting afternoon, after he had made sure that Mrs Silver had gone to work, Mr Hoppy went out on to his balcony armed with his long metal pole. He called this his tortoise-catcher. He leaned over the balcony railings and lowered the pole down on to Mrs Silver's balcony below. Alfie was basking in the pale sunlight over to one side.

"Hello Alfie," Mr Hoppy said. "You are about to go for a little ride."

He wiggled the tortoise-catcher till it was right above Alfie. He pushed the hand-lever so that the claws opened wide. Then he lowered the two claws neatly over Alfie's shell and pulled the lever. The claws closed tightly over the shell like two fingers of a hand. He hauled Alfie up on to his own balcony. It was easy.

Mr Hoppy weighed Alfie on his own kitchen scales just to make sure that Mrs Silver's figure of thirteen ounces was correct. It was.

Now, holding Alfie in one hand, he picked his way carefully through his huge collection of tortoises to find one that first of all had the same colour shell as Alfie's and secondly weighed *exactly two ounces more*.

Two ounces is not much. It is less than a smallish hen's egg weighs. But you see, the important thing in Mr Hoppy's plan was to make sure that the new tortoise was bigger than Alfie but only a *tiny bit* bigger. The difference had to be so small that Mrs Silver wouldn't notice it.

From his vast collection, it was not difficult for Mr Hoppy to find just the tortoise he wanted. He wanted one that weighed fifteen ounces exactly on his kitchen scales, no more and no less. When he had got it, he put it on the kitchen table beside Alfie, and even he could hardly tell that one was bigger than the other. But it *was* bigger. It was bigger by two ounces. This was Tortoise Number 2.

Mr Hoppy took Tortoise Number 2 out on to the balcony and gripped it in the claws of his tortoise-catcher. Then he lowered it on to Mrs Silver's balcony, right beside a nice fresh lettuce leaf.

Tortoise Number 2 had never eaten tender juicy lettuce leaves before. It had only had thick old cabbage leaves. It loved the lettuce and started chomping away at it with great gusto.

There followed a rather nervous two hours' wait for Mrs Silver to return from work.

Would she see any difference between the new tortoise and Alfie? It was going to be a tense moment.

Out on to her balcony swept Mrs Silver.

"Alfie, my darling!" she cried out. "Mummy's back! Have you missed me?"

Mr Hoppy, peering over his railing, but well hidden between two huge potted plants, held his breath.

The new tortoise was still chomping away at the lettuce.

"My my, Alfie, you do seem hungry today," Mrs Silver was saying. "It must be Mr Hoppy's magic words I've been whispering to you."

Mr Hoppy watched as Mrs Silver picked the tortoise up and stroked his shell. Then she fished Mr Hoppy's piece of paper out of her pocket, and holding the tortoise very close to her face, she whispered, reading from the paper:

"ESIO TROT, ESIO TROT,
TEG REGGIB REGGIB!
EMOC NO, ESIO TROT,
WORG PU, FFUP PU, TOOHS PU!
GNIRPS PU, WOLB PU, LLEWS PU!
EGROG! ELZZUG! FFUTS! PLUG!
TUP NO TAF, ESIO TROT, TUP NO TAF!
TEG NO, TEG NO! ELBBOG DOOF!"

Mr Hoppy popped his head out of the foliage and called out, "Good evening, Mrs Silver. How is Alfie tonight?"

"Oh, he's lovely," Mrs Silver said, looking up and beaming. "And he's developing such an appetite! I've never seen him eat like this before! It must be the magic words."

"You never know," Mr Hoppy said darkly. "You never know."

Mr Hoppy waited seven whole days before he made his next move.

On the afternoon of the seventh day, when Mrs Silver was at work, he lifted Tortoise Number 2 from the balcony below and brought it into his living-room. Number 2 had weighed exactly *fifteen* ounces. He must now find one that weighed exactly seventeen ounces, two ounces more.

From his enormous collection, he easily found a seventeen-ounce tortoise and once again he made sure the shells matched in colour. Then he lowered Tortoise Number 3 on to Mrs Silver's balcony.

As you will have guessed by now, Mr Hoppy's secret was a very simple one. If a creature grows slowly enough – I mean very very slowly indeed – then you'll never notice that it has grown at all, especially if you see it every day.

It's the same with children. They are actually growing taller every week, but their mothers never notice it until they grow out of their clothes.

Slowly does it, Mr Hoppy told himself. Don't hurry it.

So this is how things went over the next eight weeks.

In the beginning

ALFIE (weight 13 ounces)

End of first week

TORTOISE NO. 2 (weight 15 ounces)

End of second week

TORTOISE NO. 3 (weight 17 ounces)

End of third week

TORTOISE NO. 4 (weight 19 ounces)

End of fourth week

TORTOISE NO. 5 (weight 21 ounces)

End of fifth week

TORTOISE NO. 6 (weight 23 ounces)

End of sixth week

TORTOISE NO. 7 (weight 25 ounces)

End of seventh week

TORTOISE NO. 8 (weight 27 ounces)

Alfie's weight was thirteen ounces. Tortoise Number 8 was twenty-seven ounces. Very slowly, over seven weeks, Mrs Silver's pet had more than doubled in size and the good lady hadn't noticed a thing.

Even to Mr Hoppy, peering down over his railing, Tortoise Number 8 looked pretty big. It was amazing that Mrs Silver had hardly noticed anything at all during the great operation. Only once had she looked up and said, "You know, Mr Hoppy, I do believe he's getting a bit bigger. What do you think?"

"I can't see a lot of difference myself," Mr Hoppy had answered casually.

But now perhaps it was time to call a halt, and that evening Mr Hoppy was just about to go out and suggest to Mrs Silver that she ought to weigh Alfie when a startled cry from the balcony below brought him outside fast.

"Look!" Mrs Silver was shouting. "Alfie's too big to get through the door of his little house! He must have grown enormously!"

"Weigh him," Mr Hoppy ordered. "Take him in and weigh him quick."

Mrs Silver did just that, and in half a minute she was back holding the tortoise in both hands and waving it above her head and shouting, "Guess what, Mr Hoppy! Guess what! He weighs twenty-seven ounces! He's twice as big as he was before! Oh you darling!" she cried, stroking the tortoise. "Oh, you great big wonderful boy! Just look what clever Mr Hoppy has done for you!"

Mr Hoppy suddenly felt very brave. "Mrs Silver," he said. "Do you think I could pop down to your balcony and hold Alfie myself?"

"Why, of course you can!" Mrs Silver cried. "Come down at once."

Mr Hoppy rushed down the stairs and Mrs Silver opened the door to him. Together they went out on to the balcony. "Just look at him!" Mrs Silver said proudly. "Isn't he grand!"

"He's a big good-sized tortoise now," Mr Hoppy said.

"And *you* did it!" Mrs Silver cried. "You're a miracle-man, you are indeed!

"But what *am* I going to do about his house?" Mrs Silver said. "He must have a house to go into at night, but now he can't get through the door."

They were standing on the balcony looking at the tortoise who was trying to push his way into his house. But he was too big.

"I shall have to enlarge the door," Mrs Silver said.

"Don't do that," Mr Hoppy said. "You mustn't go chopping up such a pretty little house. After all, he only needs to be just a tiny bit smaller and he could get in easily."

"How can he possibly get smaller?" Mrs Silver asked.

"That's simple," Mr Hoppy said. "Change the magic words. Instead of telling him to get bigger and bigger, tell him to get a bit smaller. But in tortoise language of course."

"Will that work?"

"Of course it'll work."

"Tell me exactly what I have to say, Mr Hoppy."

Mr Hoppy got out a piece of paper and a pencil and wrote:

ESIO TROT, ESIO TROT,
TEG A TIB RELLAMS, A TIB RELLAMS.

"That'll do it, Mrs Silver," he said, handing her the paper.

"I don't mind trying it," Mrs Silver said. "But look here, I wouldn't want him to get titchy small all over again, Mr Hoppy."

"He won't, dear lady, he won't," Mr Hoppy said. "Say it only tonight and tomorrow morning and then see what happens. We might be lucky."

"If it works," Mrs Silver said, touching him softly on the arm, "then you are the cleverest man alive."

The next afternoon, as soon as Mrs Silver had gone to work, Mr Hoppy lifted the tortoise up from her balcony and carried it inside. All he had to do now was to find one that was a shade smaller, so that it would just go through the door of the little house.

He chose one and lowered it down with his tortoise-catcher.

Then, still gripping the tortoise, he tested it to see if it would go through the door. It wouldn't.

He chose another. Again he tested it. This one went through nicely. Good. He placed the tortoise in the middle of the balcony beside a nice piece of lettuce and went inside to await Mrs Silver's homecoming.

That evening, Mr Hoppy was watering his plants on the balcony when suddenly he heard Mrs Silver's shouts from below, shrill with excitement.

"Mr Hoppy! Mr Hoppy! Where are you?" she was shouting. "Just look at this!"

Mr Hoppy popped his head over the railing and said, "What's up?"

"Oh, Mr Hoppy, it's worked!" she was crying. "Your magic words have worked again on Alfie! He can now get through the door of his little house! It's a miracle!"

"Can I come down and look?" Mr Hoppy shouted back.

"Come down at once, my dear man!" Mrs Silver answered. "Come down and see the wonders you have worked upon my darling Alfie!"

Mr Hoppy turned and ran from the balcony into the living-room, jumping on tip-toe like a ballet-dancer between the sea of tortoises that covered the floor. He flung open his front door and flew down the stairs two at a time with the love-songs of a thousand cupids ringing in his ears. *This is it!* he whispered to himself under his breath. *The greatest moment of my life is coming up now! I mustn't bish it. I mustn't bosh it! I must keep very calm!* When he was three-quarters way down the stairs he caught sight of Mrs Silver already standing at the open door waiting to welcome him with a huge smile on her face. She flung her arms around him and cried out, "You really are the most wonderful man I've ever met! You can do anything! Come in at once and let me make you a cup of tea. That's the very least you deserve!"

Seated in a comfortable armchair in Mrs Silver's parlour, sipping his tea, Mr Hoppy was all of a twitter. He looked at the lovely lady sitting opposite him and smiled at her. She smiled right back at him.

That smile of hers, so warm and friendly, suddenly gave him the courage he needed, and he said, "Mrs Silver, please will you marry me?"

"Why, Mr Hoppy!" she cried. "I didn't think you'd ever get round to asking me! Of course I'll marry you!"

Mr Hoppy got rid of his teacup and the two of them stood up and embraced warmly in the middle of the room.

"It's all due to Alfie," Mrs Silver said, slightly breathless.

"Good old Alfie," Mr Hoppy said. "We'll keep him for ever."

The next afternoon, Mr Hoppy took all his other tortoises back to the pet-shops and said they could have them for nothing. Then he cleaned up his living-room, leaving not a leaf of cabbage nor a trace of tortoise.

A few weeks later, Mrs Silver became Mrs Hoppy and the two of them lived very happily ever after.

P.S. I expect you are wondering what happened to little Alfie, the first of them all. Well, he was bought a week later from one of the pet-shops by a small girl called Roberta Squibb, and he settled down in Roberta's garden. Every day she fed him lettuce and tomato slices and crispy celery, and in the winters he hibernated in a box of dried leaves in the tool-shed.

That was a long time ago. Roberta has grown up and is now married and has two children of her own. She lives in another house, but Alfie is still with her, still the much-loved family pet, and Roberta reckons that by now he must be about thirty years old. It has taken him all that time to grow to twice the size he was when Mrs Silver had him. But he made it in the end.

ROALD DAHL LOVED INVENTING THINGS.
HE INVENTED THE TORTOISE-CATCHER — WHICH
HE USED FOR PICKING UP PAPER FROM
THE FLOOR.

Hickety, Pickety

HICKETY, pickety, my black hen,
She lays eggs for gentlemen.
Not for ladies? That's absurd!
What a chauvinistic bird.

The Crocodile

from DIRTY BEASTS

No animal is half so vile
As Crocky-Wock the crocodile.
On Saturdays he likes to crunch
Six juicy children for his lunch,
And he especially enjoys
Just three of each, three girls, three boys.
He smears the boys (to make them hot)
With mustard from the mustard pot.
But mustard doesn't go with girls,
It tastes all wrong with plaits and curls.
With them, what goes extremely well
Is butterscotch and caramel.

It's such a super marvellous treat
When boys are hot and girls are sweet.
At least that's Crocky's point of view.
He ought to know. He's had a few.
That's all for now. It's time for bed
Lie down and rest your sleepy head…
Ssh! *Listen!* What is that I hear
Gallumphing softly up the stair?
Go lock the door and fetch my gun!
Go on, child, hurry! Quickly, run!
No, stop! Stand back! He's coming in!
Oh, look, that greasy greenish skin!
The shining teeth, the greedy smile!
It's CROCKY-WOCK, THE CROCODILE!

*Did any of you ever meet
A lady called Miss Violet Treat?
She lived in Rigby Hall, so grand,
With lots of servants, lots of land.
Oh, she was rich and she was fine
With cars galore and heaps of wine!
Now with the rich there is a rule,
They always build a swimming pool.
They also like (don't ask me why)
To go into the shops and buy
Most curious and expensive pets,
Like chimpanzees and marmosets.
Miss Treat did all of this and more.
She dug up all the library floor
And built a pool of gold and green,
No finer pool was ever seen.

Into this pool she put (don't smile)
A tame and friendly crocodile,
And every day she used to swim
With Crocky-Wock and play with him…

*These additional lines of 'The Crocodile' were among
Roald Dahl's papers and are previously unpublished.

147

PART TWO

Magic

Those who don't believe in magic will never find it

WE have a pair of swallows that have built their nest in exactly the same place on a wooden beam in the tool shed for the past six years, and it is amazing to me how they fly off thousands of miles to North Africa in the autumn with their young and then six months later they find their way back to the same tool shed at Gipsy House, Great Missenden, Bucks. It's a miracle and the brainiest ornithologists in the world still cannot explain how they do it.

from MY YEAR

The BFG

AN EXTRACT

The Marvellous Ears

BACK in the cave, the Big Friendly Giant sat Sophie down once again on the enormous table. "Is you quite snuggly there in your nightie?" he asked. "You isn't fridgy cold?"

"I'm fine," Sophie said.

"I cannot help thinking," said the BFG, "about your poor mother and father. By now they must be jipping and skumping all over the house shouting 'Hello hello where is Sophie gone?'"

"I don't have a mother and father," Sophie said. "They both died when I was a baby."

"Oh, you poor little scrumplet!" cried the BFG. "Is you not missing them very badly?"

"Not really," Sophie said, "because I never knew them."

"You is making me sad," the BFG said, rubbing his eyes.

"Don't be sad," Sophie said. "No one is going to be worrying too much about me. That place you took me from was the village orphanage. We are all orphans in there."

"You is a norphan?"

"Yes."

"How many is there in there?"

"Ten of us," Sophie said. "All little girls."

"Was you happy there?" the BFG asked.

"I hated it," Sophie said. "The woman who ran it was called Mrs Clonkers and if she caught you breaking any of the rules, like getting out of bed at night or not folding up your clothes, you got punished."

"How is you getting punished?"

"She locked us in the dark cellar for a day and a night without anything to eat or drink."

"The rotten old rotrasper!" cried the BFG.

"It was horrid," Sophie said. "We used to dread it. There were rats down there. We could hear them creeping about."

"The filthy old fizzwiggler!" shouted the BFG. "That is the horridest thing I is hearing for years! You is making me sadder than ever!" All at once, a huge tear that would have filled a bucket rolled down one of the BFG's cheeks and fell with a splash on the floor. It made quite a puddle.

Sophie watched with astonishment. What a strange and moody creature this is, she thought. One moment he is telling me my head is full of squashed flies and the next moment his heart is melting for me because Mrs Clonkers locks us in the cellar.

"The thing that worries *me*," Sophie said, "is having to stay in this dreadful place for the rest of my life. The orphanage was pretty awful, but I wouldn't have been there for ever, would I?"

"All is my fault," the BFG said. "I is the one who kidsnatched you." Yet another enormous tear welled from his eye and splashed on to the floor.

"Now I come to think of it, I won't actually be here all that long," Sophie said.

"I is afraid you will," the BFG said.

"No, I won't," Sophie said. "Those brutes out there are bound to catch me sooner or later and have me for tea."

"I is *never* letting that happen," the BFG said.

For a few moments the cave was silent. Then Sophie said, "May I ask you a question?"

The BFG wiped the tears from his eyes with the back of his hand and gave Sophie a long thoughtful stare. "Shoot away," he said.

"Would you please tell me what you were doing in our village last night? Why were you poking that long trumpet thing into the Goochey children's bedroom and then blowing through it?"

"Ah-ha!" cried the BFG, sitting up suddenly in his chair. "Now we is getting nosier than a parker!"

"And the suitcase you were carrying," Sophie said. "What on earth was *that* all about?"

The BFG stared suspiciously at the small girl sitting cross-legged on the table.

"You is asking me to tell you whoppsy big secrets," he said. "Secrets that nobody is ever hearing before."

"I won't tell a soul," Sophie said. "I swear it. How could I anyway? I am stuck here for the rest of my life."

"You could be telling the other giants."

"No, I couldn't," Sophie said. "You told me they would eat me up the moment they saw me."

"And so they would," said the BFG. "You is a human bean and human beans is like strawbunkles and cream to those giants."

"If they are going to eat me the moment they see me, then I wouldn't have time to tell them anything, would I?" Sophie said.

"You wouldn't," said the BFG.

"Then why did you say I might?"

"Because I is brimful of buzzburgers," the BFG said. "If you listen to everything I am saying you will be getting earache."

"Please tell me what you were doing in our village," Sophie said. "I promise you can trust me."

"Would you teach me how to make an elefunt?" the BFG asked.

"What *do* you mean?" Sophie said.

"I would dearly love to have an elefunt to ride on," the BFG said dreamily. "I would so much love to have a jumbly big elefunt and go riding through green forests picking peachy fruits off the trees all day long. This is a sizzling-hot muckfrumping country we is living in. Nothing grows in it except snozzcumbers. I would love to go somewhere else and pick peachy fruits in the early morning from the back of an elefunt."

Sophie was quite moved by this curious statement.

"Perhaps one day we will get you an elephant," she said. "And peachy fruits as well. Now tell me what you were doing in our village."

"If you is really wanting to know what I am doing in your village," the BFG said, "I is blowing a dream into the bedroom of those children."

"*Blowing a dream?*" Sophie said. "What *do* you mean?"

"I is a dream-blowing giant," the BFG said. "When all the other giants is galloping off every what way and which to swollop human beans, I is scuddling away to other places to blow dreams into the bedrooms of sleeping children. Nice dreams. Lovely golden dreams. Dreams that is giving the dreamers a happy time."

"Now hang on a minute," Sophie said. "Where do you get these dreams?"

"I collect them," the BFG said, waving an arm towards all the rows and rows of bottles on the shelves. "I has billions of them."

"You can't *collect* a dream," Sophie said. "A dream isn't something you can catch hold of."

"You is never going to understand about it," the BFG said. "That is why I is not wishing to tell you."

"Oh, please tell me!" Sophie said. "I *will* understand! Go on! Tell me how you collect dreams! Tell me everything!"

The BFG settled himself comfortably in his chair and crossed his legs. "Dreams," he said, "is very mysterious things. They is floating around in the air like little wispy-misty bubbles. And all the time they is searching for sleeping people."

"Can you see them?" Sophie asked.

"Never at first."

"Then how do you catch them if you can't see them?" Sophie asked.

"Ah-ha," said the BFG. "Now we is getting on to the dark and dusky secrets."

"I won't tell a soul."

"I is trusting you," the BFG said. He closed his eyes and sat quite still for a moment, while Sophie waited.

"A dream," he said, "as it goes whiffling through the night air, is making a tiny little buzzing-humming noise. But this little buzzy-hum is so silvery soft, it is impossible for a human bean to be hearing it."

"Can *you* hear it?" Sophie asked.

The BFG pointed up at his enormous truck-wheel ears which he now began to move in and out. He performed this exercise proudly, with a little proud smile on his face. "Is you seeing these?" he asked.

"How could I miss them?" Sophie said.

"They maybe is looking a bit propsposterous to you," the BFG said, "but you must believe me when I say they is very extra-usual ears indeed. They is not to be coughed at."

"I'm quite sure they're not," Sophie said.

"They is allowing me to hear absolutely every single twiddly little thing."

"You mean you can hear things I can't hear?" Sophie said.

"You is *deaf as a dumpling* compared with me!" cried the BFG. "You is hearing only thumping loud noises with those little earwigs of yours. But I am hearing *all the secret whisperings of the world!*"

"Such as what?" Sophie asked.

"In your country," he said, "I is hearing the footsteps of a ladybird as she goes walking across a leaf."

"*Honestly?*" Sophie said, beginning to be impressed.

"What's more, I is hearing those footsteps *very loud*," the BFG said. "When a ladybird is walking across a leaf, I is hearing her feet going *clumpety-clumpety-clump* like giants' footsteps."

"Good gracious me!" Sophie said. "What else can you hear?"

"I is hearing the little ants chittering to each other as they scuddle around in the soil."

"You mean you can hear ants talking?"

"Every single word," the BFG said. "Although I is not exactly understanding their langwitch."

"Go on," Sophie said.

"Sometimes, on a very clear night," the BFG said, "and if I is swiggling my ears in the right direction" – and here he swivelled his great ears upwards so they were facing the ceiling – "if I is swiggling them like this and the night is very clear, I is sometimes hearing faraway music coming from the stars in the sky."

A queer little shiver passed through Sophie's body. She sat very quiet, waiting for more.

"My ears is what told me you was watching me out of your window last night," the BFG said.

"But I didn't make a sound," Sophie said.

"I was hearing your heart beating across the road," the BFG said. "Loud as a drum."

"Go on," Sophie said. "Please."

"I can hear plants and trees."

"Do *they* talk?" Sophie asked.

"They is not exactly talking," the BFG said. "But they is making noises. For instance, if I come along and I is picking a lovely flower, if I is twisting the stem of the flower till it breaks, then the plant is screaming. I can hear it screaming and screaming very clear."

"You don't mean it!" Sophie cried. "How awful!"
"It is screaming just like you would be screaming
if someone was twisting *your* arm right off."

"Is that really true?" Sophie asked.

"You think I is swizzfiggling you?"

"It *is* rather hard to believe."

"Then I is stopping right here!" said the BFG sharply. "I is not wishing to be called a fibster."

"Oh no! I'm not calling you anything!" Sophie cried. "I believe you! I do really! Please go on!"

The BFG gave her a long hard stare. Sophie looked right back at him, her face open to his. "I believe you," she said softly.

She had offended him, she could see that.

"I wouldn't ever be fibbling to you," he said.

"I know you wouldn't," Sophie said. "But you must understand that it isn't easy to believe such amazing things straightaway."

"I understand that," the BFG said.

"So do please forgive me and go on," she said.

He waited a while longer, and then he said, "It is the same with trees as it is with flowers. If I is chopping an axe into the trunk of a big tree, I is hearing a terrible sound coming from inside the heart of the tree."

"What sort of sound?" Sophie asked.

"A soft moaning sound," the BFG said. "It is like the sound an old man is making when he is dying slowly."

He paused. The cave was very silent.

"Trees is living and growing just like you and me," he said. "They is alive. So is plants."

He was sitting very straight in his chair now, his hands clasped tightly together in front of him. His face was bright, his eyes round and bright as two stars.

"Such wonderful and terrible sounds I is hearing!" he said. "Some of them you would never wish to be hearing yourself! But some is like glorious music!"

He seemed almost to be transfigured by the excitement of his thoughts. His face was beautiful in its blaze of emotions.

"Tell me some more about them," Sophie said quietly.

"You just ought to be hearing the little micies talking!" he said. "Little micies is always talking to each other and I is hearing them as loud as my own voice."

"What do they say?" Sophie asked.

"Only the micies know that," he said. "Spiders is also talking a great deal. You might not be thinking it but spiders is the most tremendous natterboxes. And when they is spinning their webs they is singing all the time. They is singing sweeter than a nightingull."

"Who else do you hear?" Sophie asked.

"One of the biggest chatbags is the cattle piddlers," the BFG said.

"What do they say?"

"They is argying all the time about who is going to be the prettiest butteryfly. That is all they is ever talking about."

"Is there a dream floating around in here now?" Sophie asked.

The BFG moved his great ears this way and that, listening intently. He shook his head. "There is no dream in here," he said, "except in the bottles. I has a special place to go for catching dreams. They is not often coming to Giant Country."

"How do you catch them?"

"The same way you is catching butteryflies," the BFG answered. "With a net." He stood up and crossed over to a corner of the cave where a pole was leaning against the wall. The pole was about thirty feet long and there was a net on the end of it. "Here is the dream-catcher," he said, grasping the pole in one hand. "Every morning I is going out and snitching new dreams to put in my bottles."

Suddenly, he seemed to lose interest in the conversation. "I is getting hungry," he said. "It is time for eats."

The BFG Stamp

from THE ROYAL MAIL'S SPECIAL ISSUE
CELEBRATING CHILDREN'S LITERATURE
AND ITS ILLUSTRATORS

FEBRUARY 2ND, 1993

Snozzcumbers

from REVOLTING RECIPES

SERVES 8

YOU WILL NEED:

vegetable peeler
apple corer (round type) or melon-ball cutter
paint-brush

2 large cucumbers
1 can (3¼ oz / 95 g) tuna
1 to 2 tomatoes, deseeded and chopped
3 cocktail gherkins, finely chopped
3 tablespoons mayonnaise
2 teaspoons poppy seeds
salt and pepper

COATING:

a little extra mayonnaise
plain or cheese-flavoured popcorn
extra poppy seeds

1. Peel the cucumbers. With the point of the vegetable peeler, cut several grooves along the length of each cucumber.

2. With the pointed end of the vegetable peeler, very carefully scoop out little pits, at random, between the grooves.

3. Cut off the ends of the cucumbers about 1½ inches / 4 cm from each end and hollow out the seeds.

4. Hollow out the seeds from the body of each cucumber using a corer or melon-ball cutter, approaching from both ends. Keep 2 inches / 5 cm of the centre seed core to act as plugs later.

5. Stand the cucumbers in a tall glass and allow the excess liquids to drain (about 30 minutes).

6. Thoroughly drain the tuna, and mix in the chopped tomatoes, gherkins, mayonnaise, and poppy seeds. Season to taste with salt and pepper.

7. With a teaspoon, fill the cucumbers, packing the tuna mixture down with the teaspoon handle.

8. Replace the ends, securing with previously made plugs.

9. Paint a little mayonnaise in the grooves on the outside of the cucumbers and carefully cover with poppy seeds (a steady hand is useful!).

10. Place a small piece of popcorn in each pit, putting a little mayonnaise in first to secure the popcorn. These can also be coated in poppy seeds if wished.

N.B. There are many substitute fillings, ie taramasalata, cream cheese, or smoked salmon and chives.

Sophie said the original Snozzcumber tasted of frogskin and rotten fish. The BFG said it tasted like cockroaches and slime wanglers. I wonder what you think?

The Minpins

LITTLE Billy's mother was always telling him exactly what he was allowed to do and what he was not allowed to do.

All the things he was allowed to do were boring. All the things he was not allowed to do were exciting.

One of the things he was NEVER NEVER allowed to do, the most exciting of them all, was to go out through the garden gate all by himself and explore the world beyond.

On this sunny summer afternoon, Little Billy was kneeling on a chair in the living-room, gazing out through the window at the wonderful world beyond. His mother was in the kitchen doing the ironing and although the door was open she couldn't see him.

Every now and again his mother would call out to him saying,

"Little Billy, what are you up to in there?"

And Little Billy would always call back and say, "I'm being good, Mummy."

But Little Billy was awfully tired of being good.

Through the window, not so very far away, he could see the big black secret wood that was called The Forest of Sin. It was something he had always longed to explore.

His mother had told him that even grown-ups were frightened of going into The Forest of Sin. She recited a poem to him that was well-known in the district. It went like this:

> *Beware! Beware! The Forest of Sin!*
> *None come out, but many go in!*

"Why don't they come out?" Little Billy asked her. "What happens to them in the wood?"

"That wood," his mother said, "is full of the most blood-thirsty wild beasts in the world."

"You mean tigers and lions?" Little Billy asked.

"Much worse than that," his mother said.

"What's worse than tigers and lions, Mummy?"

"Whangdoodles are worse," his mother said, "and Hornswogglers and Snozzwanglers and Vermicious Knids. And worst of all is the Terrible Bloodsuckling Toothpluckling Stonechuckling Spittler. There's one of them in there, too."

"A Spittler, Mummy?"

"Of course. And when the Spittler chases after you, he blows clouds of hot smoke out of his nose."

"Would he eat me up?" Little Billy asked.

"In one gulp," his mother said.

Little Billy did not believe a word of this. He guessed his mother was making it all up just to frighten him and to stop him ever going out of the house alone.

And now Little Billy was kneeling on the chair, gazing with longing through the window at the famous Forest of Sin.

"Little Billy," his mother called out from the kitchen. "What are you doing?"

"I'm being good, Mummy," Little Billy called back.

Just then a funny thing happened. Little Billy began to hear somebody whispering in his ear. He knew exactly who it was. It was the Devil. The Devil always started whispering to him when he was especially bored.

"It would be easy," the Devil was whispering, "to climb out through that window. No one would see you. And in a jiffy you would be in the garden, and in another jiffy you would be through the front gate, and in yet another jiffy you would be exploring the marvellous Forest of Sin all by yourself. It is a super place. Do not believe one word of what your mother says about Whangdoodles and Hornswogglers and Snozzwanglers and Vermicious Knids and the Terrible Bloodsuckling Toothpluckling Stonechuckling Spittler. There are no such things."

"What *is* in there?" Little Billy whispered.

"Wild strawberries," the Devil whispered back. "The whole floor of the forest is carpeted with wild strawberries, every one of them luscious and red and juicy-ripe. Go and see for yourself."

These were the words the Devil whispered softly into Little Billy's ear on that sunny summer afternoon.

The next moment, Little Billy had opened the window and was climbing out.

In a jiffy he had dropped silently on to the flowerbed below.

In another jiffy he was out through the garden gate.

And in yet another jiffy he was standing on the very edge of the great big dark Forest of Sin!

He had made it! He had got there! And now the forest was all his to explore!

Was he nervous?

What?

Who said anything about being nervous?

Hornswogglers? Vermicious Knids? What sort of rubbish was that?

Little Billy hesitated.

"I'm not nervous," he said. "I'm not in the least bit nervous. Not me."

Very very slowly, he walked forward into the great forest. Giant trees were soon surrounding him on all sides and their branches made an almost solid roof high above his head, blotting out the sky. Here and there little shafts of sunlight shone through gaps in the roof.

There was not a sound anywhere. It was like being among the dead men in an enormous empty green cathedral.

When he had ventured some distance into the forest, Little Billy stopped and stood quite still, listening. He could hear nothing. Nothing at all. There was absolute silence.

Or was there?

Hold on just one second.

What was that?

Little Billy flicked his head round and stared into the everlasting gloom and doom of the forest.

There it was again! There was no mistaking it this time.

From far away, there came a very faint whoozing whiffling noise, like a small gusty wind blowing through the trees.

Then it grew louder. Every second it was growing louder, and suddenly it was no longer a small wind, it was a fearsome swooshing whooshing whiffling snorting noise that sounded as though some gigantic creature was breathing heavily through its nose as it galloped towards him.

Little Billy turned and ran.

Little Billy ran faster than he had ever run in his life before. But the swooshing whooshing whiffling snorting noise was coming after him. Worse still, it was getting louder. This meant that the *thing*, the maker of the noise, the galloping creature, was getting closer. It was catching him up!

Run, Little Billy! Run run run!

He dodged around massive trees. He skipped over roots and brambles. He bent low to flash under boughs and bushes. He had wings on his feet he ran so fast. But still the fearsome swooshing whooshing whiffling snorting noise grew louder and louder as it came closer and closer.

Little Billy glanced back quickly over his shoulder, and now, in the distance, he saw a sight that froze his blood and made icicles in his veins.

What he saw were two mighty puffs of orange-red smoke billowing and rolling through the trees in his direction. These were followed by

two more, *whoosh whoosh*, and then two more, *whoosh whoosh*, and they must surely be coming, Little Billy told himself, from the two nose-holes of some galloping panting beast that had smelled him out and was coming after him.

His mother's words began thrumming once again in his head:

> *Beware! Beware! The Forest of Sin!*
> *None come out, but many go in!*

"It's the Spittler for sure!" Little Billy cried out. "Mummy said the Spittler blows smoke when it chases you. This one is blowing smoke! It's the Terrible Bloodsuckling Toothpluckling Stonechuckling Spittler! And soon it will catch me up and I'll be bloodsuckled and toothpluckled and stonechuckled and chewed up into tiny pieces, and then the Spittler will spit me out in a cloud of smoke and that will be the end of me!"

Little Billy was running with the speed of an arrow, but each time he glanced back over his shoulder the puffs of orange-red smoky-breath had gotten closer. They were so close now he could feel the wind of them on the back of his neck. And the *noise!* It was deafening in his ears, this fearsome swooshing whooshing whiffling panting noise. *Woomph-woomph*, it went. *Woomph-woomph, woomph-woomph! Woomph-woomph!* It was like the noise made by a steam locomotive pulling out from a station.

Then suddenly he heard another noise that was somehow more fearsome still. It was the pounding of gigantic galloping hooves on the floor of the forest.

He glanced round again, but the Thing, the Beast, the Monster, or whatever it was, was hidden from his sight by the smoke it shot out as it galloped forward.

The smoky-breath was billowing all around him now. He could feel its hotness. Worse still, he could smell its smell. The smell was disgusting. It was the stench that comes from deep inside the tummy of a meat-eating animal.

"Mummy!" he cried out. "Save me!"

Suddenly, directly in front of him, Little Billy saw the trunk of an enormous tree. This tree was different from the others because it had branches hanging down very low. While still running, he made a frantic jump for its lowest branch. He caught it and pulled himself up. Then he grabbed the next branch above his head and pulled himself up again. Then again and again, climbing higher and higher to get away from the terrible snorting smoke-blowing, smelly-breathed beast down below. He stopped climbing only when he was too exhausted to climb any higher.

He looked up, but even now he couldn't see the top of the giant tree. It seemed to go on for ever. He looked down. He couldn't see the ground either. He was in a world of green leaves and thick, smooth branches with no earth or sky in sight. The snorting smelly smoke-blowing beast was miles away down below somewhere. He couldn't even hear it any more.

Little Billy found a comfortable place where two big branches came together and he sat down to rest. For the moment, at any rate, he was safe. Then something very peculiar happened. There was a huge smooth branch very close to where Little Billy was sitting and he suddenly noticed that a small square patch of bark on this branch was beginning to move. It was a very small patch, about the size of a postage stamp, and the two sides of it seemed to be splitting down the middle and opening slowly outwards, like a pair of shutters on some tiny window.

Little Billy sat staring at this extraordinary thing. And all at once, a strange uncomfortable feeling came over him. It felt as though the

tree he was sitting in and the green leaves all around him belonged to another world altogether and that he was a trespasser who had no right to be where he was. He watched intently as the tiny shutters of tree-bark opened wider and wider, and when they were fully open they revealed a small squarish window set neatly in the curve of the big branch. There was some sort of a yellowish glow coming from deep inside the window.

The very next thing Little Billy saw was a tiny face at the window. It had appeared suddenly, from nowhere, and it was the face of an extremely old man with white hair. Little Billy could see this clearly despite the fact that the whole of the tiny man's head was no larger than a pea.

This ancient miniature face was staring straight at Little Billy with the most severe expression on it. The skin on the face was deeply wrinkled all over, but the eyes were as bright as two stars.

Now something *even more* peculiar began to happen. All around him, not only on the huge main trunk of the tree but also on all the big branches that grew out of it, other tiny windows were opening and tiny faces were peering out. Some of these faces belonged to men and others were clearly women. Here and there the head of a child was seen peering over a windowsill. The heads of these children were no larger than the heads of matchsticks. In the end, there must have been more than twenty small windows all around where Little Billy was sitting, and from each window these amazing little faces were peering out. No sound came from any of the watchers.

The faces were silent, unmoving, almost ghost-like.

Now the tiny old man in the window nearest to Billy seemed to be saying something, but his voice was so soft and whispery, Little Billy had to lean right up close to catch his words.

"You're in a bit of a twizzler, aren't you?" the voice was saying. "You can't go down again because if you do you'll be guzzled up at once. But you can't possibly sit up here forever, either."

"I know, I know!" Little Billy gasped.

"Don't shout," the tiny man said.

"I'm not shouting," Little Billy said.

"Talk softer," the tiny man said. "If you talk too loud your voice will blow me away."

"But… but… who *are* you?" Little Billy asked, taking care to speak very softly this time.

"We are the Minpins," the tiny man said, "and we OWN this wood. I shall come closer, then you will hear me better." The old Minpin climbed out of his window and walked straight down the big steeply sloping branch, then up another branch until he found a place only a few inches from Little Billy's face.

It was amazing to see him walking up and down these almost vertical branches without the slightest trouble. It was like seeing someone walking up and down a wall.

"How on earth do you do that?" Little Billy asked.

"Suction-boots," the Minpin said. "We all wear them. You can't live in trees without suction-boots." On his feet he was wearing tiny green boots rather like miniature wellies.

His clothes were curiously old-fashioned, mostly brown and black, the sort of thing people wore two or three hundred years ago.

Suddenly, all the other Minpins, men, women and children, were climbing out of their windows and making their way towards Little Billy. Their suction-boots seemed to allow them to walk up and down the steepest branches with the greatest ease, and some were even walking upside-down underneath the branches. All of them were wearing these old-fashioned clothes from hundreds of years ago, and several had on very peculiar hats and bonnets. They stood or sat in groups on all the branches around Little Billy, staring at him as though he were someone from outer space.

"But do all of you actually *live* inside this tree?" Little Billy asked.

The old Minpin said, "All the trees in this forest are hollow. Not just this one, but *all* of them. And inside them thousands and thousands of Minpins are living. These great trees are filled with rooms and staircases, not just in the big main trunk but in most of the other branches as well. This is a Minpin forest. And it's not the only one in England."

"Could I peep inside?" Little Billy said.

"Of course, of course," the old Minpin said. "Put your eye close to that window." He pointed to the one he had just come out of.

Little Billy shifted his position and placed one eye right up against

the square hole that was no bigger than a postage stamp.

What he now saw was quite marvellous. He saw a room that was lit by a pale yellow light of some sort and it was furnished with beautifully made miniature chairs and a table. To one side was a four-poster bed. It was like one of the rooms Little Billy had once seen in the Queen's Dolls' House at Windsor Castle.

"It's beautiful," Little Billy said. "Are they all as lovely as this one?"

"Most are smaller," the old Minpin said. "This one is very grand because I am the Ruler of this tree. My name is Don Mini. What is yours?"

"Mine is Little Billy," Little Billy said.

"Greetings, Little Billy," Don Mini said. "You are welcome to look into some of the other rooms if you wish. We are very proud of them."

All the other Minpin families wanted to show Little Billy their own rooms. They rushed about along the branches calling out, "Come and see mine! Please come and see mine!"

Little Billy began climbing about and peeping into the tiny windows.

Through one window he saw a bathroom, just like his own at home only a thousand times smaller. And through another he saw a classroom with lots of tiny desks and a blackboard at one end.

In every room there was a stairway in one corner leading up to the room above.

As Little Billy went from window to window, the Minpins followed him, clustering round and smiling at his exclamations of wonder.

"They're all absolutely marvellous," he said. "They're much nicer than our rooms at home."

When the sightseeing tour was over, Little Billy sat down again on a large branch and said to the whole company of Minpins, "Look, I've had a lovely time with you all, but how am I ever going to get home again? My mother'll be going crazy."

"You can never get down from this tree," Don Mini said. "I've told you that. If you're stupid enough to try, you'll be eaten up in five seconds."

"Is it the Spittler?" Little Billy asked. "Is it the Terrible Bloodsuckling Toothpluckling Stonechuckling Spittler?"

"I've never heard of any Spittler," Don Mini said. "The one waiting for you down there is the fearsome Gruncher, the Red-Hot

Smoke-Belching Gruncher. He grunches up everything in the forest. That's why we have to live up here. He has grunched up hundreds of humans and literally millions of Minpins. What makes him so dangerous is his amazing and magical nose. His nose can smell out a human or a Minpin or any other animal from ten miles away. Then he gallops towards it at terrific speed. He can never see anything in front of him because of all the smoke he belches out from his nose and mouth, but that doesn't bother him. His nose tells him exactly where to go."

"Why does he blow out all that smoke?" Little Billy asked.

"Because he's got a red-hot fire in his belly," Don Mini said. "The Gruncher likes his meat roasted, and the fire roasts it as it goes down."

"Look," Little Billy said, "Gruncher or no Gruncher, I've simply got to get home somehow. I'll have to make a dash for it."

"Don't try it, I beg you," Don Mini said. "The Gruncher knows you're up here. He's down there now waiting for you. Climb down a bit with me and I'll show you."

Don Mini walked easily, straight down the side of the great treetrunk. Little Billy climbed carefully down after him, from one branch to the next.

Soon, below them, they began to smell the revolting hot stench of the Gruncher's breath, and the orange-red smoke was now billowing up into the lower branches in thick clouds.

"What does he look like?" Little Billy whispered.

"Nobody knows," Don Mini answered. "He makes so much steam and smoke you can never see him. If you are behind him you can sometimes catch a glimpse of little bits of him because all the smoke is being blown out in the front. Some Minpins say they have seen his back legs, huge and black and very hairy, shaped like lions' legs but ten times as big. And it is rumoured that his head is like an enormous crocodile's head, with rows and rows and rows of sharp pointed teeth. But nobody really knows. Mind you, he must have gigantic nose-holes to be able to blow out all that smoke."

They stayed still, listening, and they could hear the Gruncher pawing the ground at the base of the tree with his giant hooves and snorting with greed.

"He smells you," Don Mini said. "He knows you aren't far away. He'll wait for ever to get you now. He adores humans and he doesn't catch them very often. Humans are like strawberries and cream to him. You see, for months he's been living on a diet of Minpins, and a thousand Minpins is not even a snack for him. The brute is ravenous."

Little Billy and Don Mini climbed back up the tree to where all the other Minpins were gathered. They seemed glad to see Little Billy come safely back. "Stay up here with us," they said to him. "We'll look after you."

Just then, a lovely blue swallow alighted on a branch not far away, and Little Billy saw a mother Minpin and her two children climb quite casually on to the swallow's back. Then the swallow took off and flew away with its passengers seated comfortably between its wings.

"Good heavens!" cried Little Billy. "Is that a special tame bird?"

"Not at all," Don Mini said. "We know all the birds. The birds are our friends. We use them all the time for going places. That lady is taking her children to see their grandmother who lives in another forest about fifty miles away. They'll be there in less than an hour."

"Can you *talk* to them?" Little Billy asked. "To the birds, I mean?"

"Of course we can talk to them," Don Mini said. "We can summon them any time we want if we have to go somewhere. How else would we get our supplies of food up here? The Red-Hot Gruncher makes it impossible for us to walk anywhere in the wood."

"Do the birds like doing this for you?" Little Billy asked.

"They'll do anything for us," Don Mini said. "They love us and we love them. We store food for them inside the trees so they don't starve when the icy-cold winter comes along."

Suddenly all sorts of birds were alighting on the branches of the tree around where Little Billy was sitting, and the Minpins were climbing on to their backs in droves. Most of the Minpins had small sacks slung over their shoulders.

"At this time of the day they go off to collect food," Don Mini said. "All the grown-ups have to help in getting food for the community. The population of each tree looks after itself. Our large trees are like your cities and towns, and the small trees are like your villages."

It was an astonishing sight. Every kind of wonderful bird was flying in and perching on the branches of the great tree, and as soon as one landed a Minpin would climb on to its back and off they would go. There were blackbirds and thrushes and skylarks and ravens and starlings and jays and magpies and many kinds of small finches. It was all very fast and well-organised. Each bird seemed to know exactly which Minpin it was collecting, and each Minpin knew exactly which bird he or she had ordered for the morning.

"The birds are our cars," Don Mini said to Little Billy. "They are much nicer and they never crash."

Soon all the grown-up Minpins, excepting Don Mini, had flown away on birds and only the tiny children were left.

Then the robins came in and the children began climbing onto their backs and going for short flights.

Don Mini said to Little Billy, "The children all practise learning to fly on robins. Robins are sensible and careful birds and they love the little ones."

Little Billy simply stood there staring. He could hardly believe what he was seeing.

While the children were practising on the robins, Little Billy said to Don Mini, "Is there no way in the world to get rid of that disgusting Red-Hot Smoke-Belching Gruncher down below?"

"The only time a Gruncher dies," Don Mini said, "is if he falls into deep water. The water puts out the fire inside him and then he's dead. The fire to a Gruncher is like your heart is to you. Stop your heart and you die at once. Put out the fire and the Gruncher dies in five seconds. That's the only way to kill a Gruncher."

"Now hang on a minute," Little Billy said. "Is there by any chance a pond or something around here?"

"There's a big lake on the far side of the forest," Don Mini said. "But who's going to entice the Gruncher into that? Not us. And certainly not you. He'd be on you before you got within ten yards of him."

"But you did say the Gruncher can't see in front of him because of all the clouds of smoke he blows," Little Billy said.

"Quite true," Don Mini said. "But how is that going to help us? I don't think the Gruncher is ever going to fall into the lake. He never goes out of the forest."

"I think I know how to make him fall in," Little Billy said.

"What I want," Little Billy went on, "is a bird that is big enough to carry *me*."

Don Mini thought about this for a while, then he said, "You are a very small boy and because of that I think a swan could carry you quite easily."

"Call up a swan," Little Billy said. Suddenly there was a new authority in his voice.

"But… but I hope you're not going to do anything dangerous," Don Mini cried.

"Listen carefully," Little Billy said, "because you must tell the swan exactly what he has to do. With me on his back he must fly down to the Gruncher. The Gruncher will smell me and know that I am very close. But he won't see me through all the steam and the smoke. He'll go mad trying to get at me. The swan will tantalize him by flying back and forth right in front of him. Is that possible?"

"Quite possible," Don Mini said, "except that you might easily fall off. You've had no flying practice at all."

"I'll hang on somehow," Little Billy said. "Then the swan, keeping very low, will fly off through the forest with the ravenous Gruncher hotfoot in pursuit. The swan will keep just ahead of the Gruncher all the time, driving him crazy with my smell, and in the end the swan will fly straight over the big deep lake and the Gruncher, now travelling at terrific speed, will follow right behind. *Presto*, he's in the lake!"

"My boy!" Don Mini cried. "You are a genius! Will you do it?"

"Call up the swan," Little Billy ordered.

Don Mini turned to one of the robins which had just come back from

a practice flight with a child Minpin on its back. Little Billy heard him talking to the robin in a kind of curious twitter. He couldn't understand a word of it. The robin nodded its head and flew off.

Two minutes later, a truly magnificent swan, as white as snow, came swooping in and landed on a branch nearby. Don Mini walked over to it and once again a curious twittery conversation took place, a much longer one this time, with Don Mini doing nearly all the twittering and the swan nodding and nodding.

Then Don Mini turned to Little Billy and said, "Swan thinks it's a great idea. He says he can do it. But he's just a bit anxious because you have never flown before. He says you must hang on very tight to his feathers."

"Don't you worry about that," Little Billy said. "I'll hang on somehow. I don't want to be roasted alive and eaten by the Gruncher."

Little Billy climbed on to Swan's back. Many of the Minpins who had flown away a short while before were now returning on their birds. Their tiny sacks were bulging. They stood around on the branches staring in wonder at the sight of this small human preparing to take off on Swan.

"Goodbye, Little Billy!" they called out. "Good luck, good luck!" And with that, the great swan spread its wings and glided gently downward through the many branches of the big tree.

Little Billy hung on tight. Oh, it was thrilling to be flying on the back of this great swan! It was wonderful to be up in the air and to feel the air swishing past his face. He hung on very tightly to Swan's feathers.

And suddenly, there it was just below them, the huge billow of orange-red smoke and steam coming from the nostrils of the awesome Gruncher. The smoke enveloped the beast completely, and yet through the smoke, as they got very close, Little Billy could just make out the enormous black shadow of some hairy monster. The snorting grew louder, and as the brute got more and more excited by the nearness of the delicious Little Billy smell, the smoke began coming out faster and faster, *whoomph-whoomph*, *whoomph-whoomph*, *whoomph-whoomph*. Little Billy could feel the monster getting closer, *whoomph-whoomph*, *whoomph-whoomph*, *whoomph-whoomph*.

Swan was flying back and forth right in front of the snorting cloud of smoke, tempting and tantalizing the beast and driving him mad with greed. The beast, or rather the cloud of smoke, kept lunging at Little Billy, but Swan was too quick for him and jinked away every time. The snorting grew louder and more ferocious every second, and the *whoomph-whoomphs* of thick hot steam came pouring out, thicker than ever.

Once, Swan looked round to see if Little Billy was all right. Little Billy nodded and smiled, and he could swear Swan nodded and smiled back at him.

At last, Swan must have decided they had done enough teasing. The great thick orange-red cloud was leaping up and down in a frenzy of hunger and desire, and the whole forest was echoing with the snorts and growls of the awesome creature. Swan glided round and headed in a straight line towards the edge of the forest, and of course the vast cloud of smoke came hurtling after it.

Swan was very careful to fly low all the time, keeping just in front of the Gruncher, leading him on and on, threading a path carefully through the great trees in the forest. The scent of human food was very strong in the Gruncher's nostrils, and he must have been thinking that so long as he kept going flat out, he would catch his meal in the end.

Suddenly, right in front of them, on the edge of the forest, was the lake. The Gruncher, hurtling along right behind them, was interested only in the glorious human scent he was following.

Swan flew straight towards the lake. It skimmed low over the water. The Gruncher kept going.

Little Billy, looking back, saw the Gruncher plunging right into the lake, and then the whole lake seemed to erupt in a mass of boiling steaming frothing bubbling water.

For a brief moment, the terrible Red-Hot Smoke-Belching Gruncher made the lake boil and smoke like a volcano, then the fire went out and the awesome beast disappeared under the waves.

When it was all over, Swan and Little Billy flew higher and circled the lake for a last look.

And suddenly the whole sky around them was filled with birds, and every bird had one or more Minpins on its back. Little Billy recognised Don Mini riding on a fine jay and he was waving and cheering as he flew alongside them. It seemed that all the other Minpins from the big tree had turned up as well to witness the great victory over the dreaded Gruncher. Every kind of bird was circling around Little Billy and Swan, and the Minpins on their backs were waving and clapping and shouting with joy. Little Billy waved back and laughed and thought how wonderful it all was.

Then, led by Swan, all the birds and the Minpins returned to the home tree.

Back in the tree there was a tremendous celebration for Little Billy's victory over the dreaded Gruncher. Minpins from all over the forest had flown in on their birds to cheer the young hero, and all the branches and twigs of the great tree were crowded with tiny people. When the cheers and the clapping had died down at last, Don Mini stood up to make a speech.

"Minpins of the forest!" he cried, raising his small voice so that it could be heard all over the tree. "The murderous Gruncher, who has gobbled up so many thousands of us Minpins, has gone for ever! The forest floor is safe at last for us to walk on! So now we can all go down to pick blackberries and winkleberries and puckleberries and muckleberries and twinkleberries and snozzberries to our hearts' content. And our children can play among the wild flowers and the roots all day long." Don Mini paused and turned his eyes upon Little Billy who was sitting on a branch not far away.

"But ladies and gentlemen," he went on, "who is it we have to thank for this great blessing that has come upon us? Who is the saviour of the Minpins?" Don Mini paused again. The Minpins in their thousands sat listening intently.

"Our saviour," he cried out, "our hero, our wonder-boy, is, as you already know, our human visitor, Little Billy." (Cheers and shouts of "Hooray for Little Billy!" from the crowd.)

Don Mini now turned and spoke directly to Little Billy. "You, my boy, have done a wonderful thing for us and in return we wish to do something for you. I have had a word with Swan and he has agreed to become your personal private aero-plane for just as long as you remain small enough to fly on his back." (More cheers and clapping and shouts of "Good old Swan! What a great idea!")

"However," Don Mini continued, still addressing Little Billy, "you cannot go flying around all over the place on Swan's back in full daylight. Some human would be bound to see you. And then the secret would be out and you would be forced to tell your people all about us. That must never happen. If it did, crowds of enormous humans would come clumping all over our beloved forest to look for Minpins and our quiet homeland would be ruined."

"I'll never tell a soul!" Little Billy cried out.

"Even so," Don Mini said, "we cannot risk you making daylight flights. But every night, after the light in your bedroom has been switched off, Swan will come to your window to see if you'd like a ride. Sometimes he will bring you back here to see us. Other times he will take you to visit places more wonderful than you could ever dream of. Would you like Swan to take you home now? I think we can risk just one more quick daylight flight."

"Oh gosh!" Little Billy cried. "I'd clean forgotten about home! Mummy'll be in a panic! I must fly!"

Don Mini gave a signal and in five seconds Swan swooped down and landed on the tree. Little Billy climbed on to his back, and as the great swan spread his wings and flew away, the whole forest, not just the tree they were in but the whole forest from end to end, came alive with the cheering of a million Minpins.

Swan landed on the lawn of Little Billy's house, and Little Billy jumped off his back and ran to the living-room window. Very quietly he climbed in. The room was empty.

"Little Billy," came his mother's voice from the kitchen. "What are you up to in there? You've been very quiet for a long time."

"I'm being good, Mummy," Little Billy called back. "I'm being very very good."

His mother came into the room with a pile of ironing in her arms. She looked at Little Billy. "What *have* you been doing?" she cried. "Your clothes are absolutely filthy!"

"I've been climbing trees," Little Billy said.

"I can't let you out of my sight for ten minutes," his mother said. "Which tree was it?"

"Just one of those old trees outside," Little Billy said.

"If you're not careful you'll fall down and break an arm," his mother said. "Don't do it again."

"I won't," Little Billy said, smiling a little. "I'll just fly up into the branches on silver wings."

"What rubbish you talk," his mother said and she walked out of the room with her ironing.

From then on, Swan came every night to Little Billy's bedroom window. He came after Billy's mother and father had gone to sleep and the whole house was quiet. But Little Billy was never asleep. He was always wide awake and eagerly waiting. And every night, before Swan arrived, he saw to it that the curtains were drawn back and the window was open wide so that the great white bird could come gliding right into the room and land on the floor beside his bed. Then Little Billy would slip into his dressing gown and climb on to Swan's back and off they would go.

Oh, it was a wondrous secret life that Little Billy lived up there in the sky at night on Swan's back! They flew in a magical world of silence, swooping and gliding over the dark world below where all the earthly people were fast asleep in their beds.

Once, Swan flew higher than ever before and they came to an enormous billowing cloud that was shining in a pale golden light, and in the folds of this cloud Little Billy could make out creatures of some sort moving around.

Who were they?

He wanted so badly to ask Swan this question, but he couldn't speak a word of bird-language. Swan seemed unwilling to fly very close to these creatures from another world, and this made it impossible for Little Billy to see them clearly.

Another time, Swan flew through the night for what seemed like hours and hours until they came at last to a gigantic opening in the earth's surface, a sort of huge gaping hole in the ground, and Swan glided slowly round and round above this massive crater and then right down into it. Deeper and deeper they went into the dark hole. Suddenly there was a brightness like sunlight below them, and Little Billy could see a vast lake of water, gloriously blue, and on the surface of the lake thousands of swans were swimming slowly about. The pure white of the swans against the blue of the water was very beautiful.

Little Billy wondered whether this was a secret meeting place of all the swans of the world, and he wished he had been able to ask Swan

this question as well. But sometimes mysteries are more intriguing than explanations, and the swans on the blue lake, like the creatures on the golden cloud, would remain a mystery for ever in Little Billy's memory.

About once a week, Swan would fly Little Billy back to the old tree in the forest to visit the Minpins. On one of these visits, Don Mini said to him, "You are growing up fast, Little Billy. I'm afraid that soon you will be too heavy for Swan."

"I know," Little Billy said. "I can't help it."

"I'm afraid we don't have any bigger birds than Swan," Don Mini said. "But when he can't carry you any longer, I do hope you will still come up here to visit us."

"I will, I will!" Little Billy cried. "I will always keep coming to see you! I will never forget you!"

"And listen," Don Mini said, smiling. "Perhaps some of us might come down in great secrecy to visit *you*."

"Could you really do that?" Little Billy asked.

"I think we might," Don Mini said. "We could trickle silently down to your house in the dark and creep into your bedroom for a midnight feast."

"But how would you get all the way up to my bedroom window?" Little Billy asked.

"Have you forgotten our suction-boots?" Don Mini said. "We'd simply walk straight up the wall of your house."

"How lovely!" Little Billy cried. "Then we can take it in turns visiting each other!"

"Of course we can," Don Mini said.

And that is exactly what happened.

No child has ever had such an exciting young life as Little Billy, and no child has ever kept such a huge secret so faithfully. He never told a soul about the Minpins.

I myself have been very careful not to tell you where they live, and I am not about to tell you now. But if by some extraordinary chance you should one day wander into a forest and catch a glimpse of a Minpin, then hold your breath and thank your lucky stars because up to now, so far as I know, no one excepting Little Billy has ever seen one.

Watch the birds as they fly above your heads and, who knows, you might well spy a tiny creature riding high on the back of a swallow or a raven. Watch the robin especially because it always flies low, and you might see a nervous young Minpin perched on the feathers having its first flying lesson. And above all, watch with glittering eyes the whole world around you because the greatest secrets are always hidden in the most unlikely places. Those who don't believe in magic will never find it.

Cinderella

from REVOLTING RHYMES

I guess you think you know this story.
You don't. The real one's much more gory.
The phoney one, the one you know,
Was cooked up years and years ago,
And made to sound all soft and sappy
Just to keep the children happy.
Mind you, they got the first bit right,
The bit where, in the dead of night,
The Ugly Sisters, jewels and all,
Departed for the Palace Ball,
While darling little Cinderella
Was locked up in the slimy cellar,
Where rats who wanted things to eat,
Began to nibble at her feet.
She bellowed, "Help!" and "Let me out!"
The Magic Fairy heard her shout.
Appearing in a blaze of light,
She said, "My dear, are you all right?"
"*All right?*" cried Cindy. "Can't you see
  I feel as rotten as can be!"
  She beat her fist against the wall,
  And shouted, "Get me to the Ball!
  There is a Disco at the Palace!
  The rest have gone and I am jalous!
  I want a dress! I want a coach!
  And earrings and a diamond brooch!
  And silver slippers, two of those!
  And lovely nylon panty-hose!

Done up like that I'll guarantee
The handsome Prince will fall for me!"
The Fairy said, "Hang on a tick."
She gave her wand a mighty flick
And quickly, in no time at all,
Cindy was at the Palace Ball!
It made the Ugly Sisters wince
To see her dancing with the Prince.
She held him very tight and pressed
Herself against his manly chest.
The Prince himself was turned to pulp,
All *he* could do was gasp and gulp.
Then midnight struck. She shouted, "Heck!
I've got to run to save my neck!"
The Prince cried, "No! Alas! Alack!"
He grabbed her dress to hold her back.
As Cindy shouted, "Let me go!"
The dress was ripped from head to toe.
She ran out in her underwear,
And lost one slipper on the stair.
The Prince was on it like a dart,
He pressed it to his pounding heart,
"The girl this slipper fits", he cried,
"Tomorrow morn shall be my bride!
I'll visit every house in town
Until I've tracked the maiden down!"
Then rather carelessly, I fear,
He placed it on a crate of beer.
At once, one of the Ugly Sisters,
(The one whose face was blotched with blisters)
Sneaked up and grabbed the dainty shoe,
And quickly flushed it down the loo.
Then in its place she calmly put

The slipper from her own left foot.
Ah-ha, you see, the plot grows thicker,
And Cindy's luck starts looking sicker.
Next day, the Prince went charging down
To knock on all the doors in town.
In every house, the tension grew.
Who was the owner of the shoe?
The shoe was long and very wide.
(A normal foot got lost inside.)
Also it smelled a wee bit icky.
(The owner's feet were hot and sticky.)
Thousands of eager people came
To try it on, but all in vain.
Now came the Ugly Sisters' go.
One tried it on. The Prince screamed, "No!"
But she screamed, "Yes! It fits! Whoopee!
So now you've got to marry me!"
The Prince went white from ear to ear.
He muttered, "Let's get out of here."
"Oh no you don't! You've made a vow!
There's no way you can back out now!"
"Off with her head!" the Prince roared back.
They chopped it off with one big whack.
This pleased the Prince. He smiled and said,
"She's prettier without her head."
Then up came Sister Number Two,
Who yelled, "Now *I* will try the shoe!"
"Try this instead!" the Prince yelled back.
He swung his trusty sword and *smack* –
Her head went crashing to the ground.
It bounced a bit and rolled around.
In the kitchen, peeling spuds,
Cinderella heard the thuds

Of bouncing heads upon the floor,
And poked her own head round the door.
"What's all the racket?" Cindy cried.
"Mind your own bizz," the Prince replied.
Poor Cindy's heart was torn to shreds.
My Prince! she thought. He chops off *heads!*
How could I marry anyone
Who does that sort of thing for fun?
The Prince cried, "Who's this dirty slut?
Off with her nut! Off with her nut!"
Just then, all in a blaze of light,
The Magic Fairy hove in sight,
Her Magic Wand went *swoosh* and *swish!*
"Cindy!" she cried. "Come make a wish!
Wish anything and have no doubt
That I will make it come about!"
Cindy answered, "Oh kind Fairy,
This time I shall be more wary.
No more Princes, no more money.
I have had my taste of honey.
I'm wishing for a decent man.
They're hard to find. D'you think you can?"
Within a minute, Cinderella
Was married to a lovely feller,
A simple jam-maker by trade,
Who sold good home-made marmalade.
Their house was filled with smiles and laughter
And they were happy ever after.

James and the Giant Peach

AN EXTRACT

*Inside the giant peach, James crawls down
the tunnel and comes to the room at the centre.*

JAMES'S large frightened eyes travelled slowly around the room. The creatures, some sitting on chairs, others reclining on a sofa, were all watching him intently.

Creatures?

Or were they insects?

An insect is usually something rather small, is it not? A grasshopper, for example, is an insect.

So what would you call it if you saw a grasshopper as large as a dog? As large as a *large* dog. You could hardly call *that* an insect, could you?

There was an Old-Green-Grasshopper as large as a large dog sitting directly across the room from James now.

And next to the Old-Green-Grasshopper, there was an enormous Spider.

And next to the Spider, there was a giant Ladybird with nine black spots on her scarlet shell.

Each of these three was squatting upon a magnificent chair.

On a sofa near by, reclining comfortably in curled-up positions, there were a Centipede and an Earthworm.

On the floor over in the far corner, there was something thick and white that looked as though it might be a Silkworm. But it was sleeping soundly and nobody was paying any attention to it.

Every one of these 'creatures' was at least as big as James himself, and in the strange greenish light that shone down from somewhere in the ceiling, they were absolutely terrifying to behold.

"I'm hungry!" the Spider announced suddenly, staring hard at James.

"*I'm* famished!" the Old-Green-Grasshopper said.

"So am *I!*" the Ladybird cried.

The Centipede sat up a little straighter on the sofa. "*Everyone's* famished!" he said. "We need food!"

Four pairs of round black glassy eyes were all fixed upon James.

The Centipede made a wriggling movement with his body as

though he were about to glide off the sofa – but he didn't.

There was a long pause – and a long silence.

The Spider (who happened to be a female spider) opened her mouth and ran a long black tongue delicately over her lips. "Aren't *you* hungry?" she asked suddenly, leaning forward and addressing herself to James.

Poor James was backed up against the far wall, shivering with fright and much too terrified to answer.

"What's the matter with you?" the Old-Green-Grasshopper asked. "You look positively ill!"

"He looks as though he's going to faint any second," the Centipede said.

"Oh, my goodness, the poor thing!" the Ladybird cried. "I do believe he thinks it's *him* that we are wanting to eat!"

There was a roar of laughter from all sides.

"Oh dear, oh dear!" they said. "What an awful thought!"

"You mustn't be frightened," the Ladybird said kindly. "We wouldn't *dream* of hurting you. You are one of *us* now, didn't you know that? You are one of the crew. We're all in the same boat."

"We've been waiting for you all day long," the Old-Green-Grasshopper said. "We thought you were never going to turn up. I'm glad you made it."

"So cheer up, my boy, cheer up!" the Centipede said. "And meanwhile I wish you'd come over here and give me a hand with these boots. It takes me *hours* to get them all off by myself."

James decided that this was most certainly not a time to be disagreeable, so he crossed the room to where the Centipede was sitting and knelt down beside him.

"Thank you so much," the Centipede said. "You are very kind."

"You have a lot of boots," James murmured.

"I have a lot of legs," the Centipede answered proudly. "And a lot of feet. One hundred, to be exact."

"*There* he goes again!" the Earthworm cried, speaking for the first time. "He simply cannot stop telling lies about his legs! He doesn't have anything *like* a hundred of them! He's only got forty-two! The trouble is that most people don't bother to count them. They just take his word. And anyway, there is nothing *marvellous*, you know, Centipede, about having a lot of legs."

"Poor fellow," the Centipede said, whispering in James's ear. "He's blind. He can't see how splendid I look."

"In my opinion," the Earthworm said, "the *really* marvellous thing is to have no legs at all and to be able to walk just the same."

"You call that *walking!*" cried the Centipede. "You're a *slitherer*, that's all you are! You just *slither* along!"

"I glide," said the Earthworm primly.

"You are a slimy beast," answered the Centipede.

"I am *not* a slimy beast," the Earthworm said. "I am a useful and much loved creature. Ask any gardener you like. And as for you…"

"I am a pest!" the Centipede announced, grinning broadly and looking round the room for approval.

"He is *so* proud of that," the Ladybird said, smiling at James. "Though for the life of me I cannot understand why."

"I am the only pest in this room!" cried the Centipede, still grinning away. "Unless you count Old-Green-Grasshopper over there. But he is long past it now. He is too old to be a pest any more."

The Old-Green-Grasshopper turned his huge black eyes upon the Centipede and gave him a withering look. "Young fellow," he said, speaking in a deep, slow, scornful voice, "I have never been a pest in my life. I am a musician."

"Hear, hear!" said the Ladybird.

"James," the Centipede said. "Your names *is* James, isn't it?"

"Yes."

"Well, James, have you ever in your life seen such a marvellous colossal Centipede as me?"

"I certainly haven't," James answered. "How on earth did you get to be like that?"

"*Very* peculiar," the Centipede said. "*Very, very* peculiar indeed. Let me tell you what happened. I was messing about in the garden under the old peach tree and suddenly a funny little green thing came wriggling past my nose. Bright green it was, and extraordinarily beautiful, and it looked like some kind of a tiny stone or crystal..."

"Oh, but I know what that was!" cried James.

"It happened to me, too!" said the Ladybird.

"And me!" Miss Spider said. "Suddenly there were little green things everywhere! The soil was full of them!"

"I actually swallowed one!" the Earthworm declared proudly.

"So did I!" the Ladybird said.

"I swallowed three!" the Centipede cried. "But who's telling this story anyway? Don't interrupt!"

"It's too late to tell stories now," the Old-Green-Grasshopper announced. "It's time to go to sleep."

"I refuse to sleep in my boots!" the Centipede cried. "How many more are there to come off, James?"

"I think I've done about twenty so far," James told him.

"Then that leaves eighty to go," the Centipede said.

"*Twenty-two*, not *eighty*!" shrieked the Earthworm. "He's lying again."

The Centipede roared with laughter.

"Stop pulling the Earthworm's leg," the Ladybird said.

This sent the Centipede into hysterics. "Pulling his *leg!*" he cried, wriggling with glee and pointing at the Earthworm. "Which leg am I pulling? You tell me that?"

James decided that he rather liked the Centipede. He was obviously a rascal, but what a change it was to hear somebody laughing once in a while. He had never heard Aunt Sponge or Aunt Spiker laughing aloud in all the time he had been with them.

"We really *must* get some sleep," the Old-Green-Grasshopper said. "We've got a tough day ahead of us tomorrow. So would you be kind enough, Miss Spider, to make the beds?"

A few minutes later, Miss Spider had made the first bed. It was hanging from the ceiling, suspended by a rope of threads at either end so that actually it looked more like a hammock than a bed. But it was a magnificent affair, and the stuff that it was made of shimmered like silk in the pale light.

"I do hope you'll find it comfortable," Miss Spider said to the Old-Green-Grasshopper. "I made it as soft and silky as I possibly could. I spun it with gossamer. That's a much better quality thread than the one I use for my own web."

"Thank you so much, my dear lady," the Old-Green-Grasshopper said, climbing into the hammock. "Ah, this is just what I needed. Good night, everybody. Good night."

Then Miss Spider spun the next hammock, and the Ladybird got in.

After that, she spun a long one for the Centipede, and an even longer one for the Earthworm.

"And how do you like *your* bed?" she said to James when it came to his turn. "Hard or soft?"

"I like it soft, thank you very much," James answered.

"For goodness' sake stop staring round the room and get on with my boots!" the Centipede said. "You and I are never going to get any sleep at this rate! And kindly line them up neatly in pairs as you take them off. Don't just throw them over your shoulder."

James worked away frantically on the Centipede's boots. Each one had laces that had to be untied and loosened before it could be pulled off, and to make matters worse, all the laces were tied up in the most terrible complicated knots that had to be unpicked with fingernails. It was just awful. It took about two hours. And by the time James had pulled off the last boot of all and had lined them up in a row on the floor – twenty-one pairs altogether – the Centipede was fast asleep.

"Wake up, Centipede," whispered James giving him a gentle dig in the stomach. "It's time for bed."

"Thank you, my dear child," the Centipede said, opening his eyes. Then he got down off the sofa and ambled across the room and crawled into his hammock. James got into his own hammock – and oh, how soft and comfortable it was compared with the hard bare boards that his aunts had always made him sleep upon at home.

"Lights out," said the Centipede drowsily.

Nothing happened.

"Turn out the light!" he called, raising his voice.

James glanced round the room, wondering which of the others he might be talking to, but they were all asleep. The Old-Green-Grasshopper was snoring loudly through his nose. The Ladybird was making whistling noises as she breathed, and the Earthworm was coiled up like a spring at one end of his hammock, wheezing and blowing through his open mouth. As for Miss Spider, she had made a lovely web for herself across one corner of the room, and James could see her crouching right in the very centre of it, mumbling softly in her dreams.

"I said turn out the light!" shouted the Centipede angrily.

"Are you talking to me?" James asked him.

"Of course I'm not talking to you, you ass!" the Centipede answered. "That crazy Glow-worm has gone to sleep with her light on!"

For the first time since entering the room, James glanced up at the ceiling – and there he saw a most extraordinary sight. Something that looked like a gigantic fly without wings (it was at least three feet long) was standing upside down upon its six legs in the middle of the ceiling, and the tail end of this creature seemed to be literally on fire. A brilliant greenish light as bright as the brightest electric bulb was shining out of its tail and lighting up the whole room.

"Is *that* a Glow-worm?" asked James, staring at the light. "It doesn't look like a worm of any sort to me."

"Of course it's a Glow-worm," the Centipede answered. "At least that's what *she* calls herself. Although actually you are quite right. She isn't really a worm at all. Glow-worms are never worms. They are simply lady fireflies without wings. Wake up, you lazy beast!"

But the Glow-worm didn't stir, so the Centipede reached out of his hammock and picked up one of his boots from the floor. "Put out that wretched light!" he shouted, hurling the boot up at the ceiling.

The Glow-worm slowly opened one eye and stared at the Centipede. "There is no need to be rude," she said coldly. "All in good time."

"Come on, come on, come on!" shouted the Centipede. "Or I'll put it out for you!"

"Oh, hello, James!" the Glow-worm said, looking down and giving James a little wave and a smile. "I didn't see you come in. Welcome, my dear boy, welcome – and good night!"

Then *click* – and out went the light.

James Henry Trotter lay there in the darkness with his eyes wide open, listening to the strange sleeping noises that the 'creatures' were making all around him, and wondering what on earth was going to happen to him in the morning. Already, he was beginning to like his new friends very much. They were not nearly as terrible as they looked. In fact, they weren't really terrible at all. They seemed extremely kind and helpful in spite of all the shouting and arguing that went on between them.

"Good night, Old-Green-Grasshopper," he whispered. "Good night, Ladybird – Good night, Miss Spider –" But before he could go through them all, he had fallen fast asleep.

Jack and the Beanstalk

from REVOLTING RHYMES

JACK'S mother said, "We're *stony broke!*
Go out and find some wealthy bloke
Who'll buy our cow. Just say she's sound
And worth at least a hundred pound.
But don't you dare to let him know
That she's as old as billy-o."
Jack led the old brown cow away,
And came back later in the day,
And said, "Oh mumsie dear, guess what
Your clever little boy has got.
I got, I really don't know how,
A super trade-in for our cow."
The mother said, "You little creep,
I'll bet you sold her much too cheap."
When Jack produced one lousy bean,
His startled mother, turning green,
Leaped high up in the air and cried,
"I'm *absolutely stupefied!*
You crazy boy! D'you really mean
You sold our Daisy for a bean?"
She snatched the bean. She yelled, "You chump!"
And flung it on the rubbish-dump.
Then summoning up all her power,
She beat the boy for half an hour,
Using (and nothing could be meaner)
The handle of a vacuum-cleaner.

At ten p.m. or thereabout,
The little bean began to sprout.
By morning it had grown so tall
You couldn't see the top at all.
Young Jack cried, "Mum, admit it now!
It's better than a rotten cow!"
The mother said, "You lunatic!
Where are the beans that I can pick?
There's not *one bean!* It's bare as bare!"
"No no!" cried Jack. "You look up there!
Look very high and you'll behold
Each single leaf is solid gold!"
By gollikins, the boy was right!
Now, glistening in the morning light,
The mother actually perceives
A mass of lovely golden leaves!
She yells out loud, "My sainted souls!
I'll sell the Mini, buy a Rolls!
Don't stand and gape, you little clot!
Get up there quick and grab the lot!"
Jack was nimble, Jack was keen.
He scrambled up the mighty bean.
Up up he went without a stop,
But just as he was near the top,
A ghastly frightening thing occurred –
Not far above his head he heard
A big deep voice, a rumbling thing
That made the very heavens ring.
It shouted loud, "FE FI FO FUM
I SMELL THE BLOOD OF AN ENGLISHMAN!"
Jack was frightened, Jack was quick,
And down he climbed in half a tick.
"Oh Mum!" he gasped. "Believe you me

There's something nasty up our tree!
I saw him, Mum! My gizzard froze!
A Giant with a clever nose!"
"*A clever nose!*" his mother hissed.
"You must be going round the twist!"
"He smelled me out, I swear it, Mum!
He said he *smelled* an Englishman!"
The mother said, "And well he might!
I've told you every single night
To take a bath because you smell,
But would you do it? Would you hell!
You even make your mother shrink
Because of your unholy stink!"
Jack answered, "Well, if you're so clean
Why don't *you* climb the crazy bean."
The mother cried, "By gad, I will!
There's life within the old dog still!"
She hitched her skirts above her knee
And disappeared right up the tree.
Now would the Giant smell his mum?
Jack listened for the *fee-fo-fum*.
He gazed aloft. He wondered when
The dreaded words would come… And then…
From somewhere high above the ground

There came a frightful crunching sound.
He heard the Giant mutter twice,
"By gosh, that tasted very nice.
Although" (and this in grumpy tones)
"I wish there weren't so many bones."
"By Christopher!" Jack cried. "By gum!
The Giant's eaten up my mum!
He smelled her out! She's in his belly!
I had a hunch that she was smelly."
Jack stood there gazing longingly
Upon the huge and golden trcc.
He murmured softly, "Golly-gosh,
I guess I'll *have* to take a wash
If I am going to climb this tree,
Without the Giant smelling me.
In fact, a bath's my only hope…"
He rushed indoors and grabbed the soap
He scrubbed his body everywhere.
He even washed and rinsed his hair.
He did his teeth, he blew his nose
And went out smelling like a rose.
Once more he climbed the mighty bean.
The Giant sat there, gross, obscene,
Muttering through his vicious teeth
(While Jack sat tensely just beneath)
Muttering loud, "FEE FI FO FUM,
RIGHT NOW I CAN'T SMELL ANYONE."
Jack waited till the Giant slept,
Then out along the boughs he crept
And gathered so much gold, I swear
He was an instant millionaire.
"A bath," he said, "does seem to pay.
I'm going to have one every day."

The Witches

AN EXTRACT

How to recognise a Witch

THE next evening, after my grandmother had given me my bath, she took me once again into the living-room for another story.

"Tonight," the old woman said, "I am going to tell you how to recognise a witch when you see one."

"Can you always be sure?" I asked.

"No," she said, "you can't. And that's the trouble. But you can make a pretty good guess."

She was dropping cigar ash all over her lap, and I hoped she wasn't going to catch on fire before she'd told me how to recognise a witch.

"In the first place," she said, "a REAL WITCH is certain always to be wearing gloves when you meet her."

"Surely not *always*," I said. "What about in the summer when it's hot?"

"Even in the summer," my grandmother said. "She has to. Do you want to know why?"

"Why?" I said.

"Because she doesn't have finger-nails. Instead of finger-nails, she has thin curvy claws, like a cat, and she wears the gloves to hide them. Mind you, lots of very respectable women wear gloves, especially in winter, so this doesn't help you very much."

"Mamma used to wear gloves," I said.

"Not in the house," my grandmother said. "Witches wear gloves even in the house. They only take them off when they go to bed."

"How do you know all this, Grandmamma?"

"Don't interrupt," she said. "Just take it all in. The second thing to remember is that a REAL WITCH is always bald."

"*Bald?*" I said.

"Bald as a boiled egg," my grandmother said.

I was shocked. There was something indecent about a bald woman. "Why are they bald, Grandmamma?"

"Don't ask me why," she snapped. "But you can take it from me that not a single hair grows on a witch's head."

"How horrid!"

"Disgusting," my grandmother said.

"If she's bald, she'll be easy to spot," I said.

"Not at all," my grandmother said. "A REAL WITCH always wears a wig to hide her baldness. She wears a first-class wig. And it is almost impossible to tell a really first-class wig from ordinary hair unless you give it a pull to see if it comes off."

"Then that's what I'll have to do," I said.

"Don't be foolish," my grandmother said. "You can't go round pulling at the hair of every lady you meet, even if she *is* wearing gloves. Just you try it and see what happens."

"So that doesn't help much either," I said.

"None of these things is any good on its own," my grandmother said. "It's only when you put them all together that they begin to make a little sense. Mind you," my grandmother went on, "these wigs do cause a rather serious problem for witches."

"What problem, Grandmamma?"

"They make the scalp itch most terribly," she said. "You see, when

How to Recognise a Witch

a: claws hidden by gloves

b: peculiar nose

c: bald head with wig-rash

d: wig

e: sinister handbag

f: square feet with no toes

g: blue spit

an actress wears a wig, or if you or I were to wear a wig, we would be putting it on over our own hair, but a witch has to put it straight on to her naked scalp. And the underneath of a wig is always very rough and scratchy. It sets up a frightful itch on the bald skin. It causes nasty sores on the head. Wig-rash, the witches call it. And it doesn't half itch."

"What other things must I look for to recognise a witch?" I asked.

"Look for the nose-holes," my grandmother said. "Witches have slightly larger nose-holes than ordinary people. The rim of each nose-hole is pink and curvy, like the rim of a certain kind of seashell."

"Why do they have such big nose-holes?" I asked.

"For smelling with," my grandmother said. "A REAL WITCH has the most amazing powers of smell. She can actually smell out a child who is standing on the other side of the street on a pitch-black night."

"She couldn't smell me," I said. "I've just had a bath."

"Oh yes she could," my grandmother said. "The cleaner you happen to be, the more smelly you are to a witch."

"That can't be true," I said.

"An absolutely clean child gives off the most ghastly stench to a witch," my grandmother said. "The dirtier you are, the less you smell."

"But that doesn't make sense, Grandmamma."

"Oh yes it does," my grandmother said. "It isn't the *dirt* that the witch is smelling. It is *you*. The smell that drives a witch mad actually comes right out of your own skin. It comes oozing out of your skin in waves, and these waves, stink-waves the witches call them, go floating through the air and hit the witch right smack in her nostrils. They send her reeling."

"Now wait a minute, Grandmamma…"

"Don't interrupt," she said. " The point is this. When you haven't washed for a week and your skin is all covered over with dirt, then quite obviously the stink-waves cannot come oozing out nearly so strongly."

"I shall never have a bath again," I said.

"Just don't have one too often," my grandmother said. "Once a month is quite often enough for a sensible child."

It was at moments like these that I loved my grandmother more than ever.

"Grandmamma," I said, "if it's a dark night, how can a witch smell the difference between a child and a grown-up?"

"Because grown-ups don't give out stink-waves," she said. "Only children do that."

"But I don't *really* give out stink-waves, do I?" I said. "I'm not giving them out at this very moment, am I?"

"Not to me you aren't," my grandmother said. "To me you are smelling like raspberries and cream. But to a witch you would be smelling absolutely disgusting."

"What would I be smelling of?" I asked.

"Dogs' droppings," my grandmother said.

I reeled. I was stunned. "*Dogs' droppings!*" I cried. "I am *not* smelling

of dogs' droppings! I don't believe it! I *won't* believe it!"

"What's more," my grandmother said, speaking with a touch of relish, "to a witch you'd be smelling of *fresh* dogs' droppings."

"That simply is not true!" I cried. "I know I am not smelling of dogs' droppings, stale or fresh!"

"There's no point in arguing about it," my grandmother said. "It's a fact of life."

I was outraged. I simply couldn't believe what my grandmother was telling me.

"So if you see a woman holding her nose as she passes you in the street," she went on, "that woman could easily be a witch."

I decided to change the subject. "Tell me what else to look for in a witch," I said.

"The eyes," my grandmother said. "Look carefully at the eyes, because the eyes of a REAL WITCH are different from yours and mine. Look in the middle of each eye where there is normally a little black dot. If she is a witch, the black dot will keep changing colour, and you will see fire and you will see ice dancing right in the very centre of the coloured dot. It will send shivers running all over your skin."

My grandmother leant back in her chair and sucked away contentedly at her foul black cigar. I squatted on the floor, staring up at her, fascinated. She was not smiling. She looked deadly serious.

"Are there other things?" I asked her.

"Of course there are other things," my grandmother said. "You don't seem to understand that witches are not actually women at all. They *look* like women. They talk like women. And they are able to act like women. But in actual fact, they are totally different animals. They are demons in human shape. That is why they have claws and bald heads and queer noses and peculiar eyes, all of which they have to conceal as best they can from the rest of the world."

"What else is different about them, Grandmamma?"

"The feet," she said. "Witches never have toes."

"No toes!" I cried. "Then what do they have?"

"They just have feet," my grandmother said. "The feet have square ends with no toes on them at all."

"Does that make it difficult to walk?" I asked.

"Not at all," my grandmother said. "But it does give them a problem with their shoes. All ladies like to wear small rather pointed shoes, but a witch, whose feet are very wide and square at the ends, has the most awful job squeezing her feet into those neat little pointed shoes."

"Why doesn't she wear wide comfy shoes with square ends?" I asked.

"She dare not," my grandmother said. "Just as she hides her baldness with a wig, she must also hide her ugly witch's feet by squeezing them into pretty shoes."

"Isn't that terribly uncomfortable?" I said.

"Extremely uncomfortable," my grandmother said. "But she has to put up with it."

"If she's wearing ordinary shoes, it won't help me to recognise her, will it, Grandmamma?"

"I'm afraid it won't," my grandmother said. "You might possibly see her limping very slightly, but only if you were watching closely."

"Are those the only differences then, Grandmamma?"

"There's one more," my grandmother said. "Just one more."

"What is it, Grandmamma?"

"Their spit is blue."

"Blue?" I cried. "Not blue! Their spit can't be *blue!*"

"Blue as a bilberry," she said.

"You don't mean it, Grandmamma! Nobody can have blue spit!"

"Witches can," she said.

"Is it like ink?" I asked.

"Exactly," she said. "They even use it to write with. They use those old-fashioned pens that have nibs and they simply lick the nib."

"Can't you *notice* the blue spit, Grandmamma? If a witch was talking to me, would I be able to notice it?"

"Only if you looked carefully," my grandmother said. "If you looked very carefully you would probably see a slight blueish tinge on their teeth. But it doesn't show much."

"It would if she spat," I said.

"Witches never spit," my grandmother said. "They daren't."

I couldn't believe my grandmother would be lying to me. She went to church every morning of the week and she said grace before every meal, and somebody who did that would never tell lies. I was beginning to believe every word she spoke.

"So there you are," my grandmother said. "That's about all I can tell you. None of it is very helpful. You can still never be absolutely sure whether a woman is a witch or not just by looking at her. But if she is wearing the gloves, if she has the large nose-holes, the queer eyes and the hair that looks as though it might be a wig, and if she has a blueish tinge on her teeth – if she has all of these things, then you run like mad."

"Grandmamma," I said, "when you were a little girl, did *you* ever meet a witch?"

"Once," my grandmother said. "Only once."

"What happened?"

"I'm not going to tell you," she said. "It would frighten you out of your skin and give you bad dreams."

"Please tell me," I begged.

"No," she said. "Certain things are too horrible to talk about."

"Does it have something to do with your missing thumb?" I asked.

Suddenly, her old wrinkled lips shut tight as a pair of tongs and the hand that held the cigar (which had no thumb on it) began to quiver very slightly.

I waited. She didn't look at me. She didn't speak. All of a sudden she had shut herself off completely. The conversation was finished.

"Goodnight, Grandmamma," I said, rising from the floor and kissing her on the cheek.

She didn't move. I crept out of the room and went to my bedroom.

Recipe for concocting Formula 86 Delayed Action Mouse-Maker

"FIRST," said The Grand High Witch, "I had to find something that vould cause the children to become very small very qvickly."

"And what was that?" cried the audience.

"That part vos simple," said The Grand High Witch. "All you have to do if you are vishing to make a child very small is to look at him through the wrrrong end of a telescope."

"She's a wonder!" cried the audience. "Who else would have thought of a thing like that?"

"So you take the wrrrong end of a telescope," continued The Grand High Witch, "and you boil it until it gets soft."

"How long does that take?" they asked her.

"Twenty-vun hours of boiling," answered The Grand High Witch. "And vhile this is going on, you take exactly forty-five brrrown mice and you chop off their tails vith a carving-knife and you fry the tails in hair-oil until they are nice and crrrisp."

"What do we do with all those mice who have had their tails chopped off?" asked the audience.

"You simmer them in frog-juice for vun hour," came the answer. "But listen to me. So far I have only given you the easy part of the rrrecipe. The rrreally difficult problem is to put in something that will have a genuine delayed action rrree-sult, something that can be eaten by children on a certain day but vhich vill not start vurrrking on them until nine o'clock the next morning vhen they arrive at school."

"What did you come up with, O Brainy One?" they called out. "Tell us the great secret!"

"The secret," announced The Grand High Witch triumphantly, "is an *alarm-clock!*"

"An alarm-clock!" they cried. "It's a stroke of genius!"

"Of course it is," said The Grand High Witch. "You can set a

twenty-four-hour alarm-clock today and at exactly nine o'clock tomorrow it vill go off."

"But we will need five million alarm-clocks!" cried the audience. "We will need one for each child!"

"Idiots!" shouted The Grand High Witch. "If you are vonting a steak, you do not cook the whole cow! It is the same with alarm-clocks. Vun clock vill make enough for a thousand children. Here is vhat you do. You set your alarm-clock to go off at nine o'clock tomorrow morning. Then you rrroast it in the oven until it is crrrisp and tender. Are you wrrriting this down?"

"We are, Your Grandness, we are!" they cried.

"Next," said The Grand High Witch, "you take your boiled telescope and your frrried mouse-tails and your cooked mice and your rrroasted alarm-clock and all together you put them into the mixer. Then you mix them at full speed. This vill give you a nice thick paste. Vhile the mixer is still mixing you must add to it the yolk of vun grrruntle's egg."

"A gruntle's egg!" cried the audience. "We shall do that!"

Underneath all the clamour that was going on I heard one witch in the back row saying to her neighbour, "I'm getting a bit old to go bird's nesting. Those ruddy gruntles always nest very high up."

"So you mix in the egg," The Grand High Witch went on, "and vun after the other you also mix in the following items: the claw of a crrrabcrrruncher, the beak of a blabbersnitch, the snout of a grrrobblesqvirt and the tongue of a catsprrringer. I trust you are not having any trrrouble finding those."

"None at all!" they cried out. "We will spear the blabbersnitch and trap the crabcruncher and shoot the grobblesquirt and catch the cat-springer in his burrow!"

"Excellent!" said The Grand High Witch. "Vhen you have mixed everything together in the mixer, you vill have a most marvellous-looking grrreen liqvid. Put vun drop, just vun titchy droplet of this liqvid into a chocolate or a sveet, and *at nine o'clock the next morning* the child who ate it vill turn into a mouse in twenty-six seconds! But vun vurd of vorning. Never increase the dose. Never put more than vun drrrop into each sveet or chocolate. And never give more than vun sveet or chocolate to each child. An overdose of Delayed Action Mouse-Maker vill mess up the timing of the alarm-clock and cause the child to turn into a mouse too early. A large overdose might even have an instant effect, and you vouldn't vont that, vould you? You vouldn't vont the children turning into mice rrright there in your sveet-shops. That vould give the game away. So be very carrreful! Do not overdose!"

Metamorphosis

I remember thinking to myself, *There is no escape for me now! Even if I make a run for it and manage to dodge the lot of them, I still won't get out because the doors are chained and locked! I'm finished! I'm done for! Oh Grandmamma, what are they going to do to me?*

I looked round and I saw a hideous painted and powdered witch's face staring down at me, and the face opened its mouth and yelled triumphantly, "It's here! It's behind the screen! Come and get it!" The witch reached out a gloved hand and grabbed me by the hair but I twisted free and jumped away. I ran, oh how I ran! The sheer terror of it all put wings on my feet! I flew around the outside of the great Ballroom and not one of them had a chance of catching me. As I came level with the doors, I paused and tried to open them but the big chain was on them and they didn't even rattle.

The witches were not bothering to chase me. They simply stood there in small groups, watching me and knowing for certain that there was no way I could escape. Several of them were holding their noses with gloved fingers and there were cries of "Poo! What a stink! We can't stand this much longer!"

"Catch it then, you idiots!" screamed The Grand High Witch from up on the platform. "Sprrread out in a line across the room and close in on it and grab it! Corner this filthy little gumboil and seize it and bring it up here to me!"

The witches spread out as they were told. They advanced towards me, some from one end, some from the other, and some came down the middle between the rows of empty chairs. They were bound to get me now. They had me cornered.

From sheer and absolute terror, I began to scream. "*Help!*" I screamed, turning my head towards the doors in the hope that somebody outside might hear me. "Help! Help! Hel-l-l-lp!"

"Get it!" shouted The Grand High Witch. "Grrrab hold of it! Stop it yelling!"

They rushed at me then, and about five of them grabbed me by the arms and legs and lifted me clear off the ground. I went on screaming, but one of them clapped a gloved hand over my mouth and that stopped me.

"Brrring it here!" shouted The Grand High Witch. "Brrring the spying little vurm up here to me!"

I was carried on to the platform with my arms and legs held tight by many hands, and I lay there suspended in the air, facing the ceiling. I saw The Grand High Witch standing over me, grinning at me in the most horrible way. She held up the small blue bottle of Mouse-Maker and she said, "Now for a little medicine! Hold his nose to make him open his mouth!"

Strong fingers pinched my nose. I kept my mouth closed tight and held my breath. But I couldn't do it for long. My chest was bursting. I opened my mouth to get one big quick breath of air and as I did so, The Grand High Witch poured the entire contents of the little bottle down my throat!

Oh, the pain and the fire! It felt as though a kettleful of boiling water had been poured into my mouth. My throat was going up in flames! Then very quickly the frightful burning searing scorching feeling started spreading down into my chest and into my tummy and on and on into my arms and legs and all over my body! I screamed and screamed but once again the gloved hand was clapped over my lips. The next thing I felt was my skin beginning to tighten. How else can I describe it? It was quite literally a tightening and a shrinking of the skin all over my body from the top of my head to the tips of my fingers to the ends of my toes! I felt as though I was a balloon and somebody was twisting the top of the balloon and twisting and twisting and the balloon was getting smaller and smaller and the skin was getting tighter and tighter and soon it was going to burst.

Then the *squeezing* began. This time I was inside a suit of iron and somebody was turning a screw, and with each turn of the screw the iron suit became smaller and smaller so that I was squeezed like an orange into a pulpy mess with the juice running out of my sides.

After that there came a fierce prickling sensation all over my skin (or what was left of my skin) as though tiny needles were forcing their way out through the surface of the skin from the inside, and this, I realise now, was the growing of the mouse-fur.

Far away in the distance, I heard the voice of The Grand High Witch yelling, "Five hundred doses! This stinking little carbuncle has had five hundred doses and the alarm-clock has been smashed and now vee are having *instantaneous action!*" I heard clapping and cheering and I remember thinking: *I am not myself any longer! I have gone clear out of my own skin!*

I noticed that the floor was only an inch from my nose.

I noticed also a pair of little furry front paws resting on the floor. I was able to move those paws. They were mine!

At that moment, I realised that I was not a little boy any longer. I was A MOUSE.

"Now for the mouse-trrrap!" I heard The Grand High Witch yelling. "I've got it right here! And here's a piece of cheese!"

But I wasn't going to wait for *that*. I was off across the platform like a streak of lightning! I was astonished at my own speed! I leapt over witches' feet right and left, and in no time at all I was down the steps and on to the floor of the Ballroom itself and skittering off among the rows of chairs. What I especially liked was the fact that I made no sound at all as I ran. I was a swift and silent mover. And quite amazingly, the pain had all gone now. I was feeling quite remarkably well. *It is not a bad thing after all,* I thought to myself, *to be tiny as well as speedy when there is a bunch of dangerous females after your blood.* I selected the back leg of a chair and squeezed up against it and kept very still.

In the distance, The Grand High Witch was shouting, "Leave the little stinkpot alone! It is not vurth bothering about! It is only a mouse now! Somebody else vill soon catch it! Let us get out of here! The meeting is over! Unlock the doors and shove off to the Sunshine Terrace to have tea vith that idiotic Manager!"

The Heart of a Mouse

*Tricked into drinking Formula 86 Delayed Action
Mouse-Maker, the witches themselves are turned into mice.
Grandmother returns home with her grandson.*

IT was lovely to be back in Norway once again in my grandmother's
fine old house. But now that I was so small, everything looked different and it took me quite a while to find my way around. Mine was a
world of carpets and table-legs and chair-legs and the little crannies
behind large pieces of furniture. A closed door could not be opened
and nothing could be reached that was on a table.

But after a few days, my grandmother began to invent gadgets for
me in order to make life a bit easier. She got a carpenter to put
together a number of slim tall stepladders and she placed one of
these against each table in the house so that I could climb up whenever I wanted to. She herself invented a wonderful door-opening
device made out of wires and springs and pulleys, with heavy weights
dangling on cords, and soon every door in the house had a door-opener on it. All I had to do was to press my front paws on to a tiny
wooden platform and hey presto, a spring would stretch and a weight
would drop and the door would swing open.

Next, she rigged up an equally ingenious system whereby I could
switch on the light whenever I entered a room at night. I cannot
explain how it worked because I know nothing about electricity, but
there was a little button let into the floor near the door in every room
in the house, and when I pressed the button gently with one paw, the
light would come on. When I pressed it a second time, the light would
go off again.

My grandmother made me a tiny toothbrush, using a matchstick for
the handle, and into this she stuck little bits of bristle that she had
snipped off one of her hair brushes. "You *must* not get any holes in
your teeth," she said. "I can't take a *mouse* to a dentist! He'd think I was
crazy!"

234

"It's funny," I said, "but ever since I became a mouse I've hated the taste of sweets and chocolates. So I don't think I'll get any holes."

"You are still going to brush your teeth after every meal," my grandmother said. And I did.

For a bath-tub she gave me a silver sugar-basin, and I bathed in it every night before going to bed. She allowed no one else into the house, not even a servant or a cook. We kept entirely to ourselves and we were very happy in each other's com-pany.

One evening, as I lay on my grandmother's lap in front of the fire, she said to me, "I wonder what happened to that little Bruno."

"I wouldn't be surprised if his father gave him to the hall-porter to drown in the fire-bucket," I answered.

"I'm afraid you may be right," my grandmother said. "The poor little thing."

We were silent for a few minutes, my grandmother puffing away at her black cigar while I dozed comfortably in the warmth.

"Can I ask you something, Grandmamma?" I said.

"Ask me anything you like, my darling."

"How long does a mouse live?"

"Ah," she said. "I've been waiting for you to ask me that."

There was a silence. She sat there smoking away and gazing at the fire.

"Well," I said. "How long *do* we live, us mice?"

"I have been reading about mice," she said. "I have been trying to find out everything I can about them."

"Go on then, Grandmamma. Why don't you tell me?"

"If you really want to know," she said, "I'm afraid a mouse doesn't live for a very long time."

"How long?" I asked.

"Well, an *ordinary* mouse only lives for about three years," she said. "But you are not an ordinary mouse. You are a mouse-person, and that is a very different matter."

"How different?" I asked. "How long does a mouse-person live, Grandmamma?"

"Longer," she said. "Much longer."

"How much longer?" I asked.

"A mouse-person will almost certainly live for three times as long as an ordinary mouse," my grandmother said. "About nine years."

"Good!" I cried. "That's great! It's the best news I've ever had!"

"Why do you say that?" she asked, surprised.

"Because I would never want to live longer than you," I said. "I couldn't stand being looked after by anybody else."

There was a short silence. She had a way of fondling me behind the ears with the tip of one finger. It felt lovely.

"How old are *you*, Grandmamma?" I asked.

"I'm eighty-six," she said.

"Will you live another eight or nine years?"

"I might," she said. "With a bit of luck."

"You've got to," I said. "Because by then I'll be a very old mouse and you'll be a very old grandmother and soon after that we'll both die together."

"That would be perfect," she said.

I had a little doze after that. I just shut my eyes and thought of nothing and felt at peace with the world.

"Would you like me to tell you something about yourself that is very interesting?" my grandmother said.

"Yes please, Grandmamma," I said, without opening my eyes.

"I couldn't believe it at first, but apparently it's quite true," she said.

"What is it?" I asked.

"The heart of a mouse," she said, "and that means *your* heart, is beating at the rate of *five hundred times a minute!* Isn't that amazing?"

"That's not possible," I said, opening my eyes wide.

"It's as true as I'm sitting here," she said. "It's a sort of a miracle."

"That's nearly nine beats every second!" I cried, working it out in my head.

"Correct," she said. "Your heart is going so fast it's impossible to hear the separate beats. All one hears is a soft humming sound."

She was wearing a lace dress and the lace kept tickling my nose. I had to rest my head on my front paws.

"Have *you* ever heard my heart humming away, Grandmamma?" I asked her.

"Often," she said. "I hear it when you are lying very close to me on the pillow at night."

The two of us remained silent in front of the fire for a long time after that, thinking about these wonderful things.

"My darling," she said at last, "are you sure you don't mind being a mouse for the rest of your life?"

"I don't mind at all," I said. "It doesn't matter who you are or what you look like so long as somebody loves you."

It's off to work we go!

*Grandmother reveals that a new Grand High Witch and
her Assistant Witches are living in a castle in Norway. Our next
task, she says, is to destroy every witch in the place.*

"AND after that?" I said, quivering with excitement.

"After that, my darling, the greatest task of all will begin for
you and me! We shall pack our bags and go travelling all over the
world! In every country we visit, we shall seek out the houses where
the witches are living! We shall find each house, one by one, and
having found it, you will creep inside and leave your little drops of
deadly Mouse-Maker in the bread, or the cornflakes, or the rice-
pudding or whatever food you see lying about. It will be a triumph,
my darling! A colossal unbeatable triumph. We shall do it entirely by
ourselves, just you and me! That will be our work for the rest of our
lives!"

My grandmother picked me up off the table and kissed me on the
nose. "Oh, my goodness me, we're going to be busy these next few
weeks and months and years!" she cried.

"I think we are," I said. "But what fun and excitement it's going to
be!"

"You can say that again!" my grandmother cried, giving me another
kiss. "I can't wait to get started!"

The Cow

from DIRTY BEASTS

PLEASE listen while I tell you now
About a most fantastic cow.
Miss Milky Daisy was her name,
And when, aged seven months, she came
To live with us, she did her best
To look the same as all the rest.
But Daisy, as we all could see
Had some kind of deformity,
A funny sort of bumpy lump
On either side, above the rump.
Now, not so very long ago,
These bumpy lumps began to grow,
And three or maybe four months later
(I stood there, an enthralled spectator)
These bumpy lumps burst wide apart
And out there came (I cross my heart)
Of all the wondrous marvellous things,
A pair of gold and silver wings!
A cow with wings! A flying cow!
I'd never seen one up to now.
"Oh Daisy dear, can this be true?"
She flapped her wings and up she flew!
Most gracefully she climbed up high,
She fairly whizzed across the sky.
You should have seen her dive and swoop!
She even did a loop the loop!
Of course, almost immediately
Her picture was on live TV,

And millions came each day to stare
At Milky Daisy in the air.
They shouted "Jeepers Creepers! Wow!
It really is a flying cow!"
They laughed and clapped and cheered and waved,
And all of them were well-behaved
Except for one quite horrid man
Who'd travelled from Afghanistan.
This fellow, standing in the crowd,
Raised up his voice and yelled aloud,
"That silly cow! Hey, listen Daisy!
I think you're absolutely crazy!"
Unfortunately Daisy heard
Quite clearly every single word.
"By gosh," she cried, "what awful cheek!
Who is this silly foreign freak?"
She dived, and using all her power
She got to sixty miles an hour.
"Bombs gone!" she cried. "Take that!" she said,
And dropped a cowpat on his head.

Cadbury's Dairy Milk

from MY YEAR

JANUARY, I now remember, was the month when I had my first office job in London at the age of eighteen. The pay was five pounds a week and I used to travel up by train from where we lived in Kent to a station in the City of London called Cannon Street. As soon as I jumped off the train there was a mad gallop through the crowded streets in the slushy snow to reach the great hall of the Shell Company's building in order to clock-in by nine o'clock. I was one of a small group of Eastern Staff Trainees and absolute punctuality was demanded of us. If we were late, we were reported to the directors. At lunchtime I used to go to a pub for a pork pie and a beer, and on my walk back to the office I always, absolutely always, treated myself to a tuppenny bar of Cadbury's Dairy Milk chocolate. By the time I got back to the office I had eaten all the chocolate, but I never threw away the silver paper. On my very first day I rolled it into a tiny ball and left it on my desk. On the second day I rolled the second bit of silver paper around the first bit. And every day from then on I added another bit of silver paper to that little ball. The ball began to grow. In one year it had become very nearly as big as a tennis ball and just as round. It was extraordinarily heavy. When I picked it up it felt like a lump of lead and I think this was because in those days, some fifty years ago, the silver paper they used to wrap chocolate in was much thicker than it is today and very much superior all round. I never lost my chocolate silver-paper ball and today it sits, as it has done ever since I started to write, on the old pine table beside my writing chair.

Charlie and
the Chocolate Factory

AN EXTRACT

The Miracle

CHARLIE entered the shop and laid the damp fifty pence on the counter.

"One Wonka's Whipple-Scrumptious Fudgemallow Delight," he said, remembering how much he had loved the one he had on his birthday.

The man behind the counter looked fat and well-fed. He had big lips and fat cheeks and a very fat neck. The fat around his neck bulged out all around the top of his collar like a rubber ring. He turned and reached behind him for the chocolate bar, then he turned back again and handed it to Charlie. Charlie grabbed it and quickly tore off the wrapper and took an enormous bite. Then he took another... and another... and oh, the joy of being able to cram large pieces of something sweet and solid into one's mouth! The sheer blissful joy of being able to fill one's mouth with rich solid food!

"You look like you wanted that one, sonny," the shopkeeper said pleasantly.

Charlie nodded, his mouth bulging with chocolate.

The shopkeeper put Charlie's change on the counter. "Take it easy," he said. "It'll give you a tummy-ache if you swallow it like that without chewing."

Charlie went on wolfing the chocolate. He couldn't stop. And in less than half a minute, the whole thing had disappeared down his throat. He was quite out of breath, but he felt marvellously, extraordinarily happy. He reached out a hand to take the change. Then he paused. His eyes were just above the level of the counter. They were staring at the silver coins lying there. The coins were all five-penny pieces. There were nine of them altogether. Surely it wouldn't matter if he spent just one more...

"I think," he said quietly, "I think... I'll have just one more of those chocolate bars. The same kind as before, please."

"Why not?" the fat shopkeeper said, reaching behind him again and taking another Whipple-Scrumptious Fudgemallow Delight from the shelf. He laid it on the counter.

Charlie picked it up and tore off the wrapper... and *suddenly*... from underneath the wrapper... there came a brilliant flash of gold.

Charlie's heart stood still.

"It's a Golden Ticket!" screamed the shopkeeper, leaping about a foot in the air. "You've got a Golden Ticket! You've found the last Golden Ticket! Hey, would you believe it! Come and look at this, everybody! The kid's found Wonka's last Golden Ticket! There it is! It's right here in his hands!"

It seemed as though the shopkeeper might be going to have a fit. "In my shop, too!" he yelled. "He found it right here in my own little shop! Somebody call the newspapers quick and let them know! Watch out now, sonny! Don't tear it as you unwrap it! That thing's precious!"

In a few seconds, there was a crowd of about twenty people clustering around Charlie, and many more were pushing their way in from the street. Everybody wanted to get a look at the Golden Ticket and at the lucky finder.

"Where is it?" somebody shouted. "Hold it up so all of us can see it!"

"There it is, there!" someone else shouted. "He's holding it in his hands! See the gold shining!"

"How did *he* manage to find it, I'd like to know?" a large boy shouted angrily. "*Twenty* bars a day I've been buying for weeks and weeks!"

"Think of all the free stuff he'll be getting too!" another boy said enviously. "A lifetime supply!"

"He'll need it, the skinny little shrimp!" a girl said, laughing.

Charlie hadn't moved. He hadn't even unwrapped the Golden Ticket from around the chocolate. He was standing very still, holding it tightly with both hands while the crowd pushed and shouted all around him. He felt quite dizzy. There was a peculiar floating sensation coming over him, as though he were floating up in the air like a balloon. His feet didn't seem to be touching the ground at all. He could hear his heart thumping away loudly somewhere in his throat.

At that point, he became aware of a hand resting lightly on his shoulder, and when he looked up, he saw a tall man standing over him. "Listen," the man whispered. "I'll buy it from you. I'll give you fifty pounds. How about it, eh? And I'll give you a new bicycle as well. Okay?"

"Are you *crazy?*" shouted a woman who was standing equally close. "Why, I'd give him two hundred pounds for that ticket! You want to sell that ticket for two hundred pounds, young man?"

"That's *quite* enough of that!" the fat shopkeeper shouted, pushing his way through the crowd and taking Charlie firmly by the arm. "Leave the kid alone, will you! Make way there! Let him out!" And to Charlie, as he led him to the door, he whispered, "Don't you let *any-body* have it! Take it straight home, quickly, before you lose it! Run all the way and don't stop till you get there, you understand?"

Charlie nodded.

"You know something," the fat shopkeeper said, pausing a moment and smiling at Charlie, "I have a feeling you needed a break like this. I'm awfully glad you got it. Good luck to you, sonny."

"Thank you," Charlie said, and off he went, running through the snow as fast as his legs would go. And as he flew past Mr Willy Wonka's factory, he turned and waved at it and sang out, "I'll be seeing you! I'll be seeing you soon!" And five minutes later he arrived at his own home.

What It Said on the Golden Ticket

Charlie burst through the front door, shouting, "*Mother! Mother! Mother!*"

Mrs Bucket was in the old grandparents' room, serving them their evening soup.

"*Mother!*" yelled Charlie, rushing in on them like a hurricane. "Look! I've got it! Look, Mother, look! The last Golden Ticket! It's mine! I

found some money in the street and I bought two bars of chocolate and the second one had the Golden Ticket and there were *crowds* of people all around me wanting to see it and the shopkeeper rescued me and I ran all the way home and here I am! *IT'S THE FIFTH GOLDEN TICKET, MOTHER, AND I'VE FOUND IT!*"

Mrs Bucket simply stood and stared, while the four old grandparents, who were sitting up in bed balancing bowls of soup on their laps, all dropped their spoons with a clatter and froze against their pillows.

For about ten seconds there was absolute silence in the room. Nobody dared to speak or move. It was a magic moment.

Then, very softly, Grandpa Joe said, "You're pulling our legs, Charlie, aren't you? You're having a little joke?"

"I am *not!*" cried Charlie, rushing up to the bed and holding out the large and beautiful Golden Ticket for him to see.

Grandpa Joe leaned forward and took a close look, his nose almost touching the ticket. The others watched him, waiting for the verdict.

Then very slowly, with a slow and marvellous grin spreading all over his face, Grandpa Joe lifted his head and looked straight at Charlie.

The colour was rushing to his cheeks, and his eyes were wide open, shining with joy, and in the centre of each eye, right in the very centre, in the black pupil, a little spark of wild excitement was slowly dancing. Then the old man took a deep breath, and suddenly, with no warning whatsoever, an explosion seemed to take place inside him. He threw up his arms and yelled "*Yippeeeeeeee!*" And at the same time, his long bony body rose up out of the bed and his bowl of soup went flying into the face of Grandma Josephine, and in one fantastic leap, this old fellow of ninety-six and a half, who hadn't been out of bed these last twenty years, jumped on to the floor and started doing a dance of victory in his pyjamas.

"Yippeeeeeeeeee!" he shouted. "Three cheers for Charlie! Hip, hip, hooray!"

At this point, the door opened, and Mr Bucket walked into the room. He was cold and tired, and he looked it. All day long, he had been shovelling snow in the streets.

"*Cripes!*" he cried. "What's going on in here?"

It didn't take them long to tell him what had happened.

"I don't believe it!" he said. "It's not possible."

"Show him the ticket, Charlie!" shouted Grandpa Joe, who was still dancing around the floor like a dervish in his striped pyjamas. "Show your father the fifth and last Golden Ticket in the world!"

"Let me see it, Charlie," Mr Bucket said, collapsing into a chair and holding out his hand. Charlie came forward with the precious document.

It was a very beautiful thing, this Golden Ticket, having been made, so it seemed, from a sheet of pure gold hammered out almost to the thinness of paper. On one side of it, printed by some clever method in jet-black letters, was the invitation itself – from Mr Wonka.

"Read it aloud," said Grandpa Joe, climbing back into bed again at last. "Let's all hear exactly what it says."

Mr Bucket held the lovely Golden Ticket up close to his eyes. His hands were trembling slightly, and he seemed to be overcome by the whole business. He took several deep breaths. Then he cleared his throat, and said, "All right, I'll read it. Here we go:

Greetings to you, the lucky finder of this Golden Ticket, from Mr Willy Wonka! I shake you warmly by the hand! Tremendous things are in store for you! Many wonderful surprises await you! For now, I do invite you to come to my factory and be my guest for one whole day – you and all others who are lucky enough to find my Golden Tickets. I, Willy Wonka, will conduct you around the factory myself, showing you everything that there is to see, and afterwards, when it is time to leave, you will be escorted home by a procession of large trucks. These trucks, I can promise you, will be loaded with enough delicious eatables to last you and your entire household for many years. If, at any time thereafter, you should run out of supplies, you have only to come back to the factory and show this Golden Ticket, and I shall be happy to refill your cupboard with whatever you want. In this way, you will be able to keep yourself supplied with tasty morsels for the rest of your life. But this is by no means the most exciting thing that will happen on the day of your visit. I am preparing other surprises that are even more marvellous and more fantastic for you and for all my beloved Golden Ticket holders – mystic and marvellous surprises that will entrance, delight, intrigue, astonish, and perplex you beyond measure. In your wildest dreams you could not imagine that such things could happen to you! Just wait and see! And now, here are your instructions: the day I have chosen for the visit is the first day in the month of February. On this day, and on no other, you must come to the factory gates at ten o'clock sharp in the morning. Don't be late! And you are allowed to bring with you either one or two members of your own family to look after you and to ensure that you don't get into mischief. One more thing – be certain to have this ticket with you, otherwise you will not be admitted.

(Signed) Willy Wonka."

"The first day of *February!*" cried Mrs Bucket. 'But that's *tomorrow!* Today is the last day of January. *I know it is!*"

"Cripes!" said Mr Bucket. "I think you're right!"

"You're just in time!" shouted Grandpa Joe. "There's not a moment to lose. You must start making preparations at once! Wash your face, comb your hair, scrub your hands, brush your teeth, blow your nose, cut your nails, polish your shoes, iron your shirt, and for heaven's sake, get all that mud off your pants! You must get ready, my boy! You must get ready for the biggest day of your life!"

"Now don't over-excite yourself, Grandpa," Mrs Bucket said. "And don't fluster poor Charlie. We must all try to keep very calm. Now the first thing to decide is this – who is going to go with Charlie to the factory?"

"I will!" shouted Grandpa Joe, leaping out of bed once again. "I'll take him! I'll look after him! You leave it to me!"

Mrs Bucket smiled at the old man, then she turned to her husband and said, "How about you, dear? Don't you think *you* ought to go?"

"Well..." Mr Bucket said, pausing to think about it, "no... I'm not so sure that I should."

"But you *must.*"

"There's no *must* about it, my dear," Mr Bucket said gently. "Mind you, I'd *love* to go. It'll be tremendously exciting. But on the other

253

hand… I believe that the person who really *deserves* to go most of all is Grandpa Joe himself. He seems to know more about it than we do. Provided, of course, that he feels well enough…"

"Yippeeeeee!" shouted Grandpa Joe, seizing Charlie by the hands and dancing round the room.

"He certainly *seems* well enough," Mrs Bucket said, laughing. "Yes… perhaps you're right after all. Perhaps Grandpa Joe should be the one to go with him. I certainly can't go myself and leave the other three old people all alone in bed for a whole day."

"Hallelujah!" yelled Grandpa Joe. "Praise the Lord!"

At that point, there came a loud knock on the front door. Mr Bucket went to open it, and the next moment, swarms of newspapermen and photographers were pouring into the house. They had tracked down the finder of the fifth Golden Ticket, and now they all wanted to get the full story for the front pages of the morning papers. For several hours, there was complete pandemonium in the little house, and it must have been nearly midnight before Mr Bucket was able to get rid of them so that Charlie could go to bed.

Mr Willy Wonka

Mr Wonka was standing all alone just inside the open gates of the factory.

And what an extraordinary little man he was!

He had a black top hat on his head.

He wore a tail coat made of a beautiful plum-coloured velvet.

His trousers were bottle green.

His gloves were pearly grey.

And in one hand he carried a fine gold-topped walking cane.

Covering his chin, there was a small, neat, pointed black beard – a goatee. And his eyes – his eyes were most marvellously bright. They seemed to be sparkling and twinkling at you all the time. The whole face, in fact, was alight with fun and laughter.

And oh, how clever he looked! How quick and sharp and full of life! He kept making quick jerky little movements with his head, cocking it this way and that, and taking everything in with those bright twinkling eyes. He was like a squirrel in the quickness of his movements, like a quick clever old squirrel from the park.

Suddenly, he did a funny little skipping dance in the snow, and he spread his arms wide, and he smiled at the five children who were clustered near the gates, and he called out, "Welcome, my little friends! Welcome to the factory!"

His voice was high and flutey. "Will you come forward one at a time, please," he called out, "and bring your parents. Then show me your Golden Ticket and give me your name. Who's first?"

The big fat boy stepped up. "I'm Augustus Gloop," he said.

"Augustus!" cried Mr Wonka, seizing his hand and pumping it up and down with terrific force. "My *dear* boy, how *good* to see you! Delighted! Charmed! Overjoyed to have you with us! And *these* are your parents? How *nice!* Come in! Come in! That's right! Step through the gates!"

Mr Wonka was clearly just as excited as everybody else.

"My name," said the next child to go forward, "is Veruca Salt."

"My *dear* Veruca! How *do* you do? What a pleasure this is! You *do* have an interesting name, don't you? I always thought that a veruca was a sort of wart that you got on the sole of your foot! But I must be wrong, mustn't I? How pretty you look in that lovely mink coat! I'm so glad you could come! Dear me, this is going to be *such* an exciting day! I *do* hope you enjoy it! I'm sure you *will!* I *know* you *will!* Your father? How *are* you, Mr Salt? And Mrs Salt? Overjoyed to see you! Yes, the ticket is *quite* in order! Please go in!"

The next two children, Violet Beauregarde and Mike Teavee, came forward to have their tickets examined and then to have their arms practically pumped off their shoulders by the energetic Mr Wonka.

And last of all, a small nervous voice whispered, "Charlie Bucket."

"Charlie!" cried Mr Wonka. "Well, well, well! So *there* you are! You're the one who found your ticket only yesterday, aren't you? Yes, yes. I read *all* about it in this morning's papers! *Just* in time, my dear boy! I'm so glad! So happy for you! And this? Your grandfather? Delighted to meet you, sir! Overjoyed! Enraptured! Enchanted! All right! Excellent! Is everybody in now? Five children? Yes! Good! Now will you please follow me! Our tour is about to begin! But *do* keep together! *Please* don't wander off by yourselves! I shouldn't like to lose any of you at *this* stage of the proceedings! Oh, dear me, no!"

Charlie glanced back over his shoulder and saw the great iron entrance gates slowly closing behind him. The crowds on the outside were still pushing and shouting. Charlie took a last look at them. Then, as the gates closed with a clang, all sight of the outside world disappeared.

"Here we are!" cried Mr Wonka, trotting along in front of the group. "Through this big red door, please! *That's* right! It's nice and warm inside! I have to keep it warm inside the factory because of the workers! My workers are used to an *extremely* hot climate! They can't stand the cold! They'd perish if they went outdoors in this weather! They'd freeze to death!"

"But who *are* these workers?" asked Augustus Gloop.

"All in good time, my dear boy!" said Mr Wonka, smiling at Augustus. "Be patient! You shall see everything as we go along! Are all of you inside? Good! Would you mind closing the door? Thank you!"

Charlie Bucket found himself standing in a long corridor that stretched away in front of him as far as he could see. The corridor was so wide that a car could easily have been driven along it. The walls were pale pink, the lighting was soft and pleasant.

"How lovely and warm!" whispered Charlie.

"I know. And what a marvellous smell!" answered Grandpa Joe, taking a long deep sniff. All the most wonderful smells in the world seemed to be mixed up in the air around them – the smell of roasting coffee and burnt sugar and melting chocolate and mint and violets and crushed hazelnuts and apple blossom and caramel and lemon peel…

And far away in the distance, from the heart of the great factory, came a muffled roar of energy as though some monstrous gigantic machine were spinning its wheels at breakneck speed.

"Now *this*, my dear children," said Mr Wonka, raising his voice above the noise, "this is the main corridor. Will you please hang your coats and hats on those pegs over there, and then follow me. *That's* the way! Good! Everyone ready! Come on, then! Here we go!" He trotted off rapidly down the corridor with the tails of his plum-coloured velvet coat flapping behind him, and the visitors all hurried after him.

It was quite a large party of people, when you came to think of it. There were nine grown-ups and five children, fourteen in all. So you can imagine that there was a good deal of pushing and shoving as they hustled and bustled down the passage, trying to keep up with the swift little figure in front of them. "Come *on!*" cried Mr Wonka. "Get a move on, please! We'll never get round today if you dawdle like this!"

Soon, he turned right off the main corridor into another slightly narrower passage.

Then he turned left.

Then left again.

Then right.

Then left.

Then right.

Then right.

Then left.

The place was like a gigantic rabbit warren, with passages leading this way and that in every direction.

"Don't you let go my hand, Charlie," whispered Grandpa Joe.

"Notice how all these passages are sloping downwards!" called out Mr Wonka. "We are now going underground! All the most important rooms in my factory are deep down below the surface!"

"Why is that?" somebody asked.

"There wouldn't be *nearly* enough space for them up on top!" answered Mr Wonka. "These rooms we are going to see are *enormous!* They're larger than football fields! No building in the *world* would be big enough to house them! But down here, underneath the ground, I've got *all* the space I want. There's no limit – so long as I hollow it out."

Mr Wonka turned right.

He turned left.

He turned right again.

The passages were sloping steeper and steeper downhill now.

Then suddenly, Mr Wonka stopped. In front of him, there was a shiny metal door. The party crowded round. On the door, in large letters, it said:

THE CHOCOLATE ROOM

The Veruca Salt Song

from CHARLIE AND THE
CHOCOLATE FACTORY

"VERUCA Salt!" sang the Oompa-Loompas.
    "Veruca Salt, the little brute,
Has just gone down the rubbish chute
(And as we very rightly thought
That in a case like this we ought
To see the thing completely through,
We've polished off her parents, too).
Down goes Veruca! Down the drain!
And here, perhaps, we should explain
That she will meet, as she descends,
A rather different set of friends
To those that she has left behind –
These won't be nearly so refined.
A fish head, for example, cut
This morning from a halibut.
'Hello! Good morning! How d'you do?
How nice to meet you! How are you?'
And then a little further down
A mass of others gather round:

THE VERUCA SALT SONG

A bacon rind, some rancid lard,
A loaf of bread gone stale and hard,
A steak that nobody could chew,
An oyster from an oyster stew,
Some liverwurst so old and grey
One smelled it from a mile away,
A rotten nut, a reeky pear,
A thing the cat left on the stair,
And lots of other things as well,
Each with a rather horrid smell.
These are Veruca's new-found friends
That she will meet as she descends,
And *this* is the price she has to pay
For going so very far astray.
But now, my dears, we think you might
Be wondering – is it really right
That every single bit of blame
And all the scolding and the shame
Should fall upon Veruca Salt?
Is *she* the only one at fault?

For though she's spoiled, and dreadfully so,
A girl can't spoil herself, you know.
Who spoiled her, then? Ah, who indeed?
Who pandered to her every need?
Who turned her into such a brat?
Who are the culprits? *Who* did that?
Alas! You needn't look so far
To find out who these sinners are.
They are (and this is very sad)
Her loving parents, MUM and DAD.
And that is why we're glad they fell
Into the rubbish chute as well."

Treats

from REVOLTING RECIPES

TREATS were an essential part of Roald's life – never too many, never too few, and always perfectly timed. He made you feel like a king receiving the finest gift in the land.

A treat could be a wine gum lifted silently in the middle of the night out of a large sweet jar kept permanently by his bedside. It could be a lobster and oyster feast placed on the table after a secret visit to the fishmonger, his favourite shop. It could be the first new potato, broad bean, or lettuce from the garden, a basket of field mushrooms, or a superb conker. A different kind of treat would be an unannounced visit to a school, causing chaos to teachers and, I suspect, a great deal of fun for the children.

George's Marvellous Medicine

AN EXTRACT

Georges sat himself down at the table in the kitchen. He was shaking a little. Oh, how he hated Grandma! He really *hated* that horrid old witchy woman. And all of a sudden he had a tremendous urge to *do something* about her. Something *whopping*. Something *absolutely terrific*. A *real shocker*. A sort of explosion. He wanted to blow away the witchy smell that hung about her in the next room. He may have been only eight years old but he was a brave little boy. He was ready to take this old woman on.

"I'm not going to be frightened by *her*," he said softly to himself. But he *was* frightened. And that's why he wanted suddenly to explode her away.

Well… not quite away. But he did want to shake the old woman up a bit.

Very well, then. What should it be, this whopping terrific exploding shocker for Grandma?

He would have liked to put a firework banger under her chair but he didn't have one.

He would have liked to put a long green snake down the back of her dress but he didn't have a long green snake.

He would have liked to put six big black rats in the room with her and lock the door but he didn't have six big black rats.

As George sat there pondering this interesting problem, his eye fell upon the bottle of Grandma's brown medicine standing on the sideboard. Rotten stuff it seemed to be. Four times a day a large spoonful of it was shovelled into her mouth and it didn't do her the slightest bit of good. She was always just as horrid after she'd had it as she'd been before. The whole point of medicine, surely, was to make a person

better. If it didn't do that, then it was quite useless.

So-ho! thought George suddenly. *Ah-ha! Ho-hum!* I know exactly what I'll do. I shall make her a *new* medicine, one that is so strong and so fierce and so fantastic it will either cure her completely or blow off the top of her head. I'll make her a *magic medicine*, a medicine no doctor in the world has ever made before.

George looked at the kitchen clock. It said five past ten. There was nearly an hour left before Grandma's next dose was due at eleven.

"Here we go, then!" cried George, jumping up from the table. "A magic medicine it shall be!

"So give me a bug and a jumping flea,
Give me two snails and lizards three,
And a slimy squiggler from the sea,
And the poisonous sting of a bumblebee,
And the juice from the fruit of the ju-jube tree,
And the powdered bone of a wombat's knee.
And one hundred other things as well
Each with a rather nasty smell.

I'll stir them up, I'll boil them long,
A mixture tough, a mixture strong.
And then, heigh-ho, and down it goes,
A nice big spoonful (hold your nose)
Just gulp it down and have no fear.
'How do you like it, Granny dear?'
Will she go pop? Will she explode?
Will she go flying down the road?
Will she go poof in a puff of smoke?
Start fizzing like a can of Coke?
Who knows? Not I. Let's wait and see.
(I'm glad it's neither you nor me.)
Oh Grandma, if you only knew
What I have got in store for you!"

George took an enormous saucepan out of the cupboard and placed it on the kitchen table.

"George!" came the shrill voice from the next room. "What are you doing?"

"Nothing, Grandma," he called out.

"You needn't think I can't hear you just because you closed the door! You're rattling the saucepans!"

"I'm just tidying the kitchen, Grandma."

Then there was silence.

George had absolutely no doubts whatsoever about how he was going to make his famous medicine. He wasn't going to fool about wondering whether to put in a little bit of this or a little bit of that. Quite simply, he was going to put in EVERYTHING he could find. There would be no messing about, no hesitating, no wondering whether a particular thing would knock the old girl sideways or not. The rule would be this: whatever he saw, if it was runny or powdery or gooey, in it went.

Nobody had ever made a medicine like that before. If it didn't actually cure Grandma, then it would anyway cause some exciting results. It would be worth watching.

George decided to work his way round the various rooms one at a time and see what they had to offer.

He would go first to the bathroom. There are always lots of funny things in a bathroom. So upstairs he went, carrying the enormous two-handled saucepan before him.

In the bathroom, he gazed longingly at the famous and dreaded medicine cupboard. But he didn't go near it. It was the only thing in the entire house he was forbidden to touch. He had made solemn promises to his parents about this and he wasn't going to break them. There were things in there, they had told him, that could actually kill a person, and although he was out to give Grandma a pretty fiery mouthful, he didn't really want a dead body on his hands. George put the saucepan on the floor and went to work.

Number one was a bottle labelled GOLDENGLOSS HAIR SHAMPOO. He emptied it into the pan. "That ought to wash her tummy nice and clean," he said.

He took a full tube of TOOTHPASTE and squeezed out the whole lot of it in one long worm. 'Maybe that will brighten up those horrid brown teeth of hers," he said.

There was an aerosol can of SUPERFOAM SHAVING SOAP belonging to his father. George loved playing with aerosols. He pressed the button and kept his finger on it until there was nothing left. A wonderful mountain of white foam built up in the giant saucepan.

With his fingers, he scooped out the contents of a jar of VITAMIN ENRICHED FACE CREAM.

In went a small bottle of scarlet NAIL VARNISH. "If the toothpaste doesn't clean her teeth," George said, "then this will paint them as red as roses."

He found another jar of creamy stuff labelled HAIR REMOVER.

SMEAR IT ON YOUR LEGS, it said, AND ALLOW TO
REMAIN FOR FIVE MINUTES. George tipped it all into the
saucepan.

There was a bottle with yellow stuff inside it called DISH-
WORTH'S FAMOUS DANDRUFF CURE. In it went.

There was something called BRILLIDENT FOR CLEANING
FALSE TEETH. It was a white powder. In that went, too.

He found another aerosol can, NEVERMORE PONGING
DEODORANT SPRAY, GUARANTEED, it said, TO KEEP

271

AWAY UNPLEASANT BODY SMELLS FOR A WHOLE DAY. "She could use plenty of that," George said as he sprayed the entire canful into the saucepan.

LIQUID PARAFFIN, the next one was called. It was a big bottle. He hadn't the faintest idea what it did to you, but he poured it in anyway.

That, he thought, looking around him, was about all from the bathroom.

George goes round the house and out to the farm shed and the garage, adding more and more ingredients to his marvellous medicine. He boils it all up and chants a spell. Then...

"Where's that medicine of mine, boy?!" came the voice from the living-room. "You're forgetting me! You're doing it on purpose! I shall tell your mother!"

"I'm not forgetting you, Grandma," George called back. "I'm thinking of you all the time. But there are still ten minutes to go."

"You're a nasty little maggot!" the voice screeched back. "You're a lazy and disobedient little worm, and you're growing too fast."

George fetched the bottle of Grandma's real medicine from the sideboard. He took out the cork and tipped it all down the sink. He then filled the bottle with his own magic mixture by dipping a small jug into the saucepan and using it as a pourer. He replaced the cork.

Had it cooled down enough yet? Not quite. He held the bottle under the cold tap for a couple of minutes. The label came off in the wet but that didn't matter. He dried the bottle with a dishcloth.

All was now ready!

This was it!

The great moment had arrived!

"Medicine time, Grandma!" he called out.

"I should hope so, too," came the grumpy reply.

The silver tablespoon in which the medicine was always given lay ready on the kitchen sideboard. George picked it up.

Holding the spoon in one hand and the bottle in the other, he advanced into the living-room.

George's medicine has a very dramatic effect on Grandma –
she jumps to her feet and begins to grow and grow…

George stood in the farmyard looking up at the roof. The old farm-house had a fine roof of pale red tiles and tall chimneys.

There was no sign of Grandma. There was only a song-thrush sit-ting on one of the chimney-pots, singing a song. The old wurzel's got stuck in the attic, George thought. Thank goodness for that.

Suddenly a tile came clattering down from the roof and fell into the yard. The song-thrush took off fast and flew away.

Then another tile came down.

Then half a dozen more.

And then, very slowly, like some weird monster rising up from the deep, Grandma's head came through the roof…

Then her scrawny neck…

And the tops of her shoulders…

"How'm I doing, boy!" she shouted. "How's that for a bash up?"

"Don't you think you'd better stop now, Grandma?" George called out…

"I have stopped!" she answered. "I feel terrific! Didn't I tell you I had magic powers! Didn't I warn you I had wizardry in the tips of my fingers? But you wouldn't listen to me, would you? You wouldn't listen to your old Grandma!"

"*You* didn't do it, Grandma," George shouted back to her. "*I* did it! I made you a new medicine!"

"A *new medicine? You?* What rubbish!" she yelled.

"I did! I did!" George shouted.

"You're lying as usual!" Grandma yelled. "You're always lying!"

"I'm not lying. Grandma… I swear I'm not."

The wrinkled old face high up on the roof stared down suspiciously at George. "Are you telling me you actually made a new medicine all by yourself?" she shouted.

"Yes, Grandma, all by myself."

"I don't believe you," she answered. "But I'm very comfortable up here. Fetch me a cup of tea."

A brown hen was pecking about in the yard close to where George was standing. The hen gave him an idea. Quickly, he uncorked the medicine bottle and poured some of the brown stuff into the spoon. "Watch this, Grandma!" he shouted. He crouched down, holding out the spoon to the hen.

"Chicken," he said. "Chick-chick-chicken. Come here. Have some of this."

Chickens are stupid birds, and very greedy. They think everything is food. This one thought the spoon was full of corn. It hopped over. It put its head on one side and looked at the spoon. "Come on, chicken," George said. "Good chicken. Chick-chick-chick."

The brown hen stretched out its neck towards the spoon and went *peck*. It got a beakful of medicine.

The effect was electric.

"*Owee!*" shrieked the hen and it shot straight up into the air like a rocket. It went as high the house.

Then down it came again into the yard, *splosh*. And there it sat with its feathers all sticking straight out from its body. There was a look of amazement on its silly face.

George stood watching it. Grandma up on the roof was watching it, too.

The hen got to its feet. It was rather shaky. It was making funny gurgling noises in its throat. Its beak was opening and shutting. It seemed like a pretty sick hen.

"You've done it in, you stupid boy!" Grandma shouted. "That hen's going to die! Your father'll be after you now! He'll give you socks and serve you right!"

All of a sudden, black smoke started pouring out of the hen's beak.

"It's on fire!" Grandma yelled. "The hen's on fire!"

George ran to to the water-trough to get a bucket of water.

"That hen'll be roasted and ready for eating any moment!" Grandma shouted.

George sloshed the bucket of water over the hen. There was a sizzling sound and the smoke went away.

"Old hen's laid its last egg!" Grandma shouted. "Hens don't do any laying after they've been on fire!"

Now that the fire was out, the hen seemed better. It stood up properly. It flapped its wings. Then it crouched down low to the ground, as though getting ready to jump. It jumped high in the air and turned a complete somersault, then landed back on its feet.

"It's a circus hen!" Grandma shouted from the rooftop. "It's a flipping acrobat!"

Now the hen began to grow.

George had been waiting for this to happen. "It's growing!" he yelled. "It's growing, Grandma! Look, it's growing!"

Bigger and bigger... taller and taller it grew. Soon the hen was four or five times its normal size.

"Can you see it, Grandma?!" George shouted.

"I can see it, boy!" the old girl shouted back. "I'm watching it!"

George was hopping about from one foot to the other with excitement, pointing at the enormous hen and shouting, "It's had the magic medicine, Grandma, and it's growing just like you did!"

But there was a difference between the way the hen was growing and the way Grandma grew. When Grandma grew taller and taller, she got thinner and thinner. The hen didn't. It stayed nice and plump all along.

Soon it was taller than George, but it didn't stop there. It went right on growing until it was about as big as a horse. Then it stopped.

"Doesn't it look marvellous, Grandma!" George shouted.

"It's not as tall as me!" Grandma sang out. "Compared with me, that hen is titchy small! I am the tallest of them all!"

PART THREE

Family, friends and foes

Winkles for tea...

W HEN I was small my mother used always to take all of us six children to Tenby for the Easter holidays. She rented a house known as The Cabin, which was in the Old Harbour, and when the tide was in, the waves broke right up against one wall of the house. We adored Tenby… We hunted for winkles on the rocks and carried them home and boiled them and got them out of their shells with bent pins and put them on bread and butter for tea.

from MY YEAR

The Sweet-Shop

from BOY

ON the way to school and on the way back we always passed the sweet-shop. No we didn't, we never passed it. We always stopped. We lingered outside its rather small window gazing in at the big glass jars full of Bull's-eyes and Old Fashioned Humbugs and Strawberry Bonbons and Glacier Mints and Acid Drops and Pear Drops and Lemon Drops and all the rest of them. Each of us received sixpence a week for pocket-money, and whenever there was any money in our pockets, we would all troop in together to buy a pennyworth of this or that. My own favourites were Sherbet Suckers and Liquorice Bootlaces.

One of the other boys, whose name was Thwaites, told me I should never eat Liquorice Bootlaces. Thwaites's father, who was a doctor, had said that they were made from rats' blood. The father had given his young son a lecture about Liquorice Bootlaces when he had caught him eating one in bed. "Every ratcatcher in the country," the father had said, "takes his rats to the Liquorice Bootlace Factory, and the manager pays tuppence for each rat. Many a ratcatcher has become a millionaire by selling his dead rats to the Factory."

"But how do they turn the rats into liquorice?" the young Thwaites had asked his father.

"They wait until they've got ten thousand rats," the father had answered, "then they dump them all into a huge shiny steel cauldron and boil them up for several hours. Two men stir the bubbling

285

cauldron with long poles and in the end they have a thick steaming rat-stew. After that, a cruncher is lowered into the cauldron to crunch the bones, and what's left is a pulpy substance called rat-mash."

"Yes, but how do they turn that into Liquorice Bootlaces, Daddy?" the young Thwaites had asked, and this question, according to Thwaites, had caused his father to pause and think for a few moments before he answered it. At last he had said, "The two men who were doing the stirring with the long poles now put on their wellington boots and climb into the cauldron and shovel the hot rat-mash out on to a concrete floor. Then they run a steam-roller over it several times to flatten it out. What is left looks rather like a gigantic black pancake, and all they have to do after that is to wait for it to cool and to harden so they can cut it up into strips to make the Bootlaces. Don't ever eat them," the father had said. "If you do, you'll get ratitis."

"What is ratitis, Daddy?" young Thwaites had asked.

"All the rats that the rat-catchers catch are poisoned with

Ratitis!

rat-poison," the father had said. "It's the rat-poison that gives you ratitis."

"Yes, but what happens to you when you catch it?" young Thwaites had asked.

"Your teeth become very sharp and pointed," the father had answered. "And a short stumpy tail grows out of your back just above your bottom. There is no cure for ratitis. I ought to know. I'm a doctor."

We all enjoyed Thwaites's story and we made him tell it to us many times on our walks to and from school. But it didn't stop any of us except Thwaites from buying Liquorice Bootlaces. At two for a penny they were the best value in the shop. A Bootlace, in case you haven't had the pleasure of handling one, is not round. It's like a flat black tape about half an inch wide. You buy it rolled up in a coil, and in those days it used to be so long that when you unrolled it and held one end at arm's length above your head, the other end touched the ground.

Sherbet Suckers were also two a penny. Each Sucker consisted of a yellow cardboard tube filled with sherbet powder, and there was a hollow liquorice straw sticking out of it. (Rats' blood again, young Thwaites would warn us, pointing at the liquorice straw.) You sucked the sherbet up through the straw and when it was finished you ate the liquorice. They were delicious, those Sherbet Suckers. The sherbet fizzed in your mouth, and if you knew how to do it, you could make white froth come out of your nostrils and pretend you were throwing a fit.

Gobstoppers, costing a penny each, were enormous hard round balls the size of small tomatoes. One Gobstopper would provide about an hour's worth of non-stop sucking and if you took it out of your mouth and inspected it every five minutes or so, you would find it had changed colour. There was something fascinating about the way it went from pink to blue to green to yellow. We used to wonder how in the world the Gobstopper Factory managed to achieve this magic.

"How *does* it happen?" we would ask each other. "How *can* they make it keep changing colour?"

"It's your spit that does it," young Thwaites proclaimed. As the son of a doctor, he considered himself to be an authority on all things that had to do with the body. He could tell us about scabs and when they were ready to be picked off. He knew why a black eye was blue and why blood was red. "It's your spit that makes a Gobstopper change colour," he kept insisting. When we asked him to elaborate on this theory, he answered, "You wouldn't understand it if I did tell you."

Pear Drops were exciting because they had a dangerous taste. They smelled of nail-varnish and they froze the back of your throat. All of us were warned against eating them, and the result was that we ate them more than ever.

Then there was a hard brown lozenge called the Tonsil Tickler. The Tonsil Tickler tasted and smelled very strongly of chloroform. We had not the slightest doubt that these things were saturated in the dreaded anaesthetic which, as Thwaites had many times pointed out to us, could put you to sleep for hours at a stretch. "If my father has to saw off somebody's leg," he said, "he pours chloroform on to a pad and the person sniffs it and goes to sleep and my father saws his leg off without him even feeling it."

"But why do they put it into sweets and sell them to us?" we asked him.

You might think a question like this would have baffled Thwaites. But Thwaites was never baffled. "My father says Tonsil Ticklers were invented for dangerous prisoners in jail," he said. "They give them one with each meal and the chloroform makes them sleepy and stops them rioting."

"Yes," we said, "but why sell them to children?"

"It's a plot," Thwaites said. "A grown-up plot to keep us quiet."

The sweet-shop in Llandaff in the year 1923 was the very centre of our lives.

A Little Nut-Tree

from RHYME STEW

I had a little nut-tree,
Nothing would it bear,
I searched in all its branches,
But not a nut was there.

"Oh, little tree," I begged,
"Give me just a few."
The little tree looked down at me
And whispered, "Nuts to you."

Matilda's father

from MATILDA

MATILDA'S parents owned quite a nice house with three bed-rooms upstairs, while on the ground floor there was a dining-room and a living-room and a kitchen. Her father was a dealer in second-hand cars and it seemed he did pretty well at it.

"Sawdust," he would say proudly, "is one of the great secrets of my success. And it costs me nothing. I get it free from the sawmill."

"What do you use it for?" Matilda asked him.

"Ha!" the father said. "Wouldn't you like to know."

"I don't see how sawdust can help you to sell second-hand cars, Daddy."

"That's because you're an ignorant little twit," the father said. His speech was never very delicate but Matilda was used to it. She also knew that he liked to boast and she would egg him on shamelessly.

"You must be very clever to find a use for something that costs nothing," she said. "I wish I could do it."

"You couldn't," the father said. "You're too stupid. But I don't mind telling young Mike here about it seeing he'll be joining me in the busi-ness one day." Ignoring Matilda, he turned to his son and said, "I'm always glad to buy a car when some fool has been crashing the gears so badly they're all worn out and rattle like mad. I get it cheap. Then all I do is mix a lot of sawdust with the oil in the gear-box and it runs as sweet as a nut."

"How long will it run like that before it starts rattling again?" Matilda asked him.

"Long enough for the buyer to get a good distance away," the father said, grinning. "About a hundred miles."

"But that's dishonest, Daddy," Matilda said. "It's cheating."

"No one ever got rich being honest," the father said. "Customers are there to be diddled."

Mr Wormwood was a small ratty-looking man whose front teeth stuck out underneath a thin ratty moustache. He liked to wear jackets with large brightly-coloured checks and he sported ties that were usually yellow or pale green. "Now take mileage for instance," he went on. "Anyone who's buying a second-hand car, the first thing he wants to know is how many miles it's done. Right?"

"Right," the son said.

"So I buy an old dump that's got about a hundred and fifty thousand miles on the clock. I get it cheap. But no one's going to buy it with a mileage like that, are they? And these days you can't just take

the speedometer out and fiddle the numbers back like you used to ten years ago. They've fixed it so it's impossible to tamper with it unless you're a ruddy watchmaker or something. So what do I do? I use my brains, laddie, that's what I do."

"How?" young Michael asked, fascinated. He seemed to have inherited his father's love of crookery.

"I sit down and say to myself, how can I convert a mileage reading of one hundred and fifty thousand into only ten thousand without taking the speedometer to pieces? Well, if I were to run the car backwards for long enough then obviously that would do it. The numbers would click backwards, wouldn't they? But who's going to drive a flaming car in reverse for thousands and thousands of miles? You couldn't do it!"

"Of course you couldn't," young Michael said.

"So I scratch my head," the father said. "I use my brains. When you've been given a fine brain like I have, you've got to use it. And all of a sudden, the answer hits me. I tell you, I felt exactly like that other  brilliant fellow must have felt when he discovered penicillin. 'Eureka!' I cried. 'I've got it!'"

"What did you do, Dad?" the son asked him.

"The speedometer," Mr Wormwood said, "is run off a cable that is coupled up to one of the front wheels. So first I disconnect the cable where it joins the front wheel. Next, I get one of those high-speed electric drills and I couple that up to the end of the cable in such a way that when the drill turns, it turns the cable *backwards*. You got me so far? You following me?"

"Yes, Daddy," young Michael said.

"These drills run at a tremendous speed," the father said, "so when I switch on the drill the mileage numbers on the speedo spin backwards at a fantastic rate. I can knock fifty thousand miles off the clock in a few minutes with my high-speed electric drill. And by the time I've finished, the car's only done ten thousand and it's ready for sale. 'She's almost new,' I say to the customer. 'She's hardly done ten thou. Belonged to an old lady who only used it once a week for shopping.'"

"Can you really turn the mileage back with an electric drill?" young Michael asked.

"I'm telling you trade secrets," the father said. "So don't you go talking about this to anyone else. You don't want me put in jug, do you?"

"I won't tell a soul," the boy said. "Do you do this to many cars, Dad?"

"Every single car that comes through my hands gets the treatment," the father said. "They all have their mileage cut to under ten thou before they're offered for sale. And to think I invented that all by myself," he added proudly. "It's made me a mint."

Matilda, who had been listening closely, said, "But Daddy, that's even more dishonest than the sawdust. It's disgusting. You're cheating people who trust you."

"If you don't like it then don't eat the food in this house," the father said. "It's bought with the profits."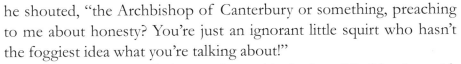

"It's dirty money," Matilda said. "I hate it."

Two red spots appeared on the father's cheeks. "Who the heck do you think you are," he shouted, "the Archbishop of Canterbury or something, preaching to me about honesty? You're just an ignorant little squirt who hasn't the foggiest idea what you're talking about!"

"Quite right, Harry," the mother said. And to Matilda she said, "You've got a nerve talking to your father like that. Now keep your nasty mouth shut so we can all watch this programme in peace."

They were in the living-room eating their suppers on their knees in front of the telly. The suppers were TV dinners in floppy aluminium containers with separate compartments for the stewed meat, the boiled potatoes and the peas...

"Mummy," Matilda said. "Would you mind if I ate my supper in the dining-room so I could read my book?"

The father glanced up sharply. "*I* would mind!" he snapped. "Supper is a family gathering and no one leaves the table till it's over!"

"But we're not at the table," Matilda said. "We never are. We're always eating off our knees and watching the telly."

"What's wrong with watching the telly, may I ask?" the father said. His voice had suddenly become soft and dangerous.

Matilda didn't trust herself to answer him, so she kept quiet. She could feel the anger boiling up inside her. She knew it was wrong to hate her parents like this, but she was finding it very hard not to do so.

Danny's father

from DANNY, THE CHAMPION OF THE WORLD

MY father, without the slightest doubt, was the most marvellous and exciting father any boy ever had. Here is a picture of him.

You might think, if you didn't know him well, that he was a stern and serious man. He wasn't. He was actually a wildly funny person. What made him appear so serious was the fact that he never smiled with his mouth. He did it all with his eyes. He had brilliant blue eyes and when he thought of something funny, his eyes would flash and if you looked carefully, you could actually see a tiny little golden spark dancing in the middle of each eye. But the mouth never moved.

I was glad my father was an eye-smiler. It meant he never gave me a fake smile because it's impossible to make your eyes twinkle if you aren't feeling twinkly yourself. A mouth-smile is different. You can fake a mouth-smile any time you want, simply by moving your lips. I've also learned that a real mouth-smile always has an eye-smile to go with it, so watch out, I say, when someone

296

smiles at you with his mouth but the eyes stay the same. It's sure to be bogus.

My father was not what you would call an educated man and I doubt if he had read twenty books in his life. But he was a marvellous story-teller. He used to make up a bedtime story for me every single night, and the best ones were turned into serials and went on for many nights running.

My father was a fine mechanic. People who lived miles away used to bring their cars to him for repair rather than take them to their nearest garage. He loved engines. "A petrol engine is sheer magic," he said to me once. "Just imagine being able to take a thousand different bits of metal... and if you fit them all together in a certain way... and then if you feed them a little oil and petrol... and if you press a little switch... suddenly those bits of metal will all come to life... and they will purr and hum and roar... they will make the wheels of a motor-car go whizzing round at fantastic speeds..."

It was impossible to be bored in my father's company. He was too sparky a man for that. Plots and plans and new ideas came flying off him like sparks from a grindstone.

"There's a good wind today," he said one Saturday morning. "Just right for flying a kite. Let's make a kite, Danny."

So we made a kite. He showed me how to splice four thin sticks together in the shape of a star, with two more sticks across the middle to brace it. Then we cut up an old blue shirt of his and stretched the material across the frame-work of the kite. We added a long tail made of thread, with little leftover pieces of the shirt tied at intervals along it. We found a ball of string in the workshop and he showed me how to attach the string to the frame-work so that the kite would be properly balanced in flight.

Together we walked to the top of the hill behind the filling-station to release the kite. I found it hard to believe that this object, made only from a few sticks and a piece of old shirt, would actually fly. I held the string while my father held the kite, and the moment he let it go, it caught the wind and soared upward like a huge blue bird.

"Let out some more, Danny!" he cried. "Go on! As much as you like!"

What I have been trying so hard to tell you all along is simply that my father, without the slightest doubt, was the most marvellous and exciting father any boy ever had.

Roald Dahl's father

from BOY

WHEN my father was fourteen, which is more than one hundred years ago, he was up on the roof of the family house replacing some loose tiles when he slipped and fell. He broke his left arm below the elbow. Somebody ran to fetch the doctor, and half an hour later this gentleman made a majestic and drunken arrival in his horse-drawn buggy. He was so drunk that he mistook the fractured elbow for a dislocated shoulder.

"We'll soon put this back into place!" he cried out and two men were called off the street to help with the pulling. They were instructed to hold my father by the waist while the doctor grabbed him by the wrist of the broken arm and shouted, "Pull men, pull! Pull as hard as you can!"

The pain must have been excruciating. The victim screamed, and his mother, who was watching the performance in horror, shouted "Stop!" But by then the pullers had done so much damage that a splinter of bone was sticking out through the skin of the forearm.

This was in 1877 and orthopaedic surgery was not what it is today. So they simply amputated the arm at the elbow, and for the rest of his life my father had to manage with one arm. Fortunately, it was the left arm that he lost and gradually, over the years, he taught himself to do more or less anything he wanted with just the four fingers and thumb of his right hand. He could tie a shoelace as quickly as you or me, and for cutting up the food on his plate, he sharpened the bottom edge of a fork so that it served as both knife and fork all in one. He kept his ingenious instrument in a slim leather case and carried it in his pocket wherever he went. The loss of an arm, he used to say, caused him only one serious inconvenience. He found it impossible to cut the top off a boiled egg.

St Peter's

Weston-super-mare.

March 17th 1926.

Dear Alfhild

Thank you very much for the letter you sent me. The barber is a very funny man, his name is Mr Lundy, when I went to have my hair cut last Monday, a lot of spiders came out from under a kind of cupboard and he stepped on them and there was a nasty squashy mess on the floor. In the Drill Display we have a Pyramid, there are a lot a boys standing in the shape of a star fish and some boys in the middle, and a boy standing on one of the boys shoulders with his hands out, it looks very nice.

Love from

Boy.

it is a picture of a kangaro it is from Austrailia from Boy

P.S Dear Mama could you fiend out the value of a 5s stamp yellow and black and let me know

The Headmaster

from BOY

THE Headmaster, while I was at Repton, struck me as being a rather shoddy bandy-legged little fellow with a big bald head and lots of energy but not much charm. Mind you, I never did know him well because in all those months and years I was at school, I doubt whether he addressed more than six sentences to me altogether. So perhaps it was wrong of me to form a judgement like that.

What is so interesting about this Headmaster is that he became a famous person later on. At the end of my third year, he was suddenly appointed Bishop of Chester and off he went to live in a palace by the River Dee. I remember at the time trying to puzzle out how on earth a person could suddenly leap from being a schoolmaster to becoming a Bishop all in one jump, but there were bigger puzzles to come.

From Chester, he was soon promoted again to become Bishop of London, and from there, after not all that many years, he bounced up the ladder once more to get the top job of them all, Archbishop of Canterbury! And not long after that it was he himself who had the task of crowning our present Queen in Westminster Abbey with half the world watching him on television. Well, well, well! And this was the man who used to deliver the most vicious beatings to the boys under his care!

By now I am sure you will be wondering why I lay so much emphasis upon school beatings in these pages. The answer is that I cannot help it. All through my school life I was appalled by the fact that masters and senior boys were allowed literally to wound other boys, and sometimes quite severely. I couldn't get over it. I never have got over it. It would, of course, be unfair to suggest that *all* masters were constantly beating the daylights out of *all* the boys in those days. They weren't. Only a few did so, but that was quite enough to leave a lasting

301

impression of horror upon me. It left another more physical impression upon me as well. Even today, whenever I have to sit for any length of time on a hard bench or chair, I begin to feel my heart beating along the old lines that the cane made on my bottom some fifty-five years ago.

There is nothing wrong with a few quick sharp tickles on the rump. They probably do a naughty boy a lot of good. But this Headmaster we were talking about wasn't just tickling you when he took out his cane to deliver a flogging. He never flogged me, thank goodness, but I

was given a vivid description of one of these ceremonies by my best friend at Repton, whose name was Michael. Michael was ordered to take down his trousers and kneel on the Headmaster's sofa with the top half of his body hanging over one end of the sofa. The great man then gave him one terrific crack. After that, there was a pause. The cane was put down and the Headmaster began filling his pipe from a tin of tobacco. He also started to lecture the kneeling boy about sin and wrongdoing. Soon, the cane was picked up again and a second tremendous crack was administered upon the trembling buttocks.

Then the pipe-filling business and the lecture went on for maybe another thirty seconds. Then came the third crack of the cane. Then the instrument of torture was put once more upon the table and a box of matches was produced. A match was struck and applied to the pipe. The pipe failed to light properly. A fourth stroke was delivered, with the lecture continuing. This slow and fearsome process went on until ten terrible strokes had been delivered, and all the time, over the pipe-lighting and the match-striking, the lecture on evil and wrong-doing and sinning and misdeeds and malpractice went on without a stop. It even went on as the strokes were being administered. At the end of it all, a basin, a sponge and a small clean towel were produced by the Headmaster, and the victim was told to wash away the blood before pulling up his trousers.

Do you wonder then that this man's behaviour used to puzzle me tremendously? He was an ordinary clergyman at that time as well as being Headmaster, and I would sit in the dim light of the school chapel and listen to him preaching about the Lamb of God and about Mercy and Forgiveness and all the rest of it and my young mind would become totally confused. I knew very well that only the night before this preacher had shown neither Forgiveness nor Mercy in flogging some small boy who had broken the rules.

So what was it all about? I used to ask myself.

Did they preach one thing and practise another, these men of God?

And if someone had told me at the time that this flogging clergy-man was one day to become the Archbishop of Canterbury, I would never have believed it.

It was all this, I think, that made me begin to have doubts about religion and even about God. If this person, I kept telling myself, was one of God's chosen salesmen on earth, then there must be something very wrong about the whole business.

The Roald Dahl
Guide to Railway Safety

AN EXTRACT

*British Rail asked Roald Dahl and Quentin Blake to produce a booklet
to help young people enjoy using the railway safely.*

I have a VERY DIFFICULT job here.
Young people are fed up with being told by grown-ups WHAT TO
DO and WHAT NOT TO DO. They get that all through their young
lives. And now I am going to have to tell you WHAT TO DO and
WHAT NOT TO DO, but this time it's a bit different because the
DOs and DON'Ts that I am going to give you may easily SAVE
YOUR LIFE. That is the only reason I agreed to write this message
to you.

But before I start with the heavy stuff, I'd like to tell you my own
theory about grown-ups and their DOs and DON'Ts and why a lot of
them are not very good at dealing with children.

I am totally convinced that most grown-ups have completely forgotten what it is like to be a child between the age of five and ten.
They all *think* they can remember. Parents think they can remember
and so do teachers. Some of course actually can, but very few. It is
after all quite difficult to remember exactly what it felt like to be a
small person when you yourself haven't been one for thirty or forty
years. That's a long time ago.

I can remember exactly what it was like. I am certain I can. If I
couldn't then I would not be able to write my sort of books for
children. Let me tell you how I see this whole difficult question
because I think it is interesting.

When you are young, you have not finished growing. You are,

therefore, physically shorter, usually by two feet or more, than the grown-ups around you. This is the first thing the grown-ups have forgotten. If a grown-up really wants to find out what it is like to live in a young person's world, let him or her get down on hands and knees and go about like that for a week. The first thing they will then discover is that all the other grown-ups in the room tower above them and they actually have to crane their necks to look at their faces. It is always like that with a small child. The child is surrounded by GIANTS, and the trouble with these beastly GIANTS is that they seem to spend most of their lives telling the child WHAT TO DO and WHAT NOT TO DO.

What the child does not understand is that unfortunately the GIANTS have to do this. It is the only way to bring up a child properly. When you are born you are an uncivilised little savage with bad habits and no manners and it is the job of the GIANTS (your parents and your teachers) to train you and discipline you. The child hates this and resists it fiercely. Yet it has to be done. It is all part of the process of turning the uncivilised and savage little child into a good citizen. "Say please... say thank you... go and wash your hands... take your elbows off the table... don't spit... don't come in here with muddy shoes... turn off the telly and do your homework..." The stream of orders is endless.

What is the result of all this? I'll tell you precisely what it is. Deep down inside the child's mind (subconsciously) the giants become THE ENEMY. Your teachers become THE ENEMY. Even your loving parents become THE ENEMY.

Not outwardly but inwardly, subconsciously. But enough of that. Having made my excuses, I must now regretfully become one of those unpopular giants who tells you WHAT TO DO and WHAT NOT TO DO.

DO NOT RIDE A BICYCLE ON A STATION PLATFORM.

DO NOT RIDE A SKATEBOARD EITHER.

Matilda

AN EXTRACT

Miss Honey

MATILDA was a little late in starting school. Most children begin Primary School at five or even just before, but Matilda's parents, who weren't very concerned one way or the other about their daughter's education, had forgotten to make the proper arrangements in advance. She was five and a half when she entered school for the first time.

The village school for younger children was a bleak brick building called Crunchem Hall Primary School. It had about two hundred and fifty pupils aged from five to just under twelve years old. The head teacher, the boss, the supreme commander of this establishment was a formidable middle-aged lady whose name was Miss Trunchbull.

Naturally Matilda was put in the bottom class, where there were eighteen other small boys and girls about the same age as her. Their teacher was called Miss Honey, and she could not have been more than twenty-three or twenty-four. She had a lovely pale oval madonna face with blue eyes and her hair was light brown. Her body was so

slim and fragile one got the feeling that if she fell over she would smash into a thousand pieces, like a porcelain figure.

Miss Jennifer Honey was a mild and quiet person who never raised her voice and was seldom seen to smile, but there is no doubt she possessed that rare gift for being adored by every small child under her care. She seemed to understand totally the bewilderment and fear that so often overwhelms young children who for the first time in their lives are herded into a classroom and told to obey orders. Some curious warmth that was almost tangible shone out of Miss Honey's face when she spoke to a confused and homesick newcomer to the class.

Miss Trunchbull, the Headmistress, was something else altogether. She was a gigantic holy terror, a fierce tyrannical monster who frightened the life out of the pupils and teachers alike. There was an aura of menace about her even at a distance, and when she came up close you could almost feel the dangerous heat radiating from her as from a red-hot rod of metal. When she marched  – Miss Trunchbull never walked, she always marched like a storm-trooper with long strides and arms aswinging – when she marched along a corridor you could actually hear her snorting as she went, and if a group of children happened to be in her path, she ploughed right on through them like a tank, with small people bouncing off her to left and right. Thank goodness we don't meet many people like her in this world, although they do exist and all of us are likely to come across at least one of them in a lifetime. If you ever do, you should behave as you would if you met an enraged rhinoceros out in the bush – climb up the nearest tree and stay there until it has gone away. This woman, in all her eccentricities and in her appearance, is almost impossible to describe, but I shall make some attempt to do so a little later on. Let us leave her for the moment and go back to Matilda and her first day in Miss Honey's class.

After the usual business of going through all the names of the children, Miss Honey handed out a brand-new exercise-book to each pupil.

"You have all brought your own pencils, I hope," she said.

"Yes, Miss Honey," they chanted.

"Good. Now this is the very first day of school for each one of you. It is the beginning of at least eleven long years of schooling that all of you are going to have to go through. And six of those years will be spent right here at Crunchem Hall where, as you know, your Headmistress is Miss Trunchbull. Let me for your own good tell you something about Miss Trunchbull. She insists upon strict discipline throughout the school, and if you take my advice you will do your very best to behave yourselves in her presence. Never argue with her. Never answer her back. Always do as she says. If you get on the wrong side of Miss Trunchbull she can liquidise you like a carrot in a kitchen blender. It's nothing to laugh about, Lavender. Take that grin off your face. All of you will be wise to remember that Miss Trunchbull deals very very severely with anyone who gets out of line in this school. Have you got the message?"

"Yes, Miss Honey," chirruped eighteen eager little voices.

"I myself," Miss Honey went on, "want to help you to learn as much as possible while you are in this class. That is because I know it will make things easier for you later on. For example, by the end of this week I shall expect every one of you to know the two-times table by heart. And in a year's time I hope you will know all the multiplication tables up to twelve. It will help you enormously if you do. Now then, do any of you happen to have learnt the two-times table already?"

Matilda put up her hand. She was the only one.

Miss Honey looked carefully at the tiny girl with dark hair and a round serious face sitting in the second row. "Wonderful," she said. "Please stand up and recite as much of it as you can."

Matilda stood up and began to say the two-times table. When she

got to twice twelve is twenty-four she didn't stop. She went right on with twice thirteen is twenty-six, twice fourteen is twenty-eight, twice fifteen is thirty, twice sixteen is…"

"Stop!" Miss Honey said. She had been listening slightly spellbound to this smooth recital, and now she said, "How far can you go?"

"How far?" Matilda said. "Well, I don't really know, Miss Honey. For quite a long way, I think."

Miss Honey took a few moments to let this curious statement sink in. "You mean," she said, "that you could tell me what two times twenty-eight is?"

"Yes, Miss Honey."

"What is it?"

"Fifty-six, Miss Honey."

"What about something much harder, like two times four hundred and eighty-seven? Could you tell me that?"

"I think so, yes," Matilda said.

"Are you sure?"

"Why yes, Miss Honey, I'm fairly sure."

"What is it then, two times four hundred and eighty-seven?"

"Nine hundred and seventy-four," Matilda said immediately. She spoke quietly and politely and without any sign of showing off.

Miss Honey gazed at Matilda with absolute amazement, but when next she spoke she kept her voice level. "That is really splendid," she said. "But of course multiplying by two is a lot easier than some of the bigger numbers. What about the other multiplication tables? Do you know any of those?"

"I think so, Miss Honey. I think I do."

"Which ones, Matilda? How far have you got?"

"I... I don't quite know," Matilda said. "I don't know what you mean."

"What I mean is do you for instance know the three-times table?"

"Yes, Miss Honey."

"And the four-times?"

"Yes, Miss Honey."

"Well, how many *do* you know, Matilda? Do you know all the way up to the twelve-times table?"

"Yes, Miss Honey."

"What are twelve sevens?"

"Eighty-four," Matilda said.

Miss Honey paused and leaned back in her chair behind the plain table that stood in the middle of the floor in front of the class. She was considerably shaken by this exchange but took care not to show it. She had never come across a five-year-old before, or indeed a ten-year-old, who could multiply with such facility.

"I hope the rest of you are listening to this," she said to the class. "Matilda is a very lucky girl. She has wonderful parents who have already taught her to multiply lots of numbers. Was it your mother, Matilda, who taught you?"

"No, Miss Honey, it wasn't."

"You must have a great father then. He must be a brilliant teacher."

"No, Miss Honey," Matilda said quietly. "My father did not teach me."

"You mean you taught yourself?"

"I don't quite know," Matilda said truthfully. "It's just that I don't find it very difficult to multiply one number by another."

Miss Honey took a deep breath and let it out slowly. She looked again at the small girl with bright eyes standing beside her desk so sensible and solemn. "You say you don't find it difficult to multiply one number by another," Miss Honey said. "Could you try to explain that a little bit?"

"Oh dear," Matilda said. "I'm not really sure."

Miss Honey waited. The class was silent, all listening.

"For instance," Miss Honey said, "if I asked you to multiply fourteen by nineteen... No, that's too difficult..."

"It's two hundred and sixty-six," Matilda said softly.

Miss Honey stared at her. Then she picked up a pencil and quickly worked out the sum on a piece of paper. "What did you say it was?" she said, looking up.

"Two hundred and sixty-six," Matilda said.

Miss Honey put down her pencil and removed her spectacles and began to polish the lenses with a piece of tissue. The class remained quiet, watching her and waiting for what was coming next. Matilda was still standing up beside her desk.

"Now tell me, Matilda," Miss Honey said, still polishing, "try to tell me exactly what goes on inside your head when you get a multiplication like that to do. You obviously have to 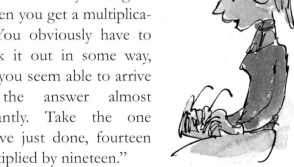 work it out in some way, but you seem able to arrive at the answer almost instantly. Take the one you've just done, fourteen multiplied by nineteen."

"I... I... I simply put the fourteen down in my head and multiply it by nineteen," Matilda said.

"I'm afraid I don't know how else to explain it. I've always said to myself that if a little pocket calculator can do it why shouldn't I?"

"Why not indeed," Miss Honey said. "The human brain is an amazing thing."

"I think it's a lot better than a lump of metal," Matilda said. "That's all a calculator is."

Throwing the Hammer

*Before the first week of term was up, awesome tales
about the Headmistress, Miss Trunchbull, began to filter through
to the newcomers. As Matilda and Lavender stood in the
corner of the playground during morning break on the
third day, something strange happened.*

THE playground, which up to then had been filled with shrieks and the shouting of children at play, all at once became silent as the grave. "Watch out," Hortensia whispered. Matilda and Lavender glanced round and saw the gigantic figure of Miss Trunchbull advancing through the crowd of boys and girls with menacing strides. The children drew back hastily to let her through and her progress across the asphalt was like that of Moses going through the Red Sea when the waters parted. A formidable figure she was too, in her belted smock and green breeches. Below the knees her calf muscles stood out like grapefruits inside her stockings. "Amanda Thripp!" she was shouting. "You, Amanda Thripp, come here!"

"Hold your hats," Hortensia whispered.

"What's going to happen?" Lavender whispered back.

"That idiot Amanda," Hortensia said, "has let her long hair grow even longer during the hols and her mother has plaited it into pigtails. Silly thing to do."

"Why silly?" Matilda asked.

"If there's one thing the Trunchbull can't stand it's pigtails," Hortensia said.

Matilda and Lavender saw the giant in green breeches advancing upon a girl of about ten who had a pair of plaited golden pigtails hanging over her shoulders. Each pigtail had a blue satin bow at the end of it and it all looked very pretty. The girl wearing the pigtails, Amanda Thripp, stood quite still, watching the advancing giant, and the expression on her face was one that you might find on the face of a person who is trapped in a small field with an enraged bull which is charging flat-out towards her. The girl was glued to the spot, terror-struck, pop-eyed, quivering, knowing for certain that the Day of Judgement had come for her at last.

Miss Trunchbull had now reached the victim and stood towering over her. "I want those filthy pigtails off before you come back to school tomorrow!" she barked. "Chop 'em off and throw 'em in the dustbin, you understand?"

Amanda, paralysed with fright, managed to stutter, "My m-m-mummy likes them. She p-p-plaits them for me every morning."

"Your mummy's a twit!" the Trunchbull bellowed. She pointed a finger the size of a salami at the child's head and shouted, "You look like a rat with a tail coming out of its head!"

"My m-m-mummy thinks I look lovely, Miss T-T-Trunchbull,"
Amanda stuttered, shaking like a blancmange.

"I don't give a tinker's toot what your mummy thinks!"
the Trunchbull yelled, and with that she lunged forward
and grabbed hold of Amanda's pigtails in her right
fist and lifted the girl clear off the ground.
Then she started swinging her round and
round her head, faster and faster and
Amanda was screaming bluc
murder and the Trunchbull
was yelling, "I'll give
you pigtails, you
little rat!"

"Shades of the Olympics," Hortensia murmured. "She's getting up speed now just like she does with the hammer. Ten to one she's going to throw her."

And now the Trunchbull was leaning back against the weight of the whirling girl and pivoting expertly on her toes, spinning round and round, and soon Amanda Thripp was travelling so fast she became a blur, and suddenly, with a mighty grunt, the Trunchbull let go of the pigtails and Amanda went sailing like a rocket right over the wire fence of the playground and high into the sky.

"Well thrown, sir!" someone shouted from across the playground, and Matilda, who was mesmerised by the whole crazy affair, saw Amanda Thripp descending in a long graceful parabola on the playing-field beyond. She landed on the grass and bounced three times and finally came to rest. Then, amazingly, she sat up. She looked a trifle dazed and who could blame her, but after a minute or so she was on her feet again and tottering back towards the playground.

The Trunchbull stood in the playground dusting off her hands. "Not bad," she said, "considering I'm not in strict training. Not bad at all." Then she strode away.

"She's mad," Hortensia said.

"But don't the parents complain?" Matilda asked.

"Would yours?" Hortensia asked. "I know mine wouldn't. She treats the mothers and fathers just the same as the children and they're all scared to death of her. I'll be seeing you some time, you two." And with that she sauntered away.

When We
Acquired the Motor-Boat

from BOY

EVERYONE has some sort of a boat in Norway. Nobody sits around in front of the hotel. Nor does anyone sit on the beach because there aren't any beaches to sit on. In the early days, we had only a row-boat, but a very fine one it was. It carried all of us easily, with places for two rowers. My mother took one pair of oars and my fairly ancient half-brother took the other, and off we would go.

My mother and the half-brother (he was somewhere around eighteen then) were expert rowers. They kept in perfect time and the oars went *click-click*, *click-click* in their wooden rowlocks, and the rowers never paused once during the long forty-minute journey. The rest of us sat in the boat trailing our fingers in the clear water and looking for jellyfish. We skimmed across the sound and went whizzing through narrow channels with rocky islands on either side, heading as always for a very secret tiny patch of sand on a distant island that only we knew about. In the early days we needed a place like this where we could paddle and play about because my youngest sister was only one, the next sister was three and I was four. The rocks and the deep water were no good to us.

Every day, for several summers, that tiny secret sand patch on that tiny secret island was our regular destination. We would stay there for three or four hours, messing about in the water and in the rockpools and getting extraordinarily sunburnt.

In later years, when we were all a little older and could swim, the daily routine became different. By then, my mother had acquired a motor-boat, a small and not very seaworthy white wooden vessel which sat far too low in the water and was powered by an unreliable

one-cylinder engine. The fairly ancient half-brother was the only one who could make the engine go at all. It was extremely difficult to start, and he always had to unscrew the sparking-plug and pour petrol into the cylinder. Then he swung a flywheel round and round, and with a bit of luck, after a lot of coughing and spluttering, the thing would finally get going.

When we first acquired the motor-boat, my youngest sister was four and I was seven, and by then all of us had learnt to swim. The exciting new boat made it possible for us to go much farther afield, and every day we would travel far out into the fjord, hunting for a different island. There were hundreds of them to choose from. Some were very small, no more than thirty yards long. Others were quite large, maybe half a mile in length. It was wonderful to have such a choice of places, and it was terrific fun to explore each island before we went swimming off the rocks. There were the wooden skeletons of ship-wrecked boats on those islands, and big white bones (were they human bones?) and wild raspberries, and mussels clinging to the rocks, and some of the islands had shaggy long-haired goats on them, and even sheep.

Now and again, when we were out in the open water beyond the chain of islands, the sea became very rough, and that was when my mother enjoyed herself most. Nobody, not even the tiny children, bothered with lifebelts in those days. We would cling to the sides of our funny little white motor-boat, driving through mountainous white-capped waves and getting drenched to the skin, while my mother calmly handled the tiller. There were times, I promise you, when the waves were so high that as we slid down into a trough the whole world disappeared from sight. Then up and up the little boat would climb, standing almost vertically on its tail, until we reached the crest of the next wave, and then it was like being on top of a foaming mountain. It requires great skill to handle a small boat in seas like these. The thing can easily capsize or be swamped if the bows do not meet the great combing breakers at just the right angle. But my mother knew exactly how to do it, and we were never afraid. We loved every minute of it, all of us except for our long-suffering Nanny, who would bury her face in her hands and call aloud upon the Lord to save her soul.

In the early evenings we nearly always went out fishing. We collected mussels from the rocks for bait, then we got into either the row-boat or the motor-boat and pushed off to drop anchor later in some likely spot. The water was very deep and often we had to let out two hundred feet of line before we touched bottom. We would sit silent and tense, waiting for a bite, and it always amazed me how even a little nibble at the end of that long line would be transmitted to one's fingers. "A bite!" someone would shout, jerking the line. "I've got him! It's a big one! It's a whopper!" And then came the thrill of hauling in the line hand over hand and peering over the side into the clear water to see how big the fish really was as he neared the surface. Cod, whiting, haddock and mackerel, we caught them all and bore them back triumphantly to the hotel kitchen where the cheery fat woman who did the cooking promised to get them ready for our supper.

I tell you, my friends, those were the days.

A Dahl Invention

from MY YEAR

As I write, I am remembering something I did during the Christmas holidays when I was either nine or ten, I can't be sure which. We lived in Kent then, in a fairly large house that had a wide lane and a public footpath running through our land at the back of the house. For Christmas that year I had been given a fine Meccano set as my main present, and I lay in bed that night after the celebrations were over thinking that I must build something with my new Meccano that had never been built before. In the end I decided I would make a device that was capable of 'bombing' from the air the pedestrians using the public footpath across our land.

Briefly my plan was as follows: I would stretch a wire all the way from the high roof of our house to the old garage on the other side of the footpath. Then I would construct from my Meccano a machine that would hang from the wire by a grooved wheel (there was such a wheel in my Meccano box) and this machine would hopefully run down the wire at great speed dropping its bombs on the unwary walkers underneath.

Next morning, filled with the enthusiasm that grips all great inventors, I climbed on to the roof of our house by the skylight and wrapped one end of the long roll of wire around a chimney. I threw the rest of the wire into the garden below and went back down myself through the skylight. I carried the wire across the garden, over the fence, across the footpath, over the next fence and into our land on the other side. I now pulled the wire very tight and fixed it with a big nail to the top of the door of the old garage. The total length of the wire was about one hundred yards. So far so good.

Next I set about constructing from the Meccano my bombing

322

machine, or chariot as I called it. I put the wheel at the top, and then running down from the wheel I made a strong column about two feet long. At the lower end of this column, I fixed two arms that projected outwards at right angles, one on either side, and along these arms I suspended five empty Heinz soup tins. The whole thing looked something like this:

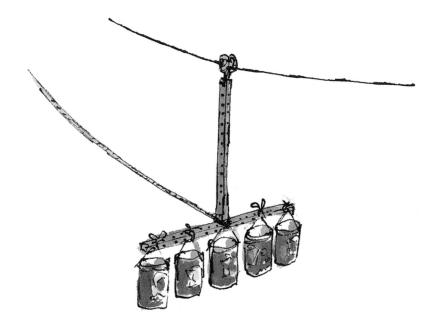

I carried it up to the roof and hung it on the wire. Then I attached one end of a ball of string to the lower end of the chariot and let it rip, playing out the string as it went. It was wonderful. Because the wire sloped steeply from the roof of the house all the way to the other end, the chariot careered down the wire at terrific speed, across the garden and over the footpath, and it didn't stop until it hit the old garage door on the far side. Great. I was ready to go.

With the string, I hauled the chariot back to the roof. And now, from a jug I filled all the five soup tins with water. I lay flat on the roof waiting for a victim. I knew I wouldn't have to wait long because the footpath was much used by people taking their dogs for walks in the wood beyond.

Soon two ladies dressed in tweed skirts and jackets and each wearing a hat, came strolling up the path with a revolting little Pekinese dog on a lead. I knew I had to time this carefully, so when they were very nearly but not quite directly under the wire, I let my chariot go. Down she went, making a wonderful screeching-humming noise as the metal wheel ran down the wire and the string ran through my fingers at great speed. Bombing from a height is never easy. I had to guess when my chariot was directly over the target, and when that moment came, I jerked the string. The chariot stopped dead and the tins swung upside down and all the water tipped out. The ladies, who had halted and looked up on hearing the rushing noise of my chariot overhead, caught the cascade of water full in their faces. It was tremendous. A bull's-eye first time. The women screamed. I lay flat on the roof so as not to be seen, peering over the edge, and I saw the women shouting and waving their arms. Then they came marching straight into our garden through the gate at the back and crossed the garden and hammered on the door. I nipped down smartly through the skylight and did a bunk.

Later on, at lunch, my mother fixed me with a steely eye and told me she was confiscating my Meccano set for the rest of the holidays. But for days afterwards I experienced the pleasant warm glow that comes to all of us when we have brought off a major triumph.

A poem in reply to schoolchildren

MY teacher loved using the cane
He would thrash us again and again
I'd be raised in the air
By the roots of my hair,
While he shouted "It's good for the brain!"

I used to wear pants extra thick
To lessen the sting from his stick.
When he saw what I'd done,
He yelled, "This is no fun!
Take them off altogether and quick!"

From your letters to me it would seem
That your teacher is clearly a dream.
There's no whacks on the bum
When you can't do a sum,
Instead you get strawberries and cream.

Danny,
The Champion of the World
AN EXTRACT

Danny and his father have filled 200 raisins with powder from sleeping
pills and are off to scatter them in the woods. They plan to immobilise pheasants
belonging to Mr Victor Hazell, a greedy bully of a landowner who is trying to
turn the two of them out of their caravan.

MY father came out of the caravan wearing the old navy-blue sweater and the brown cloth-cap with the peak pulled down low over his eyes.

"What's under there, Dad?" I asked, seeing the bulge at his waistline.

He pulled up his sweater and showed me two thin but very large white cotton sacks. They were bound neat and tidy round his belly. "To carry the stuff," he said darkly.

"Ah-ha."

"Go and put on your sweater," he said. "It's brown, isn't it?"

"Yes," I said.

"That'll do. But take off those white sneakers and wear your black shoes instead."

I went into the caravan and changed my shoes and put on my sweater. When I came out again, my father was standing by the pumps squinting anxiously up at the sun which was now only the width of a man's hand above the line of trees along the crest of the ridge on the far side of the valley.

"I'm ready, Dad."

"Good boy. Off we go!"

"Have you got the raisins?" I asked.

"In here," he said, tapping his trouser pocket where yet another bulge was showing. "I've put them all in one bag."

It was a calm sunny evening with little wisps of brilliant white cloud hanging motionless in the sky, and the valley was cool and very quiet as the two of us began walking together along the road that ran between the hills towards Wendover. The iron thing underneath my father's foot made a noise like a hammer striking a nail each time it hit the road.

"This is it, Danny. We're on our way now," he said. "By golly, I wish my old dad were coming with us on this one. He'd have given his right teeth to be here at this moment."

"Mum, too," I said.

"Ah, yes," he said, giving a little sigh. "Your mother would have *loved* this one."

Then he said, "Your mother was a great one for walking, Danny. And she would always bring something home with her to brighten up the caravan. In summer it was wild flowers or grasses. When the grass was in seed she could make it look absolutely beautiful in a jug of water, especially with some stalks of wheat or barley in between. In the autumn she would pick branches of leaves, and in the winter it was berries or old man's beard."

We kept going. Then he said, "How do you feel, Danny?"

"Terrific," I said. And I meant it. For although the snakes were still wriggling in my stomach, I wouldn't have swopped places with the King of Arabia at that moment.

"Do you think they might have dug any more of those pits for us to fall into?" I asked.

"Don't you go worrying about pits, Danny," my father said. "I'll be on the lookout for them this time. We shall go very carefully and very slowly once we're in the wood."

"How dark will it be in there when we arrive?"

"Not too dark," he said. "Quite light in fact."

"Then how do we stop the keepers from seeing us?"

"Ah," he said. "That's the fun of the whole thing. That's what it's all about. It's hide-and-seek. It's the greatest game of hide-and-seek in the world."

"You mean because they've got guns?"

"Well," he said, "that does add a bit of a flavour to it, yes."

We didn't talk much after that. But as we got closer and closer to the wood, I could see my father becoming more and more twitchy as the excitement began to build up in him. He would get hold of some awful old tune and instead of using the words, he would go "Tum-tiddely-um-tum-tum-tum-tum" over and over again. Then he would get hold of another tune and go "Pom-piddely-om-pom-pom-pom-

pom, pom-piddely-om, pom-piddely-om." As he sang, he tried to keep time with the tap-tap of his iron foot on the roadway.

When he got tired of that, he said to me, "I'll tell you something interesting about pheasants, Danny. The law says they're wild birds, so they only belong to you when they're on your own land, did you know that?"

"I didn't know that, Dad."

"So if one of Mr Hazell's pheasants flew over and perched on our filling-station," he said, "it would belong to us. No one else would be allowed to touch it."

"You mean even if Mr Hazell had bought it himself as a chick?" I said. "Even if he had bought it and reared it in his own wood?"

"Absolutely," my father said. "Once it flies off his own land, he's lost it. Unless, of course, it flies back again. It's the same with fish. Once a trout or a salmon has swum out of your stretch of the river into somebody else's, you can't very well say, 'Hey, that's mine. I want it back,' can you?"

"Of course not," I said. "But I didn't know it was like that with pheasants."

"It's the same with all game," my father said. "Hare, deer, partridge, grouse. You name it."

We had been walking steadily for about an hour and a quarter and we were coming to the gap in the hedge where the cart-track led up the hill to the big wood where the pheasants lived. We crossed over the road and went through the gap.

We walked on up the cart-track and when we reached the crest of the hill we could see the wood ahead of us, huge and dark with the sun going down behind the trees and little sparks of gold shining through.

"No talking, Danny, once we're inside," my father said. "Keep very close to me, and try not to go snapping any branches."

Five minutes later we were there. The wood skirted the edge of the track on the right-hand side with only the hedge between it and us.

"Come on," my father said. "In we go." He slipped through the hedge on all fours and I followed.

It was cool and murky inside the wood. No sunlight came in at all. My father took me by the hand, and together we started walking forward between the trees. I was very grateful to him for holding my hand. I had wanted to take hold of his the moment we entered the wood, but I thought he might disapprove.

My father was very tense. He was picking his feet up high and putting them down gently on the brown leaves. He kept his head moving all the time, the eyes sweeping slowly from side to side, searching for danger. I tried doing the same, but soon I began to see a keeper behind every tree, so I gave it up.

We went on like this for maybe four or five minutes, going slowly deeper and deeper into the wood.

Then a large patch of sky appeared ahead of us in the roof of the forest, and I knew that this must be the clearing. My father had told me that the clearing was the place where the young birds were introduced into the wood in early July, where they were fed and watered and guarded by the keepers, and where many of them stayed from force of habit until the shooting began. "There's always plenty of pheasants in the clearing," my father had said.

"And keepers, Dad?"

"Yes," he had said. "But there's thick bushes all around and that helps."

The clearing was about a hundred yards ahead of us. We stopped behind a big tree while my father let his eyes travel very slowly all round. He was checking each little shadow and every part of the wood within sight.

"We're going to have to crawl the next bit," he whispered, letting go of my hand. "Keep close behind me all the time, Danny, and do exactly as I do. If you see me lie flat on my face, you do the same. Right?"

"Right," I whispered back.

"Off we go then. This is it!"

My father got down on his hands and knees and started crawling. I followed. He moved surprisingly fast on all fours and I had quite a job to keep up with him. Every few seconds he would glance back at me to see if I was all right, and each time he did so, I gave him a nod and a smile.

We crawled on and on, and then at last we were kneeling safely behind a big clump of bushes right on the edge of the clearing. My father was nudging me with his elbow and pointing through the branches at the pheasants.

The place was absolutely stiff with them. There must have been at least two hundred huge birds strutting around among the tree-stumps.

"You see what I mean?" he whispered.

It was a fantastic sight, a poacher's dream come true. And how close they were! Some of them were not ten paces from where we knelt.

The hens were plump and creamy-brown. They were so

fat their breast-feathers almost brushed the ground as they walked. The cocks were slim and elegant, with long tails and brilliant red patches round the eyes, like scarlet spectacles. I glanced at my father. His face was transfixed in ecstasy. The mouth was slightly open and the eyes were sparkling bright as they stared at the pheasants.

"There's a keeper," he said softly.

I froze. At first I didn't even dare to look.

"Over there," my father whispered.

I mustn't move, I told myself. Not even my head.

"Look carefully," my father whispered. "Over the other side, by that big tree."

Slowly, I swivelled my eyeballs in the direction he indicated. Then I saw him.

"Dad!" I whispered.

"Don't move now, Danny. Stay well down."

"Yes but Dad…"

"It's all right. He can't see *us*."

We crouched close to the ground, watching the keeper. He was a smallish man with a cap on his head and a big double-barrelled shotgun under his arm. He never moved. He was like a little post standing there.

"Should we go?" I whispered.

The keeper's face was shadowed by the peak of his cap, but it seemed to me he was looking straight at us.

"Should we go, Dad?"

"Hush," my father said.

Slowly, never taking his eyes from the keeper, he reached into his pocket and brought out a single raisin. He placed it in the palm of his right hand, and then quickly with a little flick of the wrist he threw the raisin high into the air. I watched it as it went sailing over the bushes and I saw it land within a yard of two hen birds standing beside an old tree-stump. Both birds turned their heads sharply at the drop of the raisin. Then one of them hopped over and made a quick peck at the ground and that must have been it.

I looked at the keeper. He hadn't moved.

I could feel a trickle of cold sweat running down one side of my forehead and across my cheek. I didn't dare lift a hand to wipe it away.

My father threw a second raisin into the clearing… then a third… and a fourth… and a fifth.

It takes guts to do that, I thought. Terrific guts. If I'd been alone I would never have stayed there for one second. But my father was in a sort of poacher's trance. For him, this was it. This was the moment of danger, the biggest thrill of all.

He kept on throwing the raisins into the clearing, swiftly, silently, one at a time. Flick went his wrist, and up went the raisin, high over the bushes, to land among the pheasants.

Then all at once, I saw the keeper turn away his head to inspect the wood behind him.

My father saw it too. Quick as a flash, he pulled the bag of raisins out of his pocket and tipped the whole lot into the palm of his right hand.

"Dad!" I whispered. "Don't!"

But with a great sweep of the arm he flung the entire handful way over the bushes into the clearing.

They fell with a soft little patter, like raindrops on dry leaves, and every single pheasant in the place must have heard them fall. There was a flurry of wings and a rush to find the treasure.

The keeper's head flicked round as though there were a spring inside his neck. The birds were all pecking away madly at the raisins. The keeper took two quick paces forward, and for a moment I thought he was going in to investigate. But then he stopped, and his face came up and his eyes began travelling slowly round the edge of the clearing.

"Lie down flat!" my father whispered. "Stay there! Don't move an inch!"

I flattened my body against the ground and pressed one side of my face into the brown leaves. The soil below the leaves had a queer pungent smell, like beer. Out of one eye, I saw my father raise his head just a tiny bit to watch the keeper. He kept watching him.

"Don't you *love* this?" he whispered to me.

I didn't dare answer him.

We lay there for what seemed like a hundred years.

At last I heard my father whisper, "Panic's over. Follow me, Danny. But be extra careful, he's still there. And *keep down low all the time.*"

He started crawling away quickly on his hands and knees. I went after him. I kept thinking of the keeper who was somewhere behind us. I was very conscious of that keeper, and I was also very conscious of my own backside, and how it was sticking up in the air for all to see. I could understand now why 'poacher's bottom' was a fairly common complaint in this business.

We went along on our hands and knees for about a hundred yards.

"Now run!" my father said.

We got to our feet and ran, and a few minutes later we came out through the hedge into the lovely open safety of the cart-track.

"It went marvellously!" my father said, breathing heavily. "Didn't it go absolutely marvellously?" His face was scarlet and glowing with triumph.

"Did the keeper see us?" I asked.

"Not on your life!" he said. "And in a few minutes the sun will be going down and the birds will all be flying up to roost and that keeper will be sloping off home to his supper. Then all we've got to do is go back in again and help ourselves. We'll be picking them up off the ground like pebbles!"

He sat down on the grassy bank below the hedge. I sat down close to him. He put an arm round my shoulders and gave me a hug. "You did well, Danny," he said. "I'm right proud of you."

We sat on the grassy bank below the hedge, waiting for darkness to fall. The sun had set now and the sky was a pale smoke blue, faintly glazed with yellow. In the wood behind us the shadows and the spaces in between the trees were turning from grey to black.

"You could offer me anywhere in the world at this moment," my father said, "and I wouldn't go."

His whole face was glowing with happiness.

"We did it, Danny," he said, laying a hand gently on my knee. "We pulled it off. Doesn't that make you feel good?"

"Terrific," I said. "But it was a bit scary while it lasted."

"Ah, but that's what poaching's all about," he said. "It scares the pants off us. That's why we love it. Look, there's a hawk!"

I looked where he was pointing and saw a kestrel hawk hovering superbly in the darkening sky above the ploughed field across the track.

"It's his last chance for supper tonight," my father said. "He'll be lucky if he sees anything now."

Except for the swift fluttering of its wings, the hawk remained absolutely motionless in the sky. It seemed to be suspended by some invisible thread, like a toy bird hanging from the ceiling. Then suddenly it folded its wings and plummeted towards the earth at an incredible speed. This was a sight that always thrilled me.

"What do you think he saw, Dad?"

"A young rabbit perhaps," my father said. "Or a vole or a field-mouse. None of them has a chance when there's a kestrel overhead."

We waited to see if the hawk would fly up again. He didn't, which meant he had caught his prey and was eating it on the ground.

"How long does a sleeping pill take to work?" I asked.

"I don't know the answer to that one," my father said. "I imagine it's about half an hour."

"It might be different with pheasants though, Dad."

"It might," he said. "We've got to wait a while anyway, to give the keepers time to go home. They'll be off as soon as it gets dark. I've brought an apple for each of us," he added, fishing into one of his pockets.

"A Cox's Orange Pippin," I said, smiling. "Thank you very much."

We sat there munching away.

"One of the nice things about a Cox's Orange Pippin," my father said, "is that the pips rattle when it's ripe. Shake it and you can hear them rattling."

I shook my half-eaten apple. The pips rattled.

"Look out!" he whispered sharply. "There's someone coming."

The man had appeared suddenly and silently out of the dusk and was quite close before my father saw him. "It's another keeper," he whispered. "Just sit tight and don't say a word."

We both watched the keeper as he came down the track towards us. He had a shotgun under his arm and there was a black Labrador walking at his heel. He stopped when he was a few paces away and the dog stopped with him and stayed behind him, watching us through the keeper's legs.

"Good evening," my father said, nice and friendly.

This one was a tall bony man with a hard eye and a hard cheek and hard dangerous hands.

"I know you," he said, coming closer, "I know the both of you."

My father didn't answer this.

"You're from the fillin'-station. Right?"

His lips were thin and dry with some sort of a brownish crust over them.

"You're from the fillin'-station and that's your boy and you live in that filthy old caravan. Right?"

"What are we playing?" my father said. "Twenty Questions?"

The keeper spat out a big gob of spit and I saw it go sailing through the air and land with a plop on a patch of dry dust six inches from my father's plaster foot. It looked like a little baby oyster lying there.

"Beat it," the man said. "Go on. Get out."

When he spoke, his upper lip lifted above the gum and I could see a row of small discoloured teeth. One of them was black. The others were brownish-yellow, like the seeds of a pomegranate.

"This happens to be a public footpath," my father said. "Kindly do not molest us."

The keeper shifted the gun from his left arm to his right.

"You're loiterin'," he said, "with intent to commit a nuisance. I could run you in for that."

"No you couldn't," my father said.

All this made me rather nervous.

"I see you broke your foot," the keeper said. "You didn't by any chance fall into a hole in the ground, did you?"

"It's been a nice walk, Danny," my father said, putting a hand on my knee, "but it's time we went home for our supper." He stood up and so did I. We wandered off down the track the way we had come, leaving the keeper standing there, and soon he was out of sight in the half-darkness behind us.

"That's the head keeper," my father said. "His name is Rabbetts."

"Do we have to go home, Dad?"

"Home!" my father cried. "My dear boy, we're just beginning! Come in here."

There was a gate on our right leading into a field, and we climbed over it and sat down behind the hedge.

"Mr Rabbetts is also due for his supper," my father said. "You mustn't worry about him."

We sat quietly behind the hedge waiting for the keeper to walk past us on his way home. A few stars were showing, and a bright three-quarter moon was coming up over the hills behind us in the east.

"We have to be careful of that dog," my father said. "When they come by, hold your breath and don't move a muscle."

"Won't the dog smell us out anyway?" I asked.

"No," my father said. "There's no wind to carry the scent. Look out! Here they come! Don't move!"

The keeper came loping softly down the track with the dog padding quick and soft-footed at his heel. I took a deep breath and held it as they went by.

When they were some distance away, my father stood up and said, "It's all clear. He won't be coming back tonight."

"Are you sure?"

"I'm positive, Danny."

"What about the other one, the one in the clearing?"

"He'll be gone too."

"Mightn't one of them be waiting for us at the bottom of the track?" I asked. "By the gap in the hedge?"

"There wouldn't be any point in him doing that," my father said. "There's at least twenty different ways of reaching the road when you come out of Hazell's Wood. Mr Rabbetts knows that."

We stayed behind the hedge for a few minutes more just to be on the safe side.

"Isn't it a marvellous thought though, Danny," my father said, "that there's two hundred pheasants at this very moment roosting up in those trees and already they're beginning to feel groggy. Soon they'll be falling out of the branches like raindrops!"

The three-quarter moon was well above the hills now, and the sky was filled with stars as we climbed back over the gate and began walking up the track towards the wood.

It was not as dark as I had expected it to be inside the wood this time. Little glints and glimmers from the brilliant moon outside shone through the leaves and gave the place a cold eerie look.

"I brought a light for each of us," my father said. "We're going to need it later on." He handed me one of those small pocket torches shaped like a fountain-pen. I switched mine on. It threw a long narrow beam of surprising brightness, and when I moved it around it was like waving a very long white wand among the trees. I switched it off.

We started walking back towards the clearing where the pheasants had eaten the raisins.

"This," my father said, "will be the first time in the history of the world that anyone has ever tried to poach roosting pheasants. Isn't it marvellous though, to be able to walk around without worrying about keepers?"

"You don't think Mr Rabbetts might have sneaked back again just to make sure?"

"Never," my father said. "He's gone home to his supper."

I couldn't help thinking that if *I* had been Mr Rabbetts, and if *I* had seen two suspicious-looking characters lurking just outside my precious pheasant wood, I certainly would not have gone home to *my* supper. My father must have sensed my fears because once again he reached out and took my hand in his, folding his long warm fingers around mine.

Hand in hand, we threaded our way through the trees towards the

clearing. In a few minutes we were there. "Here's where we threw the raisins," my father said.

I peered through the bushes. The clearing lay pale and milky in the moonlight.

"What do we do next?" I asked.

"We stay here and wait," my father said. I could just make out his face under the peak of his cap, the lips pale, the cheeks flushed, the eyes shining bright.

"Are they all roosting, Dad?"

"Yes. They're all around us. They don't go far."

"Could I see them if I shone my light up into the branches?"

"No," he said. "They go up pretty high and they hide in among the leaves."

We stood waiting for something to happen.

Nothing happened. It was very quiet there in the wood.

"Danny," my father said.

"Yes, Dad?"

"I've been wondering how a bird manages to keep its balance sitting on a branch when it's asleep."

"I don't know," I said. "Why?"

"It's very peculiar," he said.

"What's peculiar?"

"It's peculiar that a bird doesn't topple off its perch as soon as it goes to sleep. After all, if *we* were sitting on a branch and we went to sleep, we would fall off at once, wouldn't we?"

"Birds have claws and long toes, Dad. I expect they hold on with those."

"I know that, Danny. But I still don't understand why the toes keep gripping the perch once the bird is asleep. Surely everything goes limp when you fall asleep."

I waited for him to go on.

"I was just thinking," he said, "that if a bird can keep its balance when it's asleep, then surely there isn't any reason why the pills should make it fall down."

"It's doped," I said. "Surely it will fall down if it's doped."

"But isn't that simply a *deeper* sort of sleep?" he said. "Why should we expect it to fall down just because it's in a *deeper* sleep?"

There was a gloomy silence.

"I should have tested it with roosters," my father added. Suddenly the blood seemed to have drained right out of his cheeks. His face was so pale I thought he might be going to faint. "My dad would have tested it with roosters before he did anything else," he said.

At that moment there came a soft thump from the wood behind us.

"What was that?" I asked.

"Ssshh!"

We stood listening.

Thump!

"There's another!" I said.

It was a deep muffled sound as though a bag of sand had been dropped to the ground.

Thump!

"They're pheasants!" I cried.

"Wait!"

"They must be pheasants, Dad!"

Thump! Thump!

"You may be right, Danny!"

We switched on our torches and ran towards the sounds.

"Where were they?" my father said.

"Over here, Dad! Two of them were over here!"

"I thought they were this way. Keep looking! They can't be far!"

We searched for about a minute.

"Here's one!" my father called.

When I got to him he was holding a magnificent cock bird in both hands. We examined it closely with our torches.

"It's doped to high heaven," my father said. "It won't wake up for a week."

Thump!

"There's another!" I cried.

Thump! Thump!

"Two more!" my father yelled.

Thump!

Thump! Thump! Thump!

"Jeepers!" my father said.

Thump! Thump! Thump! Thump!

Thump! Thump!

All around us the pheasants were starting to rain down out of the trees. We began rushing round madly in the dark, sweeping the ground with our torches.

Thump! Thump! Thump! This lot fell almost on top of me. I was right under the tree as they came down and I found all three of them immediately – two cocks and a hen. They were limp and warm, the feathers wonderfully soft in the hand.

"Where shall I put them, Dad?" I called out.

"Lay them here, Danny! Just pile them up here where it's light!"

My father was standing on the edge of the clearing with the moonlight streaming down all over him and a great bunch of pheasants in each hand. His face was bright, his eyes big and bright and wonderful, and he was staring around him like a child who has just discovered that the whole world is made of chocolate.

Thump!

Thump! Thump!

"It's too many!" I said.

"It's beautiful!" he cried. He dumped the birds he was carrying and ran off to look for more.

Thump! Thump! Thump! Thump!

Thump!

It was easy to find them now. There were one or two lying under every tree. I quickly collected six more, three in each hand, and ran back and dumped them with the others. Then six more. Then six more after that.

And still they kept falling.

My father was in a whirl of excitement now, dashing about like a mad ghost under the trees. I could see the beam of his torch waving round in the dark, and every time he found a bird he gave a little yelp of triumph.

Thump! Thump! Thump!

"Hey Danny!" he shouted.

"Yes, I'm over here! What is it, Dad?"

"What do you think the great Mr Victor Hazell would say if he could see this?"

"Don't talk about it," I said.

For three or four minutes, the pheasants kept on falling. Then suddenly they stopped.

"Keep searching!" my father shouted. "There's plenty more on the ground!"

"Dad," I said, "don't you think we ought to get out while the going's good?"

"Never!" he shouted. "Not on your life!"

We went on searching. Between us we looked under every tree within a hundred yards of the clearing, north, south, east and west, and I think we found most of them in the end. At the collecting-point there was a pile of pheasants as big as a bonfire.

"It's a miracle," my father was saying. "It's an absolute miracle." He was staring at them in a kind of trance.

"Shouldn't we just take about six each and get out quick?" I said.

"I would like to count them, Danny."

"Dad! Not now!"

"I *must* count them."

"Can't we do that later?"

"One…

"Two…

"Three…

"Four…"

He began counting them very carefully, picking up each bird in turn and laying it carefully to one side. The moon was directly overhead now, and the whole clearing was brilliantly lit up. I felt as though I was standing in the glare of powerful headlamps.

"A hundred and seventeen… a hundred and eighteen… a hundred and nineteen… *one hundred and twenty!*" he cried. "It's an all-time record!" He looked happier than I had ever seen him in his life. "The most my dad ever got was fifteen and he was drunk for a week afterwards!" he said. "But this… this, my dear boy, is an all-time *world record!*"

"I expect it is," I said.

"And *you* did it, Danny! The whole thing was your idea in the first place!"

"I didn't do it, Dad."

"Oh yes you did! And you know what that makes you, my dear boy? It makes you the champion of the world!" He pulled up his sweater and unwound the two big cotton sacks from round his belly. "Here's yours," he said, handing one of them to me. "Fill it up quick!"

The light of the moon was so strong I could read the print across the front of the sack, J. W. CRUMP, it said, KESTON FLOUR MILLS, LONDON S.W.17.

"You don't think that keeper with the brown teeth is watching us this very moment from behind a tree?" I said.

"No chance," my father said. "If he's anywhere he'll be down at the filling-station waiting to catch us coming home with the loot."

We started loading the pheasants into the sacks. They were soft and floppy-necked and the skin underneath the feathers was still warm.

"We can't possibly carry this lot all the way home," I said.

"Of course not. There'll be a taxi waiting for us on the track outside the wood."

"A *taxi!*" I said.

"My dad always made use of a taxi on a big job," he said.

"Why a taxi, for heaven's sake?"

"It's more secret, Danny. Nobody knows who's inside a taxi except the driver."

"Which driver?" I asked.

"Charlie Kinch. He's only too glad to oblige."

"Does *he* know about poaching, too?"

"Old Charlie Kinch? Of course he does. He's poached more pheasants in his time than we've sold gallons of petrol."

We finished loading the sacks and my father humped his on to his shoulders. I couldn't do that with mine. It was too heavy for me. "Drag it," my father said. "Just drag it along the ground." My sack had sixty

birds inside it and it weighed a ton. But it slid quite easily over the dry leaves with me walking backwards and pulling it with both hands.

We came to the edge of the wood and peered through the hedge on to the track. My father said "Charlie boy" very softly, and the old man behind the wheel of the taxi poked his head out into the moonlight and gave us a sly toothless grin. We slid through the hedge, dragging the sacks after us along the ground.

"Hello-hello-hello," Charlie Kinch said. "What's all this then?"

Two minutes later we were safely inside the taxi and cruising slowly down the bumpy track towards the road.

My father was bursting with pride and excitement. He kept leaning forward and tapping Charlie Kinch on the shoulder and saying, "How about it, Charlie? How about this for a haul?" And Charlie kept glancing back pop-eyed at the huge bulging sacks. "Cripes, man!" he kept saying. "How did you do it?"

"Danny did it!" my father said proudly. "My son Danny is the champion of the world."

Hansel and Gretel

from RHYME STEW

MUM said to Dad, "Those kids of ours!
The food that each of them devours!
That Hansel! Cripes, that little tick!
To watch him eat, it makes me sick!
And as for ghastly greedy Gretel –
I'm turning round to boil the kettle
And while I'm at it she's been able
To guzzle all that's on the table!"
The father merely shrugged and sighed.
Mum waved her frying-pan and cried,
"My motto is that *we* come first,
Them kids should *always* get the worst.
Now look, if we could rub them out,
There'd be more beans and sauerkraut
And stuff for you and me to eat.
Mind you, we'd have to be discreet."
The father said, "Well, what's to do?
We can't just flush them down the loo."
To which the mother answered "No,
They're much too big. They wouldn't go."
"What if," the father said, "they fell,
Quite accidentally, down the well?"
"Oh no," Mum said, "I doubt we oughta,
It might pollute the drinkin' water.
I think it's better, on the whole,
To take them for a little stroll
And lose them in among the trees.
Now surely that's a better wheeze?"
"Let's do it!" Dad cried out. "And then

We'll never see the pigs again!"
"Walkies!" the parents cried. "It's spring!
Let's go and hear the birdies sing!
Let's look for robins in the trees!
Let's pick some wild anemones!"
Now Hansel suddenly espies
His mother's shrewd and shifty eyes.
He whispers softly, "Listen, Sis,
I don't much like the smell of this.
I think our loving mum and dad
Are plotting something rather bad.
I think I'd better mark our track
To help us on the journey back."
So on the walk, when outward bound,
He scatters breadcrumbs on the ground.

They walk, all four, for hours and hours,
They see no robins, pick no flowers.
The wood is dark and cold and bare,
And Dad says, "Children, stay right here,
Your mum and I have things to do.
We'll see you later, toodle-oo."
They sidled off with perfect ease
And disappeared among the trees.
"They're going to dump us!" Gretel cried.
"They won't succeed," the boy replied.
"We'll get back home, we cannot fail,
By following the breadcrumb trail.
Just take my hand and come with me,
We'll find our way, you wait and see."
But oh! Alas! Where crumbs had been
There now was nothing to be seen.
Young Gretel cried, "You silly twit,
The crows have eaten every bit."

Poor little children all alone,
The foul and filthy parents flown.
Poor little children all forlorn
To face the dismal murky morn.
"We'll starve to death!" young Hansel cried,
When all at once the youth espied
A funny little snow-white bird
Who spoke as follows, word for word:
"Come follow me, you troubled things,
I'll take you on my silver wings
To safety, to a lovely place
Where you can live in peace and grace!"

355

This wondrous bird then led them forth
For miles and miles towards the north
Until at last there hove in sight
A lovely cottage painted white,
And there before the cottage door
These two enraptured children saw
A sweet old dame with rosy skin
Who smiled and said, "Oh, do come in.
You must be hungry, little lambs."
She fed them treacle tarts and hams
And sugar-buns and gorgeous jam.
The children cried, "Oh, thank you, ma'am!"
The woman with the rosy cheeks
Now smiles again and softly speaks:
"My darling children, as you see,

You eat extremely well with me."
She then serves up the second treat,
A very curious roast of meat,
All sizzling hot and crispy brown.
The happy children wolf it down.
The hostess says, "Do have some more.
I doubt you've tasted this before."
Young Hansel asks her, "Is it lamb?
Or is it beef or is it ham?
Whate'er it is, I must admit
It's awfully tender, isn't it?"
The woman said, "This special meat
S'the only kind I like to eat."
Then Gretel says, "I'll make a bid –
This meat is either goat or kid."
The woman says, "Well, no-o-o and yes-s-s,
I must say *kid*'s a clever guess."
She smiled and chewed and chewed and smiled
And looked so innocent and mild.

As soon as they had left the table
The woman led them to a stable.
Stable? they wondered, turning pale.
The place looked like a sort of jail
With bars and bolts and horrid things
Like manacles and iron rings.
The woman said, "Go in and look,
It's such a cosy little nook."
So Hansel, wanting to explore,
Went boldly through the open door.
The woman quickly slammed it, BANG!
The bars and locks and bolts went CLANG!

"Hey, let me out!" young Hansel cried.
"You stay in there!" the dame replied.
"I'm going to feed you up a treat
Until you're fat enough to eat."
(The Brothers Grimm who wrote this story
Made it a thousand times more gory.
I've taken out the foulest scene
In order that you won't turn green.
It is beyond me how it came
To merit such enormous fame.
Did parents really, in those days,
Agree to read such gruesome plays
To little children in the night?
And did they never die of fright?
It might have been okay, who knows,
If there'd been humour in the prose.
Did I say humour? Wilhelm Grimm?
There's not a scrap of it in him.)
I'll cut the grizzly ending short,
But even so I think I ought
To tell you gently what came next.
I'll make it brief so don't be vexed.

Just when the stove is nice and hot
And water's boiling in the pot
(The pot's for boiling Hansel in,
The stove for crisping up his skin),
Young Gretel in her pinafore
Flings open wide the oven door.
"The fire is going out!" she cried.
The woman pokes her head inside
And Gretel with a springy jump
Takes aim and kicks her on the rump.
She totters forward, in she goes

Head first, and last of all her toes.
Now Gretel with a gleeful roar
Slams shut the open oven door.
The temperature inside, she sees,
Is just on four-five-o degrees,
And soon this red-hot oven heat
Gives out the smell of roasting meat.

The child runs fast as she is able
To open up the prison-stable.
"Hansel!" she shouts. "We're free at last!
The foul old dame is roasting fast!"
Young Hansel cried, "Oh, well done you!
Oh, what a splendid thing to do!
But then again, you must admit
You always liked to cook a bit."

Hansel and Gretel Spare Ribs

from REVOLTING RECIPES

SERVES 4

YOU WILL NEED:

roasting pan

1¹/₂ lb / 675 g spare ribs
1 tablespoon Worcestershire sauce
1 tablespoon soy sauce
1 tablespoon prepared mustard
1 tablespoon tomato ketchup
1 tablespoon honey
1 medium onion, finely chopped
salt and pepper

1. Preheat the oven to 425°F/220°C/gas mark 7.

2. Place the ribs in a roasting pan in one layer.

3. Mix all the remaining ingredients together and spread the mixture on the ribs with a knife.

4. Place the pan of ribs in the oven and bake for about 1¹/₂ hours, turning them over every half hour and basting them with the juices.

NOTE: These must be well cooked and crunchy, as in the picture.

Conkers!

from MY YEAR

I have always loved September. As a schoolboy I loved it because it is the Month of the Conker. It is no good knocking down conkers in August because they are still soft and white. But in September, ah, yes, then they are a deep rich brown colour and shining as though they have been polished and that is the time to gather them by the bucketful. I recently wrote a letter to *The Times* newspaper bemoaning the fact that children weren't playing conkers with the same fervour as when I was young. This caused an explosion of angry letters from young enthusiasts all over the country. Nearly one thousand people wrote to me, both boys *and* girls, telling of their love for the sport and of the great contests that were taking place all over the country in the autumn. I received press clippings about the World Conker Championships held at Ashton in Cambridgeshire, and about the All England Conker Championships that were held at Henley. From these letters I learnt that the whole of Britain is still alive with ardent conker players. Many girls wrote to me saying they were just as good as the boys and I was delighted to hear it.

We all know, of course, that a great conker is one that has been stored in a dry place for at least a year. This matures it and makes it rock hard and therefore very formidable. We also know about the short cuts that less dedicated players take to harden their conkers. Some soak them in vinegar for a week. Others bake them in the oven at a low temperature for six hours. But such methods are not for the true conker player. No world-champion conker has ever been produced by short cuts.

I could go on for hours about the best shape to select for a fighting conker – always, the flat sharp-edged one, never the big round fellow

365

– and I could talk about the relative merits of using thin and thick string. I could write several pages on the various aiming methods to use and the best swing to adopt when delivering the blow, and the importance of keeping your head still throughout the stroke, and the necessity of a correct stance, but there is no space for all of that here. Suffice it to say that it is a splendid game to play during the winter months and one that requires a cool head and a keen eye.

When I was nine, I made myself a Conker Practising Machine on which I would string up six conkers in a row and work at busting them one after the other. Let's face it, you don't become top class at any sport, be it golf or tennis or snooker or conkers, unless you prac- tise long and hard. The best conker I ever had was a conker 109, and I can still remember that frosty morning in the school playground when my one-o-nine was finally shattered by Perkins's conker 74 in an epic contest that lasted over half an hour. After it, I felt even more shat- tered than my conker.

October 11th 1925

S? Peters
Weston-super-mare

Dear Mama

I am sorry I have not writting before. ~~We~~ There was a foot-ball match yestarday, ~~so to~~ agenst clarence, and The first eleven ~~lost~~ by 1 goals, The score was 3 goals to 2, but The ~~se~~ second eleven won by 5 goals The score Was 5 nill. We playd Brien house on Wedensday, and The score was 1 all. I hope none of you have got coalds. It is quite a nice day To-day, I am just going To church. I hope mike is quite all right now, and Buzz. Major Cottam is going To recite something caled "as you like it" To night. Plese could you send me some conkers as quick as you can, but ~~dont~~ dont send To meny, ~~the~~ Just send them in a Tin and wrap it up in paper

Love from
BOY

From the very first Sunday at St Peter's until the day my mother died thirty-two years later, I wrote to her once a week, sometimes more often. My mother, for her part, kept every one of these letters, binding them carefully in neat bundles with green tape, but this was her own secret. She never told me she was doing it.

A Drive in the Motor-Car

from BOY

ONE amazing morning our whole family got ready to go for our first drive in the first motor-car we had ever owned. This new motor-car was an enormous long black French automobile called a De Dion-Bouton which had a canvas roof that folded back. The driver was to be that twelve-years-older-than-me half-sister (now aged twenty-one) who had recently had her appendix removed.

She had received two full half-hour lessons in driving from the man who delivered the car, and in that enlightened year of 1925 this was considered quite sufficient. Nobody had to take a driving-test. You were your own judge of competence, and as soon as you felt you were ready to go, off you jolly well went.

As we all climbed into the car, our excitement was so intense we could hardly bear it.

368

"How fast will it go?" we cried out. "Will it do fifty miles an hour?"

"It'll do sixty!" the ancient sister answered. Her tone was so confident and cocky it should have scared us to death, but it didn't.

"Oh, let's make it do sixty!" we shouted. "Will you promise to take us up to sixty?"

"We shall probably go faster than that," the sister announced, pulling on her driving-gloves and tying a scarf over her head in the approved driving-fashion of the period.

The canvas hood had been folded back because of the mild weather, converting the car into a magnificent open tourer. Up front, there were three bodies in all, the driver behind the wheel, my half-brother (aged eighteen) and one of my sisters (aged twelve). In the back seat there were four more of us, my mother (aged forty), two small sisters (aged eight and five) and myself (aged nine). Our machine possessed one very special feature which I don't think you see on the cars of today. This was a second windscreen in the back solely to keep the breeze off the faces of the back-seat passengers when the hood was down. It had a long centre section and two little end sections that could be angled backwards to deflect the wind.

We were all quivering with fear and joy as the driver let out the clutch and the great long black automobile leaned forward and stole into motion.

"Are you sure you know how to do it?" we shouted. "Do you know where the brakes are?"

"Be quiet!" snapped the ancient sister. "I've got to concentrate!"

Down the drive we went and out into the village of Llandaff itself. Fortunately there were very few vehicles on the roads in those days. Occasionally you met a small truck or a delivery-van and now and again a private car, but the danger of colliding with anything else was fairly remote so long as you kept the car on the road.

The splendid black tourer crept slowly through the village with the driver pressing the rubber bulb of the horn every time we passed a human being, whether it was the butcher-boy on his bicycle or just a pedestrian strolling on the pavement. Soon we were entering a countryside of green fields and high hedges with not a soul in sight.

"You didn't think I could do it, did you?" cried the ancient sister, turning round and grinning at us all.

"Now you keep your eyes on the road," my mother said nervously.

"Go faster!" we shouted. "Go on! Make her go faster! Put your foot down! We're only doing *fifteen miles an hour!*"

Spurred on by our shouts and taunts, the ancient sister began to increase the speed. The engine roared and the body vibrated. The driver was clutching the steering-wheel as though it were the hair of a drowning man, and we all watched the speedometer needle creeping up to twenty, then twenty-five, then thirty. We were probably doing about thirty-five miles an hour when we came suddenly to a sharpish bend in the road. The ancient sister, never having been faced with a situation like this before, shouted "Help!" and slammed on the brakes and swung the wheel wildly round. The rear wheels locked and went into a fierce sideways skid, and then, with a marvellous crunch of mudguards and metal, we went crashing into the hedge. The front passengers all shot through the front windscreen and the back passengers all shot through the back windscreen. Glass (there was no Triplex then) flew in all directions and so did we. My brother and one sister landed on the bonnet of the car, someone else was catapulted out on to the road and at least one small sister landed in the middle of the hawthorn hedge. But miraculously nobody was hurt very much except me. My nose had been cut almost clean off my face as I went through the rear windscreen and now it was hanging on only by a single small thread of skin. My mother disentangled herself from the scrimmage and grabbed a handkerchief from her purse. She clapped the dangling nose back into place fast and held it there.

Not a cottage or a person was in sight, let alone a telephone. Some kind of bird started twittering in a tree farther down the road, otherwise all was silent.

My mother was bending over me in the rear seat and saying, "Lean back and keep your head still." To the ancient sister she said, "Can you get this thing going again?"

The sister pressed the starter and to everyone's surprise, the engine fired.

"Back it out of the hedge," my mother said. "And hurry."

The sister had trouble finding reverse gear. The cogs were grinding against one another with a fearful noise of tearing metal.

"I've never actually driven it backwards," she admitted at last.

Everyone with the exception of the driver, my mother and me was out of the car and standing on the road. The noise of gear-wheels grinding against each other was terrible. It sounded as though a lawn-mower was being driven over hard rocks. The ancient sister was using bad words and going crimson in the face, but then my brother leaned his head over the driver's door and said, "Don't you have to put your foot on the clutch?"

The harassed driver depressed the clutch-pedal and the gears meshed and one second later the great black beast leapt backwards out of the hedge and careered across the road into the hedge on the other side.

"Try to keep cool," my mother said. "Go forward slowly."

At last the shattered motor-car was driven out of the second hedge and stood sideways across the road, blocking the highway. A man with a horse and cart now appeared on the scene and the man dismounted from his cart and walked across to our car and leaned over the rear door. He had a big drooping moustache and he wore a small black bowler-hat.

"You're in a fair old mess 'ere, ain't you?" he said to my mother.

"Can you drive a motor-car?" my mother asked him.

"Nope," he said. "And you're blockin' up the 'ole road. I've got a thousand fresh-laid heggs in this cart and I want to get 'em to market before noon."

"Get out of the way," my mother told him. "Can't you see there's a child in here who's badly injured?"

"One thousand fresh-laid heggs," the man repeated, staring straight at my mother's hand and the blood-soaked handkerchief and the blood running down her wrist. "And if I don't get 'em to market by noon today I won't be able to sell 'em till next week. Then they won't be fresh-laid any more, will they? I'll be stuck with one thousand stale ole heggs that nobody wants."

"I hope they all go rotten," my mother said. "Now back that cart out of our way this instant!" And to the children standing on the road she cried out, "Jump back into the car! We're going to the doctor!"

"There's glass all over the seats!" they shouted.

"Never mind the glass!" my mother said. "We've got to get this boy to the doctor fast!"

The passengers crawled back into the car. The man with the horse and cart backed off to a safe distance. The ancient sister managed to straighten the vehicle and get it pointed in the right direction, and then at last the once magnificent automobile tottered down the highway and headed for Dr Dunbar's surgery in Cathedral Road, Cardiff.

"I've never driven in a city," the ancient and trembling sister announced.

"You are about to do so," my mother said. "Keep going."

Proceeding at no more than four miles an hour all the way, we finally made it to Dr Dunbar's house. I was hustled out of the car and in through the front door with my mother still holding the blood-stained handkerchief firmly over my wobbling nose.

"Good heavens!" cried Dr Dunbar. "It's been cut clean off!"

"It hurts," I moaned.

"He can't go round without a nose for the rest of his life!" the doctor said to my mother.

"It looks as though he may have to," my mother said.

"Nonsense!" the doctor told her. "I shall sew it on again."

"Can you do that?" my mother asked him.

"I can try," he answered. "I shall tape it on tight for now and I'll be up at your house with my assistant within the hour."

Huge strips of sticking-plaster were strapped across my face to hold the nose in position. Then I was led back into the car and we crawled the two miles home to Llandaff.

About an hour later I found myself lying upon that same nursery table my ancient sister had occupied some months before for her appendix operation. Strong hands held me down while a mask stuffed with cotton-wool was clamped over my face. I saw a hand above me holding a bottle with white liquid in it and the liquid was being poured on to the cotton-wool inside the mask. Once again I smelled the sickly stench of chloroform and ether, and a voice was saying, "Breathe deeply. Take some nice deep breaths."

I fought fiercely to get off that table but my shoulders were pinned down by the full weight of a large man. The hand that was holding the bottle above my face kept tilting it farther and farther forward and the white liquid dripped and dripped on to the cotton-wool. Blood-red circles began to appear before my eyes and the circles started to spin round and round until they made a scarlet whirlpool with a deep black hole in the centre, and miles away in the distance a voice was saying, "That's a good boy. We're nearly there now…we're nearly there… just close your eyes and go to sleep…"

I woke up in my own bed with my anxious mother sitting beside me, holding my hand. "I didn't think you were ever going to come round," she said. "You've been asleep for more than eight hours."

"Did Dr Dunbar sew my nose on again?" I asked her.

"Yes," she said.

"Will it stay on?"

"He says it will. How do you feel, my darling?"

"Sick," I said.

After I had vomited into a small basin, I felt a little better.

"Look under your pillow," my mother said, smiling.

I turned and lifted a corner of my pillow, and underneath it, on the snow-white sheet, there lay a beautiful golden sovereign with the head of King George V on its uppermost side.

"That's for being brave," my mother said. "You did very well. I'm proud of you."

When you grow up
and have children of your own
do please remember something important

a stodgy parent is *no fun* at all

What a child wants
and deserves
is a parent who is

SPARKY

PART FOUR

Matters
of Importance

The biggest hip bone ever

As I sit here in my comfortable chair with my writing board across my lap, I can see scattered over the table top the following things: One of my own hip bones (the head of the femur)… which the surgeon gave me after he had sawed it off and stuck a steel one into me instead. He said it was worth keeping because it was the biggest hip bone he had ever seen.

A glass bottle in which lies the tiny mechanism or valve which I helped to invent for draining off excess fluid from the ventricles of the brains of children who suffer from a type of brain injury known as hydrocephalus…

from MY YEAR

379

Lucky Break

APART from the masters, there was another man in the school [St Peter's] who frightened us considerably. This was Mr Pople. Mr Pople was a paunchy, crimson-faced individual who acted as school-porter, boiler superintendent and general handyman. His power stemmed from the fact that he could (and he most certainly did) report us to the headmaster upon the slightest provocation. Mr Pople's moment of glory came each morning at seven-thirty precisely, when he would stand at the end of the long main corridor and 'ring the bell'. The bell was huge and made of brass, with a thick wooden handle, and Mr Pople would swing it back and forth at arm's length in a special way of his own, so that it went *clangetty-clang-clang, clangetty-clang-clang, clangetty-clang-clang*. At the sound of the bell, all the boys in the school, one hundred and eighty of us, would move smartly to our positions in the corridor. We lined up against the walls on both sides and stood stiffly to attention awaiting the headmaster's inspection.

But at least ten minutes would elapse before the headmaster arrived on the scene, and during this time, Mr Pople would conduct a ceremony so extraordinary that to this day I find it hard to believe it ever took place. There were six lavatories in the school, numbered on their doors from one to six. Mr Pople, standing at the end of the long corridor, would have in the palm of his hand six small brass discs, each with a number on it, one to six. There was absolute silence as he allowed his eye to travel down the two lines of stiffly-standing boys. Then he would bark out a name, "Arkle!"

Arkle would fall out and step briskly down the corridor to where Mr Pople stood. Mr Pople would hand him a brass disc. Arkle would

then march away toward the lavatories, and to reach them he would have to walk the entire length of the corridor, past all the stationary boys, and then turn left. As soon as he was out of sight, he was allowed to look at his disc and see which lavatory number he had been given.

"Highton!" barked Mr Pople, and now Highton would fall out to receive his disc and march away.

"Angel!"...

"Williamson!"...

"Gaunt!"...

"Price!"...

In this manner, six boys selected at Mr Pople's whim were dispatched to the lavatories to do their duty. Nobody asked them if they might or might not be ready to move their bowels at seven-thirty in the morning before breakfast. They were simply ordered to do so. But we considered it a great privilege to be chosen because it meant that during the headmaster's inspection we would be sitting safely out of reach in blessed privacy.

In due course, the headmaster would emerge from his private quarters and take over from Mr Pople. He walked slowly down one side of the corridor, inspecting each boy with the utmost care, strapping his wristwatch on to his wrist as he went along. The morning inspection was an unnerving experience. Every one of us was terrified of the two sharp brown eyes under their bushy eyebrows as they travelled slowly up and down the length of one's body.

"Go away and brush your hair properly. And don't let it happen again or you'll be sorry."

"Let me see your hands. You have ink on them. Why didn't you wash it off last night?"

"Your tie is crooked, boy. Fall out and tie it again. And do it properly this time."

"I can see mud on that shoe. Didn't I have to talk to you about that last week? Come and see me in my study after breakfast."

And so it went on, the ghastly early-morning inspection. And by the end of it all, when the headmaster had gone away and Mr Pople started marching us into the dining-room by forms, many of us had lost our appetites for the lumpy porridge that was to come.

Photography

from BOY

THERE was one other thing [apart from playing games] that gave me great pleasure at this school and that was photography. I was the only boy who practised it seriously, and it was not quite so simple a business fifty years ago as it is today. I made myself a little darkroom in a corner of the music building, and in there I loaded my glass plates and developed my negatives and enlarged them.

Our Arts Master was a shy retiring man called Arthur Norris who kept himself well apart from the rest of the staff. Arthur Norris and I became close friends and during my last year he organised an exhibition of my photographs. He gave the whole of the Art School over to this project and helped me to get my enlargements framed. The exhibition was rather a success, and masters who had hardly ever spoken to me over the past four years would come up and say things like, "It's quite extraordinary"… "We didn't know we had an artist in our midst"… "Are they for sale?"

Arthur Norris would give me tea and cakes in his flat and would talk to me about painters like Cézanne and Manet and Matisse, and I have a feeling that it was there, having tea with the gentle soft-spoken Mr Norris in his flat on Sunday afternoons, that my great love of painters and their work began.

After leaving school, I continued for a long time with photography and I became quite good at it. Today, given a 35mm camera and a built-in exposure-meter, anyone can be an expert photographer, but it was not so easy fifty years ago. I used glass plates instead of film, and each of these had to be loaded into its separate container in the darkroom before I set out to take pictures. I usually carried with me six loaded plates, which allowed me only six exposures, so that clicking the shutter even once was a serious business that had to be carefully thought out beforehand.

You may not believe it, but when I was eighteen I used to win prizes and medals from the Royal Photographic Society in London, and from other places like the Photographic Society of Holland. I even got a lovely big bronze medal from the Egyptian Photographic Society in Cairo, and I still have the photograph that won it. It is a picture of one of the so-called Seven Wonders of the World, the Arch of Ctesiphon in Iraq. This is the largest unsupported arch on earth and I took the photograph while I was training out there for the RAF in 1940. I was flying over the desert solo in an old Hawker Hart biplane and I had my camera round my neck. When I spotted the huge arch standing alone in a sea of sand, I dropped one wing and hung in my straps and let go of the stick while I took aim and clicked the shutter. It came out fine.

Motorbikes

from MY YEAR

I had bought my motorbike soon after I was sixteen. It was a second-hand Ariel 500cc and it cost me twenty-two pounds. It was a wonderful big powerful machine and when I rode upon it, it gave me an amazing feeling of winged majesty and of independence that I had never known before. Wherever I wished to go, my mighty Ariel would take me. Up to then, I had either had to walk or bicycle or buy a ticket for a bus or a train and it was a slow business. But now all I had to do was sling one leg over the saddle, kick the starter and away I went. I got the same feeling a few years later when I flew single-seater fighter planes in the war. Anyway, my plan now was to enliven the last term at Repton by secretly taking my motorbike with me. So on the first day of that summer term I rode it the hundred and fifty miles from our house in Kent to the village of Wilmington, which is about three miles from Repton. There I left it with a friendly garage owner together with my waders and helmet and goggles and wind jacket. Then I walked the rest of the way to school with my little suitcase.

Sunday afternoons were the only times we had free throughout the school week and most boys went for long walks in the countryside. But I took no long Sunday afternoon walks during my last term. My walks took me only as far as the garage in Wilmington where my lovely motorbike was hidden. There I would put on my disguise – my waders and helmet and goggles and wind jacket – and go sailing in a state of absolute bliss through the highways and byways of Derbyshire. But the greatest thrill of all was to ride at least once every Sunday afternoon slap through the middle of Repton village, sailing past the pompous prefects and the masters in their gowns and mortarboards. I felt pretty safe with my big goggles covering half of my face, although I will admit that on one famous occasion I got a twist in my stomach when I found myself motoring within a couple of yards of the terrifying figure of the headmaster, Dr Geoffrey Fisher himself, as he strode with purposeful step towards the chapel. He glared at me as I rode past, but I don't think that it would have entered his brainy head for one moment that I was a member of the school. Don't forget that those were the days when schools like mine were merciless places where serious misdemeanours were punished by savage beatings that drew blood from your backside. I am quite sure that if I had ever been caught, that same headmaster would have thrashed me within an inch of my life and would probably have expelled me into the bargain. That is what made it so exciting. I never told anyone, not even my best friend, where I went on my Sunday walks. I had learnt even at that tender age that there are no secrets unless you keep them to yourself, and this was the greatest secret I had ever had to keep in my life so far.

The Twits

AN EXTRACT

IF a person has ugly thoughts, it begins to show on the face. And when that person has ugly thoughts every day, every week, every year, the face gets uglier and uglier until it gets so ugly you can hardly bear to look at it.

A person who has good thoughts cannot ever be ugly. You can have a wonky nose and a crooked mouth and a double chin and stick-out teeth, but if you have good thoughts they will shine out of your face like sunbeams and you will always look lovely.

The Emperor's New Clothes

from RHYME STEW

THE Royal Tailor, Mister Ho,
  Had premises on Savile Row,
And thence the King would make his way
At least a dozen times a day.
His passion was for gorgeous suits
And sumptuous cloaks and fur-lined boots
And brilliant waistcoats lined in red,
Hand-sewn with gold and silver thread.
Within the Palace things were grand,
With valets everywhere on hand
To hang the clothes and clean and press
And help the crazy King to dress.
But clothes are very dangerous things,
Especially for wealthy kings.
This King had gone to pot so fast,
His clothes came first, his people last.
One valet who was seen to leave
A spot of gravy on a sleeve
Was hung from rafters by his hair
And left forever dangling there.
Another who had failed to note
A fleck of dust upon a coat
Was ordered to be boiled alive,
A fate not easy to survive.
And one who left a pinch of snuff
Upon a pale-blue velvet cuff

Was minced inside a large machine
And reappeared as margarine.
Oh, what a beastly horrid King!
The people longed to do him in!
And so a dozen brainy men
Met secretly inside a den
To formulate a subtle plot
To polish off this royal clot.
Up spake the very brainiest man
Who cried, "I've got a wizard plan.
Please come with me. We all must go
To see the royal tailor, Ho.
We'll tell him very strong and true
Exactly what he's got to do."
So thus the secret plans were laid
And all arrangements quickly made.

T'was winter-time with lots of snow
And every day the King would go
To ski a bit before he dined
In ski-suits specially designed.
But even on these trips he'd stop
To go into the tailor's shop.
"O Majesty!" cried Mister Ho,
"I cannot wait to let you know
That I've contrived at last to get
From secret weavers in Tibet
A cloth so magical and fine,
So unbelievably divine,
You've never seen its like before
And never will do any more!"
The King yelled out, "I'll buy the lot!
I'll purchase every yard you've got!"
The tailor smiled and bowed his head.
"O honoured sire," he softly said,
"This marvellous magic cloth has got
Amazing ways to keep you hot,
And even when it's icy cold
You still feel warm as molten gold.
However hard the north wind blows
You still won't need your underclothes."
The King said, "If it's all that warm,
I'll have a ski-ing uniform!
I want ski-trousers and a jacket!
I don't care if it costs a packet!
Produce the cloth. I want to see
This marvellous stuff you're selling me."
The tailor, feigning great surprise,
Said, "Sire, it's here before your eyes."
The King said, "Where? Just tell me where."

"It's in my hands, o King, right here!"
The King yelled, tearing at his hair,
"Don't be an ass! There's nothing there!"
The tailor cried, "Hold on, I pray!
There's something I forgot to say!
This cloth's invisible to fools
And nincompoops and other ghouls.
For brainless men who're round the twist
This cloth does simply not exist!
But seeing how you're wise and bright,
I'm sure it glistens in your sight."
Now right on cue, exactly then,
In burst the dozen brainy men.
They shouted, "Oh, what lovely stuff!
We want some too! D'you have enough?"
Extremely calm, the tailor stands,
With nothing in his empty hands,
And says, "No, no! this gorgeous thing
Is only for my lord, the King."
The King, not wanting to admit
To being a proper royal twit
Cried out, "Oh, isn't it divine!
I want it all! It's mine! It's mine!
I want a ski-ing outfit most
So I can keep as warm as toast!"
The brainy men all cried, "Egad!
Oh, Majesty, you lucky lad!
You'll feel so cosy in the snow
With temps at zero and below!"
Next day the tailor came to fit
The costume on the royal twit.
The brainy men all went along
To see that nothing should go wrong.

The tailor said, "Strip naked, sire.
This suit's so warm you won't require
Your underclothes or pants or vest
Or even hair upon your chest."
And now the clever Mister Ho
Put on the most terrific show
Of dressing up the naked King
In nothing – not a single thing.

"That's right sir, slip your arm in there,
And now I'll zip you up right here.
Do you feel comfy? Does it fit?
Or should I take this in a bit?"

Now during this absurd charade,
And while the King was off his guard,
The brainy men, so shrewd and sly,
Had turned the central heating high.
The King, although completely bare,
With not a stitch of underwear,
Began to sweat and mop his brow,
And cried, "I do believe you now!
I feel as though I'm going to roast!
This suit will keep me warm as toast!"
The Queen, just then, came strolling through
With ladies of her retinue.
They stopped. They gasped. There stood the King
As naked as a piece of string,
As naked as a popinjay,
With not a fig-leaf in the way.

He shouted, striking up a pose,
"Behold my marvellous ski-ing clothes!
These clothes will keep me toasty-warm
In hail or sleet or snow or storm!"
Some ladies blushed and hid their eyes
And uttered little plaintive cries.
But some, it seemed, enjoyed the pleasures
Of looking at the royal treasures.
A brazen wench cried, "Oh my hat!
Hey girls, just take a look at that!"
The Queen, who'd seen it all before,
Made swiftly for the nearest door.

The King cried, "Now I'm off to ski!
You ladies want to come with me?"
They shook their heads, so off he went,
A madman off on pleasure bent.
The crazy King put on his skis,
And now, oblivious to the freeze
He shot outdoors and ski'd away,
Still naked as a popinjay.
And thus this fool, so lewd and squalid,
In half an hour was frozen solid.
And all the nation cried, "Heigh-ho!
The King's deep-frozen in the snow!"

Wild Mushrooms

from MY YEAR

YOU may think it odd that hunting for wild mushrooms is truly one of my favourite pastimes. Nothing has a more seductive flavour than the fresh wild mushroom gently fried in butter. It is even better with eggs and bacon. And to me the wonder of it is that these treasures are to be had free and for nothing. But you must know where to look. You must know which is a mushroom field and which is not because mushrooms are mysterious things. They will grow in one field but not another and there is no explanation for it. But walk slowly across a green field in the autumn and spot suddenly ahead of you that little pure white dome nestling in the grass, that, I tell you, is exciting. And where there is one, there are usually many more. When you have carefully lifted your mushroom out of the grass and turned it upside down, the delicate pale pink gills are beautiful to behold.

Interestingly enough, it is no crime to pick mushrooms in somebody else's field. The owner cannot prosecute you for stealing. Mushrooms are not like apples or cherries. They have not been cultivated by the owner of the field. They are a freak of nature. Nor can you be prosecuted for trespassing. No farmer can ever prosecute for trespassing. He can only prosecute you for damaging his property, for breaking down fences or damaging trees or crops. But he can ask you to leave his land, and if he does so and is polite about it then you should go at once. But don't forget to take your mushrooms with you.

Simba

from GOING SOLO

After leaving school, Roald Dahl joined the Shell Oil Company and in 1938 was sent out to Africa on a three-year assignment.

THE Sanford house was on a hill outside the town. It was a white wooden two-storey building with a roof of green tiles. The eaves of the house projected far out beyond the walls to provide extra shade, and this gave the building a sort of Japanese pagoda appearance. The surrounding countryside was to me a very pleasant sight. It was a vast brown plain with many quite large knolls and hummocks dotted all over it, and although the plain itself was mostly burnt-up scrubland, the hills were covered with all sorts of huge jungle trees, and their dense foliage made little emerald-green dots all over the plain. On the burnt-up plain itself there grew nothing but those bare spiky thorn trees that you find all over East Africa, and there were about six huge vultures sitting quite motionless on every thorn tree in sight. The vultures were brown with curved orange beaks and orange feet, and they spent their whole lives sitting and watching and waiting for some animal to die so they could pick its bones.

"Do you like this sort of life?" I said to Robert Sanford.

"I love the freedom," he said. "I administer about two thousand square miles of territory and I can go where I want and do more or less exactly as I please. That part of it is marvellous. But I do miss the company of other white men. There aren't many even moderately intelligent Europeans in the town."

We sat there watching the sun go down behind the flat brown plain that was covered with thorn trees, and we could see the sinister vultures waiting like feathered undertakers for death to come along and give them something to work on.

"Keep the children a bit closer to the house!" Mary Sanford called out to the nurse. "Bring them closer, please!"

Robert Sanford said, "My mother sent me out Beethoven's Third Symphony from England last week. HMV, two records, four sides in all, Toscanini conducting. I'm using a thorn needle instead of a steel one so as not to wear out the grooves. It seems to work."

"Don't you find the records warp a lot out here?" I asked.

"I keep them lying flat with a pile of books on top of them," he said. "What I'm terrified of is dropping one and breaking it."

The sun had gone down now and a lovely soft light was spreading over the landscape. I could see a group of zebra grazing among the thorn trees about half a mile away. Robert Sanford was also watching the zebras.

"I keep wondering," he said, "if it wouldn't be possible to catch a young zebra and break it in for riding, just like a horse. After all, they are only wild horses with stripes on."

"Has anyone ever tried?" I asked.

"Not that I know," he said. "Mary's a good rider..What do you think, darling? How would you like to have a private zebra to ride on?"

"It might be fun," she said. Even though she had a bit of a jaw, she was a handsome woman. I didn't mind the jaw. The shape of it gave her the look of a fighter.

"Perhaps we could cross one with a horse," Robert Sanford said, "and call it a zorse."

"Or a hebra," Mary Sanford said.

"Right," her husband said, smiling.

"Shall we try it?" Mary Sanford said. "It would be rather splendid to have a baby zorse or hebra. Oh darling, *shall* we try it?"

"The children could ride it," he said. "A black zorse with white stripes all over it."

"Please can we play your Beethoven after supper?" I said.

"Absolutely," Robert Sanford said. "I'll put the gramophone out here on the veranda and then those tremendous chords can go booming out through the night over the plain. It's terrific. The only trouble is I have to wind the thing up twice for each side."

"I'll wind it for you," I said.

Suddenly, the voice of a man yelling in Swahili exploded into the quiet of the evening. It was my boy, Mdisho. "Bwana! Bwana! Bwana!" he was yelling from somewhere behind the house. "Simba, bwana! Simba! Simba!"

Simba is Swahili for lion. All three of us leapt to our feet, and the next moment Mdisho came tearing round the corner of the house yelling at us in Swahili, "Come quick, bwana! Come quick! Come quick! A huge lion is eating the wife of the cook!"

That sounds pretty funny when you put it on paper back here in England, but to us, standing on a veranda in the middle of East Africa, it was not funny at all.

Robert Sanford flew into the house and came out again in five seconds flat holding a powerful rifle and ramming a cartridge into the breech. "Get those children indoors!" he shouted to his wife as he ran down off the veranda with me behind him.

Mdisho was dancing about and pointing towards the back of the house and yelling in Swahili, "The lion has taken the wife of the cook and the lion is eating her and the cook is chasing the lion and trying to save his wife!"

The servants lived in a series of low whitewashed outbuildings at the back of the house, and as we came running round the corner we saw four or five house-boys leaping about and pointing and shrieking, "Simba! Simba! Simba!" The boys were all clothed in spotless white cotton robes that looked like long nightshirts, and each had a fine scarlet tarboosh on his head. The tarboosh is a sort of top-hat without a brim, and there is often a black tassel on it. The women had come out of their huts as well and were standing in a separate group, silent, immobile and staring.

"Where is it?" Robert Sanford shouted, but he had no need to ask, for we very quickly spotted the massive sandy-coloured lion not more than eighty or ninety yards off and trotting away from the house. He had a fine bushy collar of fur around his neck, and in his jaws he was holding the wife of the cook.

The lion had the woman by the waist so that her head and arms hung down on one side and her legs on the other, and I could see that she was wearing a red and white spotted dress. The lion, so startlingly close, was loping away from us in the calmest possible manner with a slow, long-striding, springy lope, and behind the lion, not more than the length of a tennis court behind, ran the cook himself in his white cotton robe and with his red hat on his head, running most bravely and waving his arms like a whirlwind, leaping, clapping his hands, screaming, shouting, shouting, shouting, "Simba! Simba! Simba! Simba! Let go of my wife! Let go of my wife!"

Oh, it was a scene of great tragedy and comedy both mixed up together, and now Robert Sanford was running full speed after the cook who was running after the lion. He was holding his rifle in both hands and shouting to the cook, "Pingo! Pingo! Get out of the way, Pingo! Lie down on the ground so I can shoot the simba! You are in my way! You are *in my way*, Pingo!"

But the cook ignored him and kept on running, and the lion ignored everybody, not altering his pace at all but continuing to lope along with slow springy strides and with the head held high and carrying the woman proudly in his jaws, rather like a dog who is trotting off with a good bone.

Both the cook and Robert Sanford were travelling faster than the lion who really didn't seem to care about his pursuers at all. And as for me, I didn't know what to do to help them so I ran after Robert Sanford. It was an awkward situation because there was no way that Robert Sanford could take a shot at the lion without risking a hit on the cook's wife, let alone on the cook himself who was still right in his line of fire.

The lion was heading for one of those hillocks that was densely covered with jungle trees and we all knew that once he got in there, we would never be able to get at him. The incredibly brave cook was actually catching up on the lion and was now not more than ten yards behind him, and Robert Sanford was thirty or forty yards behind the cook. "Ayee!" the cook was shouting. "Simba! Simba! Simba! Let go my wife! I am coming after you, simba!"

Then Robert Sanford stopped and raised his rifle and took aim, and I thought surely he is not risking a shot at a moving lion when it's got a woman in its jaws. There was an almighty crack as the big gun went off and I saw a spurt of dust just ahead of the lion. The lion stopped dead and turned his head, still holding the woman in his jaws. He saw the arm-waving shouting cook and he saw Robert Sanford and he saw me and he had certainly heard the rifle shot and seen the spurt of dust. He must have thought an army was coming after him because instantaneously he dropped the cook's wife on to the ground and broke for cover. I have never seen anything accelerate so fast from a standing start. With great leaping bounding strides he was in among the jungle trees on the hillock before Robert Sanford could ram another cartridge into his gun.

The cook reached the wife first, then Robert Sanford, then me. I couldn't believe what I saw. I was certain that the grip of those terrible jaws would have ripped the woman's waist and stomach almost in two, but there she was sitting up on the ground and smiling at the cook, her husband.

"Where are you hurt?" shouted Robert Sanford, rushing up.

The cook's wife looked up at him and kept smiling, and she said in Swahili, "That old lion he couldn't scare me. I just lay there in his mouth pretending I was dead and he didn't even bite through my clothes." She stood up and smoothed down her red and white spotted dress which was wet with the lion's saliva, and the cook embraced her and the two of them did a little dance of joy in the twilight out there on the great brown African plain.

Robert Sanford just stood there gaping at the cook's wife. So, for that matter, did I.

"Are you absolutely sure the simba didn't hurt you?" he asked her. "Did not his teeth go into your body?"

"No, bwana," the woman said, laughing. "He carried me as gently as if I had been one of his own cubs. But now I shall have to wash my dress."

We walked slowly back to the group of astonished onlookers. "Tonight," Robert Sanford said, addressing them all, "nobody is to go far from the house, you understand me?"

"Yes, bwana," they said. "Yes, yes, we understand you."

"That old simba is hiding over there in the wood and he may come back," Robert Sanford said. "So be very careful. And Pingo, please continue to cook our dinner. I am getting hungry."

The cook ran into the kitchen, clapping his hands and leaping for joy. We walked over to where Mary Sanford was standing. She had come round to the back of the house soon after us and had witnessed the whole scene. The three of us then returned to the veranda and fresh drinks were poured.

"I don't believe anything like this has ever happened before," Robert Sanford said as he sat down once again in his cane armchair. There was a little round slot in one of the arms of the chair to carry his glass and he put the whisky and soda carefully into it. "In the first place," he went on, "lions do not attack people around here unless you go near their cubs. They can get all the food they want. There's plenty of game on the plain."

"Perhaps he's got a family in that patch of wood on the hill," Mary Sanford said.

"That could be," Robert Sanford said. "But if he had thought the woman was threatening his family, he would have killed her on the spot. Instead of that, he carries her off as soft and gentle as a good gun-dog with a partridge. If you want my opinion, I do not believe he ever meant to hurt her."

We sat there sipping our drinks and trying to find some sort of an explanation for the astonishing behaviour of the lion.

"Normally," Robert Sanford said, "I would get together a bunch of hunters first thing tomorrow morning and we'd flush out that old lion and kill him. But I don't want to do it. He doesn't deserve it. In fact, I'm not going to do it."

"Good for you, darling," his wife said.

The story of this strange happening with the lion spread in the end all over East Africa and it became a bit of a legend. And when I got back to Dar es Salaam about two weeks later, there was a letter waiting for me from the *East African Standard* (I think it was called) up in Nairobi asking if I would write my own eye-witness description of the incident. This I did and in time I received a cheque for five pounds from the newspaper for my first published work.

There followed a long correspondence in the columns of the paper from the white hunters and other experts all over Uganda, Kenya and Tanganyika, each offering his or her different and often bizarre explanation. But none of them made any sense. The matter has remained a mystery ever since.

Ideas to help
aspiring writers

Collecting Ideas

WHEN I wake up in the morning after having had a dream, I lie in bed thinking about it. Every crazy detail is vivid in my memory. But, five minutes later, by the time I've got out of bed and brushed my teeth, it's all gone. It's impossible to remember what the dream was about. That happens with everybody. So the only way to remember your dreams is to keep a pencil and paper beside your bed and write them down the moment you wake.

With me, exactly the same thing happens with ideas for stories. A story idea is liable to come flitting into the mind at any moment of the day, and if I don't make a note of it at once, right then and there, it will be gone forever. So I must find a pencil, a pen, a crayon, a lipstick, anything that will write, and scribble a few words that will later on remind me of the idea. Then as soon as I get the chance, I go straight to my hut and write the idea down in an old red-coloured school exercise book. Sometimes I write one line; sometimes I'll write out a conversation between two people; sometimes I'll write a question.

Notes and Clippings

I collect pictures of people because I find them helpful when I'm trying to describe characters in my books. When you are creating characters you've got to see the eyes, the nose, the teeth and then the whole general expression of the face. Every little detail is important.

I also find it useful to jot down interesting facts that I come across and that might be useful for my future work. On the inside of the back cover of my notebook there is a chart listing the number of breaths per minute and heartbeats per minute of various animals.

Begin collecting pictures and facts that you think might be useful for your future writing.

Enthrall Your Reader

The reason I collect good ideas is because plots themselves are very difficult indeed to come by. Every month they get scarcer and scarcer. Any good story must start with a strong plot that gathers momentum all the way to the end. My main preoccupation when I am writing a story is a constant unholy terror of boring the reader. Consequently, as I write my stories I always try to create situations that will cause my reader to

> 1) Laugh (actual loud belly laughs)
> 2) Squirm
> 3) Become enthralled
> 4) Become TENSE and EXCITED and say, "Read on! Please read on! Don't stop!"

There must be an element of farce. The wilder the better. You must always go a bit further than you initially meant to go. When I first thought about writing the book *Charlie and the Chocolate Factory*, I never originally meant to have children in it at all!

All good books have to have a mixture of extremely nasty people – which are always fun – and some nice people. Can you imagine how boring *The BFG* would be if he were the only giant in Giantland? Early on in that story, I realised that if he was a Big·Friendly Giant somewhere he had to have an antagonist or a threat. So I gradually invented the other giants. "How many of these beasts am I going to have?" I thought. "Four? Five? Six?" I finally settled on eight because I had a lot of fun inventing their names.

In every book or story there has to be somebody you can loathe. In

James it is the aunts. In *Danny* it is Mr Hazell. In *Charlie* it is the spoiled and filthy children. In *The Twits* it is Mr and Mrs Twit. The fouler and more filthy a person is, the more fun it is to watch him getting scrunched.

Whether it is with a group of characters or an idea for the plot, begin to write. Everything develops under the pencil as you begin to write. It really does. Once someone said to Stravinsky, a great composer, "Maestro, where do you get your ideas? In the bath? Shaving? Or, exploring the woods in the moonlight?" And he responded, "At the piano."

Charlie's Story

One of the most difficult books for me to write was *Charlie and the Chocolate Factory*. At first I got too carried away describing horrid little children, which is always fun. I had 15 children in the first draft. I gave the manuscript to my young nephew and said, "What do you think of this?" He read it and then came back and said, "Uncle Roald, I think it's rotten. I don't like it at all."

So I rewrote it all over again. You'll find when you rewrite you pick out the best material from what you have written.

The Green Mamba

from GOING SOLO

OH, those snakes! How I hated them! They were the only fearful thing about Tanganyika, and a newcomer very quickly learnt to identify most of them and to know which were deadly and which were simply poisonous. The killers, apart from the black mambas, were the green mambas, the cobras and the tiny little puff adders that looked very much like small sticks lying motionless in the middle of a dusty path, and so easy to step on.

One Sunday evening I was invited to go and have a sundowner at the house of an Englishman called Fuller who worked in the Customs office in Dar es Salaam. He lived with his wife and two small children in a plain white wooden house that stood alone some way back from the road in a rough grassy piece of ground with coconut trees scattered about. I was walking across the grass towards the house and was about twenty yards away when I saw a large green snake go gliding straight up the veranda steps of Fuller's house and in through the open front door. The brilliant yellowy-green skin and its great size made me certain it was a green mamba, a creature almost as deadly as

the black mamba, and for a few seconds I was so startled and dumb-founded and horrified that I froze to the spot. Then I pulled myself together and ran round to the back of the house shouting, "Mr Fuller! Mr Fuller!"

Mrs Fuller popped her head out of an upstairs window. "What on earth's the matter?" she said.

"You've got a large green mamba in your front room!" I shouted. "I saw it go up the veranda steps and right in through the door!"

"Fred!" Mrs Fuller shouted, turning round. "Fred! Come here!"

Freddy Fuller's round red face appeared at the window beside his wife. "What's up?" he asked.

"There's a green mamba in your living-room!" I shouted.

Without hesitation and without wasting time with more questions, he said to me, "Stay there. I'm going to lower the children down to you one at a time." He was completely cool and unruffled. He didn't even raise his voice.

A small girl was lowered down to me by her wrists and I was able to catch her easily by the legs. Then came a small boy. Then Freddy Fuller lowered his wife and I caught her by the waist and put her on the ground. Then came Fuller himself. He hung by his hands from the window-sill and when he let go he landed neatly on his two feet.

We stood in a little group on the grass at the back of the house and I told Fuller exactly what I had seen.

The mother was holding the two children by the hand, one on each side of her. They didn't seem to be particularly alarmed.

"What happens now?" I asked.

"Go down to the road, all of you," Fuller said. "I'm off to fetch the snake-man." He trotted away and got into his small ancient black car and drove off. Mrs Fuller and the two small children and I went down to the road and sat in the shade of a large mango tree.

"Who is this snake-man?" I asked Mrs Fuller.

"He is an old Englishman who has been out here for years," Mrs Fuller said. "He actually *likes* snakes. He understands them and never kills them. He catches them and sells them to zoos and laboratories all over the world. Every native for miles around knows about him and whenever one of them sees a snake, he marks its hiding place and runs, often for great distances, to tell the snake-man. Then the snake-man comes along and captures it. The snake-man's strict rule is that he will never buy a captured snake from the natives."

"Why not?" I asked.

"To discourage them from trying to catch snakes themselves," Mrs Fuller said. "In his early days he used to buy caught snakes, but so many natives got bitten trying to catch them, and so many died, that he decided to put a stop to it. Now any native who brings in a caught snake, no matter how rare, gets turned away."

"That's good," I said.

"What is the snake-man's name?" I asked.

"Donald Macfarlane," she said. "I believe he's Scottish."

"Is the snake in the house, Mummy?" the small girl asked.

"Yes, darling. But the snake-man is going to get it out."

"He'll bite Jack," the girl said.

"Oh, my God!" Mrs Fuller cried, jumping to her feet. "I forgot about Jack!" She began calling out, "Jack! Come here, Jack! Jack!... Jack!... Jack!"

The children jumped up as well and all of them started calling to the dog. But no dog came out of the open front door.

"He's bitten Jack!" the small girl cried out. "He must have bitten him!" She began to cry and so did her brother who was a year or so younger than she was. Mrs Fuller looked grim.

"Jack's probably hiding upstairs," she said. "You know how clever he is."

Mrs Fuller and I seated ourselves again on the grass, but the children remained standing. In between their tears they went on calling to the dog.

"Would you like me to take you down to the Maddens' house?" their mother asked.

"No!" they cried. "No, no, no! We want Jack!"

"Here's Daddy!" Mrs Fuller cried, pointing at the tiny black car coming up the road in a swirl of dust. I noticed a long wooden pole sticking out through one of the car windows.

The children ran to meet the car. "Jack's inside the house and he's been bitten by the snake!" they wailed. "We know he's been bitten! He doesn't come when we call him!"

Mr Fuller and the snake-man got out of the car. The snake-man was small and very old, probably over seventy. He wore leather boots made of thick cowhide and he had long gauntlet-type gloves on his hands made of the same stuff. The gloves reached above his elbows. In his right hand he carried an extraordinary implement, an eight-foot-long wooden pole with a forked end. The two prongs of the fork were made, so it seemed, of black rubber, about an inch thick and quite flexible, and it was clear that if the fork was pressed against the ground the two prongs would bend outwards, allowing the neck of the fork to go down as close to the ground as necessary. In his left hand he carried an ordinary brown sack.

Donald Macfarlane, the snake-man, may have been old and small but he was an impressive-looking character. His eyes were pale blue, deep-set in a face round and dark and wrinkled as a walnut. Above the blue eyes, the eyebrows were thick and startlingly white but the hair on his head was almost black. In spite of the thick leather boots, he moved like a leopard, with soft slow cat-like strides, and he came straight up to me and said, "Who are you?"

"He's with Shell," Fuller said. "He hasn't been here long."

"You want to watch?" the snake-man said to me.

"Watch?" I said, wavering. "Watch? How do you mean, watch? I mean where from? Not in the house?"

"You can stand out on the veranda and look through the window," the snake-man said.

"Come on," Fuller said. "We'll both watch."

"Now don't do anything silly," Mrs Fuller said.

The two children stood there forlorn and miserable, with tears all over their cheeks.

The snake-man and Fuller and I walked over the grass towards the house, and as we approached the veranda steps the snake-man whispered, "Tread softly on the wooden boards or he'll pick up the vibration. Wait until I've gone in, then walk up quietly and stand by the window."

The snake-man went up the steps first and he made absolutely no sound at all with his feet. He moved soft and cat-like on to the veranda and straight through the front door and then he quickly but very quietly closed the door behind him.

I felt better with the door closed. What I mean is I felt better for myself. I certainly didn't feel better for the snake-man. I figured he was committing suicide. I followed Fuller on to the veranda and we both crept over to the window. The window was open, but it had a fine mesh mosquito-netting all over it. That made me feel better still. We peered through the netting.

The living-room was simple and ordinary, coconut matting on the floor, a red sofa, a coffee-table and a couple of armchairs. The dog was sprawled on the matting under the coffee-table, a large Airedale with curly brown and black hair. He was stone dead.

The snake-man was standing absolutely still just inside the door of the living-room. The brown sack was now slung over his left shoulder and he was grasping the long pole with both hands, holding it out in front of him, parallel to the ground. I couldn't see the snake. I didn't think the snake-man had seen it yet either.

A minute went by... two minutes... three... four... five. Nobody moved. There was death in that room. The air was heavy with death and the snake-man stood as motionless as a pillar of stone, with the long rod held out in front of him.

And still he waited. Another minute... and another... and another.

And now I saw the snake-man beginning to bend his knees. Very slowly he bent his knees until he was almost squatting on the floor, and from that position he tried to peer under the sofa and the armchairs.

And still it didn't look as though he was seeing anything.

Slowly he straightened his legs again, and then his head began to swivel around the room. Over to the right, in the far corner, a staircase led up to the floor above. The snake-man looked at the stairs, and I knew very well what was going through his head. Quite abruptly, he took one step forward and stopped.

Nothing happened.

A moment later I caught sight of the snake. It was lying full-length along the skirting of the right-hand wall, but hidden from the snake-man's view by the back of the sofa. It lay there like a long, beautiful, deadly shaft of green glass, quite motionless, perhaps asleep. It was facing away from us who were at the window, with its small triangular head resting on the matting near the foot of the stairs.

I nudged Fuller and whispered, "It's over there against the wall." I pointed and Fuller saw the snake. At once, he started waving both hands, palms outward, back and forth across the window, hoping to get the snake-man's attention. The snake-man didn't see him. Very softly, Fuller said, "Pssst!" and the snake-man looked up sharply. Fuller pointed. The snake-man understood and gave a nod.

Now the snake-man began working his way very very slowly to the back wall of the room so as to get a view of the snake behind the sofa. He never walked on his toes as you or I would have done. His feet remained flat on the ground all the time. The cowhide boots were like moccasins, with neither soles nor heels. Gradually, he worked his way over to the back wall, and from there he was able to see at least the head and two or three feet of the snake itself.

But the snake also saw him. With a movement so fast it was invisible, the snake's head came up about two feet off the floor and the front of the body arched backwards, ready to strike. Almost simultaneously, it bunched its whole body into a series of curves, ready to flash forward.

The snake-man was just a bit too far away from the snake to reach it with the end of his pole. He waited, staring at the snake and the snake stared back at him with two small malevolent black eyes.

Then the snake-man started speaking to the snake. "Come along, my pretty," he whispered in a soft wheedling voice. "There's a good boy. Nobody's going to hurt you. Nobody's going to harm you, my pretty little thing. Just lie still and relax…" He took a step forward towards the snake, holding the pole out in front of him.

What the snake did next was so fast that the whole movement couldn't have taken more than a hundredth of a second, like the flick of a camera shutter. There was a green flash as the snake darted forward at least ten feet and struck at the snake-man's leg. Nobody could have got out of the way of that one. I heard the snake's head strike against the thick cowhide boot with a sharp little *crack*, and then at once the head was back in that same deadly backward-curving position, ready to strike again.

"There's a good boy," the snake-man said softly. "There's a clever boy. There's a lovely fellow. You mustn't get excited. Keep calm and everything's going to be all right." As he was speaking, he was slowly lowering the end of the pole until the forked prongs were about twelve inches above the middle of the snake's body. "There's a lovely fellow," he whispered. "There's a good kind little chap. Keep still now, my beauty. Keep still, my pretty. Keep quite still. Daddy's not going to hurt you."

I could see a thin dark trickle of venom running down the snake-man's right boot where the snake had struck.

The snake, head raised and arcing backwards, was as tense as a tight-wound spring and ready to strike again. "Keep still, my lovely," the snake-man whispered. "Don't move now. Keep still. No one's going to hurt you."

Then *wham*, the rubber prongs came down right across the snake's body, about midway along its length, and pinned it to the floor. All I could see was a green blur as the snake thrashed around furiously in an effort to free itself. But the snake-man kept up the pressure on the prongs and the snake was trapped.

What happens next? I wondered. There was no way he could catch hold of that madly twisting flailing length of green muscle with his hands, and even if he could have done so, the head would surely have flashed around and bitten him in the face.

Holding the very end of the eight-foot pole, the snake man began to work his way round the room until he was at the tail end of the snake. Then, in spite of the flailing and the thrashing, he started pushing the prongs forward along the snake's body towards the head. Very very slowly he did it, pushing the rubber prongs forward over the snake's flailing body, keeping the snake pinned down all the time and pushing, pushing, pushing the long wooden rod forward millimetre by millimetre. It was a fascinating and frightening thing to watch, the little man with white eyebrows and black hair carefully manipulating his long implement and sliding the fork ever so slowly along the length of the twisting snake towards the head. The snake's body was thumping against the coconut matting with such a noise that if you had been upstairs you might have thought two big men were wrestling on the floor.

Then at last the prongs were right behind the head itself, pinning it down, and at that point the snake-man reached forward with one gloved hand and grasped the snake very firmly by the neck.

He threw away the pole. He took the sack off his shoulder with his free hand. He lifted the great still twisting length of the deadly green snake and pushed the head into the sack. Then he let go the head and bundled the rest of the creature in and closed the sack. The sack started jumping about as though there were fifty angry rats inside it, but the snake-man was now totally relaxed and he held the sack casually in one hand as if it contained no more than a few pounds of potatoes. He stooped and picked up his pole from the floor, then he turned and looked towards the window where we were peering in.

"Pity about the dog," he said. "You'd better get it out of the way before the children see it."

Where art thou, Mother Christmas?

This is the original poem and drawing submitted to Great Ormond Street Hospital for Sick Children for a fund-raising Christmas card.

WHERE art thou, Mother Christmas?
  I only wish I knew
Why Father should get all the praise
And no one mentions you.

I'll bet you buy the presents
And wrap them large and small
While all the time that rotten swine
Pretends he's done it all.

So Hail To Mother Christmas
Who shoulders all the work!
And down with Father Christmas,
That unmitigated jerk!

Hot and Cold

from RHYME STEW

A woman who my mother knows
Came in and took off all her clothes.
Said I, not being very old,
"By golly gosh, you must be cold!"

"No, no!" she cried. "Indeed I'm not!
I'm feeling devilishly hot!"

The Price of Debauchery

from RHYME STEW

MY mother said, "There are no joys
In ever kissing silly boys.
Just one small *kiss* and one small squeeze
Can land you with some foul disease."

"But Mum, d'you mean from just a *kiss?*"

"You know quite well my meaning, miss."

Last week when coming home from school
I clean forgot Mum's golden rule.
I let Tom Young, that handsome louse,
Steal one small kiss behind my house.

Oh, woe is me! I've paid the price!
I should have listened to advice.
My mum was right one hundredfold!
I've caught Tom's horrid runny cold!

Dar es Salaam to Nairobi by Ford Prefect

from GOING SOLO

Roald Dahl's work in Africa was interrupted
by the outbreak of World War II.

IN November 1939, when the war was two months old, I told the Shell Company that I wanted to join up and help in the fight against Bwana Hitler, and they released me with their blessing. In a wonderfully magnanimous gesture, they told me that they would continue to pay my salary into the bank wherever I might happen to be in the world and for as long as the war lasted and I remained alive. I thanked them very much indeed and got into my ancient little Ford Prefect and set off on the 600-mile journey from Dar es Salaam to Nairobi to enlist in the RAF.

When one is quite alone on a lengthy and slightly hazardous journey like this, every sensation of pleasure and fear is enormously intensified,

and several incidents from that strange two-day safari up through central Africa in my little black Ford have remained clear in my memory.

A frequent and always wonderful sight was the astonishing number of giraffe that I passed on the first day. They were usually in groups of three or four, often with a baby alongside, and they never ceased to enthral me. They were surprisingly tame. I would see them ahead of me nibbling green leaves from the tops of acacia trees by the side of the road, and whenever I came upon them I would stop the car and get out and walk slowly towards them, shouting inane but cheery greetings up into the sky where their small heads were waving about on their long long necks. I often amazed myself by the way I behaved when I was certain that there were no other human beings within fifty miles. All my inhibitions would disappear and I would shout, "Hello, giraffes! Hello! Hello! Hello! How are you today?" And the giraffes would incline their heads very slightly and stare down at me with languorous demure expressions, but they never ran away. I found it exhilarating to be able to walk freely

among such huge graceful wild creatures and talk to them as I wished.

The road northwards through Tanganyika was narrow and often deeply rutted, and once I saw a very large thick greenish-brown cobra gliding slowly over the ruts in the road about thirty yards ahead of me. It was seven or eight feet long and was holding its flat spoon-shaped head six inches up in the air and well clear of the dusty road. I stopped the car smartly so as not to run it over, and to be truthful I was so frightened I went quickly into reverse and kept backing away until the fearsome thing had disappeared into the undergrowth. I never lost my fear of snakes all the time I was in the tropics. They gave me the shivers.

At the Wami river the natives put my car on a raft and six strong men on the opposite bank started to pull me across the hundred yards or so of water with a rope, chanting as they pulled. The river was running swiftly and in midstream the slim raft upon which my car and I were balanced began to get carried down-river by the current. The six strong men chanted louder and pulled harder and I sat helpless in the car watching the crocodiles swimming around the raft, and the crocodiles stared up at me with their cruel black eyes. I was bobbing about on that river for over an hour, but in the end the six strong men won their battle with the currents and pulled me across. "That will be three shillings, bwana," they said, laughing.

Only once did I see any elephant. I saw a big tusker and his cow and their one baby moving slowly forward in line astern about fifty yards from the road on the edge of the forest. I stopped the car to watch them but I did not get out. The elephants never saw me and I was able to stay gazing at them for quite a while. A great sense of peace and serenity seemed to surround these massive, slow-moving, gentle beasts. Their skin hung loose over their bodies like suits they had inherited from larger ancestors, with the trousers ridiculously baggy. Like the giraffes they were vegetarians and did not have to hunt or kill in order to survive in the jungle, and no other wild beast would ever dare to threaten them. Only the foul humans in the shape of an occasional big-game hunter or an ivory poacher were to be feared, but this small elephant family did not look as though they had yet met any of these horrors. They seemed to be leading a life of absolute contentment. They are better off than me, I told myself, and a good deal wiser. I myself am at this moment on my way to kill Germans or to be killed by them, but those elephants have no thought of murder in their minds.

At the frontier between Tanganyika and Kenya there was a wooden gate across the road with an old shack alongside it, and in command

of this great outpost of Customs and Immigration was an ancient and toothless black man who told me he had been there for thirty-seven years. He gave me a cup of tea and said he was sorry he did not have any sugar to put into it. I asked him if he wished to see my passport but he shook his head and said all passports looked the same to him. In any event, he added, smiling secretly, he could not read without spectacles and he did not possess any.

Outside the Customs shack, a group of enormous Masai tribesmen holding spears were crowding round my car. They stared at me curiously and patted the car with their hands, but we were unable to understand each other's language.

A little later on, I was bumping along on a particularly narrow bit of road through some very thick jungle when all of a sudden the sun went down and in ten minutes darkness descended over the jungle land. My headlamps were very dim. It would have been foolish to push on through the night. So I parked just off the road in a scrubby patch of thorn trees to wait for the dawn, and I sat in the car with the window down and poured myself a tot of whisky with water. I drank it slowly, listening to the jungle noises all around me and I was not afraid. A car is good protection against almost any wild animal. I had with me a sandwich with hard cheese inside it and I ate that with my whisky. Then I wound up the two windows, leaving just a half-inch gap at the top of each, and got into the back seat and curled up and went to sleep.

I reached Nairobi at about three o'clock the next afternoon and drove straight to the aerodrome where the small RAF headquarters was situated. There I was given a medical examination by an affable English doctor who remarked that six feet six inches was not the ideal height for a flier of aeroplanes.

"Does that mean you can't pass me for flying duties?" I asked him fearfully.

"Funnily enough," he said, "there is no mention of a height limit in my instructions, so I can pass you with a clear conscience. Good luck, my boy."

Nairobi

4 December 1939

Dear Mama,

I'm having a lovely time, have never enjoyed
myself so much. I've been sworn in to the
R.A.F, proper and am definitely in it now
until the end of the war. My rank - a Leading
Aircraftsman, with every opportunity of
becoming a pilot officer in a few months if I
don't make a B.F. of myself. No boys to do
everything for me anymore. Get your own
food, wash your own knives and forks, fold up
your own clothes, and in short, do everything
for yourself. I suppose I'd better not say too
much about what we do or when we are going
because the letter would probably be torn up
by the censor, but we wake at 5.30 a.m., drill
before breakfast till 7 a.m., fly and attend
lectures till 12.30. 12.30/1.30 lunch - 1.30
to 6.00 p.m. flying and lectures. The flying
is grand and our instructors are extremely
pleasant and proficient. With any luck I'll be
flying solo by the end of this week...

Survival

from GOING SOLO

Roald Dahl was posted to 80 Squadron in the Western Desert.

I flew straight for the point where the 80 Squadron airfield should have been. It wasn't there. I flew around the area to north, south, east and west, but there was not a sign of an airfield. Below me there was nothing but empty desert, and rather rugged desert at that, full of large stones and boulders and gullies.

At this point, dusk began to fall and I realised that I was in trouble. My fuel was running low and there was no way I could get back to Fouka on what I had left. I couldn't have found it in the dark anyway.

The only course open to me now was to make a forced landing in the desert and make it quickly, before it was too dark to see.

I skimmed low over the boulder-strewn desert searching for just one small strip of reasonably flat sand on which to land. I knew the direction of the wind so I knew precisely the direction that my approach should take. But where, oh where was there one little patch of desert that was clear of boulders and gullies and lumps of rock. There simply wasn't one. It was nearly dark now. I *had* to get down somehow or other. I chose a piece of ground that seemed to me to be as boulder-free as any and I made an approach. I came in as slowly as I dared, hanging on the prop, travelling just above my stalling speed of eighty miles an hour. My wheels touched down. I throttled back and prayed for a bit of luck.

I didn't get it. My undercarriage hit a boulder and collapsed completely and the Gladiator buried its nose in the sand at what must have been about seventy-five miles an hour.

My injuries in that bust-up came from my head being thrown forward violently against the reflector-sight when the plane hit the ground (in spite of the fact that I was strapped tightly, as always, into the cockpit), and apart from the skull fracture, the blow pushed my nose in and knocked out a few teeth and blinded me completely for days to come.

It is odd that I can remember very clearly quite a few of the things that followed seconds after the crash. Obviously I was unconscious for some moments, but I must have recovered my senses very quickly because I can remember hearing a mighty *whoosh* as the petrol tank in the port wing exploded, followed almost at once by another mighty *whoosh* as the starboard tank went up in flames. I could see nothing at all, and I felt no pain. All I wanted was to go gently off to sleep and to hell with the flames. But soon a tremendous heat around my legs galvanised my soggy brain into action. With great difficulty I managed to undo first my seat-straps and then the straps of my parachute, and I can even remember the desperate effort it took to push myself upright in the cockpit and roll out head first on to the sand below. Again I wanted to lie down and doze off, but the heat close by was terrific and had I stayed where I was I should simply have been roasted alive. I began very very slowly to drag myself away from the awful hotness. I heard my machine-gun ammunition exploding in the flames and the bullets were pinging about all over the place but that didn't worry me. All I wanted was to get away from the tremendous heat and rest in peace. The world about me was divided sharply down the middle into two halves. Both of these halves were pitch black, but one was scorching-hot and the other was not. I had to keep on dragging myself away from the scorching-hot side and into the cooler one, and this took a long time and enormous effort, but in the end the temperature all around me became bearable. When that happened I collapsed and went to sleep.

It was revealed at an inquiry into my crash held later that the CO at Fouka had given me totally wrong information. Eighty Squadron had never been in the position I was sent to. They were fifty miles to the south, and the place to which I had been sent was actually no-man's-land, which was a strip of sand in the Western Desert about half a mile wide dividing the front lines of the British and Italian armies. I am told that the flames from my burning aircraft lit up the sand dunes for miles around, and of course not only the crash but also the subsequent bonfire were witnessed by the soldiers of both sides. The watchers in the trenches had been observing my antics for some time, and both sides knew that it was an RAF fighter and not an Italian plane that had come down. The remains, if any, were therefore of more interest to our people than to the enemy.

When the flames had died down and the desert was dark, a little patrol of three brave men from the Suffolk Regiment crawled out from the British lines to inspect the wreck. They did not think for one moment that they would find anything but a burnt-out fuselage and a charred skeleton, and they were apparently astounded when they came upon my still-breathing body lying in the sand nearby.

When they turned me over in the dark to get a better look, I must have swum back into consciousness because I can distinctly remember hearing one of them asking me how I felt, but I was unable to reply. Then I heard them whispering together about how they were going to get me back to the lines without a stretcher.

The next thing I can remember a long time later was a man's voice speaking loudly to me and telling me that he knew I was unable to see him or to answer him, but he thought there was a chance I could hear him. He told me he was an English doctor and that I was in an underground first-aid post in Mersah Matrûh. He said they were going to take me to the train by ambulance and send me back to Alexandria.

First
Encounter with a Bandit

After six months spent recovering in hospital in Alexandria,
Roald Dahl flew to Greece to rejoin his squadron.

A T exactly ten o'clock I was strapped into my Hurricane ready for
take-off. Several others had gone off singly before me during
the past half-hour and had disappeared into the blue Grecian sky. I
took off and climbed to 5,000 feet and started circling above the
flying field while somebody in the Ops Room tried to contact me on
his amazingly inefficient apparatus. My code-name was Blue Four.

Through a storm of static a far-away voice kept saying in my earphones, "Blue Four, can you hear me? Can you hear me?" And I kept
replying, "Yes, but only just."

"Await orders," the faint voice said. "Listen out."

I cruised around admiring the blue sea to the south and the great
mountains to the north, and I was just beginning to think to myself
that this was a very nice way to fight a war when the static erupted
again and the voice said, "Blue Four, are you receiving me?"

"Yes," I said, "but speak louder please."

"Bandits over shipping at Khalkis," the voice said. "Vector 035
forty miles angels eight."

"Received," I said. "I'm on my way."

The translation of this simple message, which even I could understand, told me that if I set a course on my compass of thirty-five
degrees and flew for a distance of forty miles, I would then, with a bit
of luck, intercept the enemy at 8,000 feet, where he was trying to sink
ships off a place called Khalkis, wherever that might be.

I set my course and opened the throttle and hoped I was doing
everything right. I checked my ground speed and calculated that it
would take me between ten and eleven minutes to travel forty miles to

this place called Khalkis. I cleared the top of the mountain range with 500 feet to spare, and as I went over it I saw a single solitary goat, brown and white, wandering on the bare rock. "Hello goat," I said aloud into my oxygen mask, "I'll bet you don't know the Germans are going to have you for supper before you're very much older."

To which, as I realised as soon as I'd said it, the goat might very well have answered, "And the same to you, my boy. You're no better off than I am."

Then I saw below me in the distance a kind of waterway or fjord and a little cluster of houses on the shore. Khalkis, I thought. It must be Khalkis. There was one large cargo ship in the waterway and as I was looking at it I saw an enormous fountain of spray erupting high in the air close to the ship. I had never seen a bomb exploding in the water before, but I had seen plenty of photographs of it happening. I looked up into the sky above the ship, but I could see nothing there. I kept staring. I figured that if a bomb had been dropped, someone must be up there dropping it. Two more mighty cascades of water leapt up around the ship. Then suddenly I spotted the bombers. I saw the small black dots wheeling and circling in the sky high above the ship. It gave me quite a shock. It was my first-ever sight of the enemy from my own plane. Quickly I turned the brass ring of my firing button from 'safe' to 'fire'. I switched on my reflector-sight and a pale red circle of light with two crossbars appeared suspended in the air in front of my face. I headed straight for the little dots.

Half a minute later, the dots had resolved themselves into black twin-engine bombers. They were Ju 88s. I counted six of them. I glanced above and around them but I could see no fighters protecting them. I remember being absolutely cool and unafraid. My one wish was to do my job properly and not to make a hash of it.

There are three men in a Ju 88, which gives it three pairs of eyes. So six Ju 88s have no less than eighteen pairs of eyes scanning the sky. Had I been more experienced, I would have realised this much earlier on and before going any closer I would have swung round so that the sun was behind me. I would also have climbed very fast to get well above them before attacking. I did neither of these things. I simply went straight for them at the same height as they were and with the strong Grecian sun right in my own eyes.

They spotted me while I was still half a mile away and suddenly all six bombers banked away steeply and dived straight for a great mass of mountains behind Khalkis.

I had been warned never to push my throttle 'through the gate' except in a real emergency. Going 'through the gate' meant that the big Rolls-Royce engine would produce absolute maximum revs, and three minutes was the limit of time it could tolerate such stress. OK, I thought, this is an emergency. I rammed the throttle right 'through the gate'. The engine roared and the Hurricane leapt forward. I began to catch up fast on the bombers. They had now gone into a line abreast formation which, as I was soon to discover, allowed all six of their rear-gunners to fire at me simultaneously.

The mountains behind Khalkis are wild and black and very rugged and the Germans were right in among them flying well below the summits. I followed, and sometimes we flew so close to the cliffs I could see the startled vultures taking off as we roared past. I was still gaining on them, and when I was about 200 yards behind them, all six rear-gunners in the Ju 88s began shooting at me. As David Coke had

warned, they were using tracer and out of each one of the six rear turrets came a brilliant shaft of orange-red flame. Six different shafts of bright orange-red came arcing towards me from six different turrets. They were like very thin streams of coloured water from six different hosepipes. I found them fascinating to watch. The deadly orange-red streams seemed to start out quite slowly from the turrets and I could see them bending in the air as they came towards me and then suddenly they were flashing past my cockpit like fireworks.

I was just beginning to realise that I had got myself into the worst possible position for an attacking fighter to be in when suddenly the passage between the mountains on either side narrowed and the Ju 88s were forced to go into line astern. This meant that only the last one in the line could shoot at me. That was better. Now there was only a single stream of orange-red bullets coming towards me. David Coke had said, "Go for one of his engines." I went a little closer and by jiggling my plane this way and that I managed to get the starboard engine of the bomber into my reflector-sight. I aimed a bit ahead of the engine and pressed the button. The Hurricane gave a small shudder as the eight Brownings in the wings all opened up together, and a second later I saw a huge piece of his metal engine-cowling the size of a dinner-tray go flying up into the air. Good heavens, I thought, I've hit him! I've actually hit him! Then black smoke came pouring out of his engine and very slowly, almost in slow motion, the bomber winged over to starboard and began to lose height. I throttled back. He was well below me now. I could see him clearly by squinting down out of my cockpit. He wasn't diving and he wasn't spinning either. He was turning slowly over and over like a leaf, the black smoke pouring out from the starboard engine. Then I saw one…two…three people jump out of the fuselage and go tumbling earthwards with legs and arms outstretched in grotesque attitudes, and a moment later one…two… three parachutes billowed open and began floating gently down between the cliffs towards the narrow valley below.

I watched spellbound. I couldn't believe that I had actually shot down a German bomber. But I was immensely relieved to see the parachutes.

I opened the throttle again and began to climb up above the mountains. The five remaining Ju 88s had disappeared. I looked around me and all I could see were craggy peaks in every direction. I set a course due south and fifteen minutes later I was landing at Elevsis. I parked my Hurricane and clambered out. I had been away for exactly one hour. It seemed like ten minutes. I walked slowly all the way round my Hurricane looking for damage. Miraculously the fuselage seemed to be completely unscathed. The only mark those six rear-gunners had been able to make on a sitting duck like me was a single neat round hole in one of the blades of my wooden propeller. I shouldered my parachute and walked across to the Ops Rooms hut. I was feeling pretty good.

As before, the Squadron-Leader was in the hut and so was the wireless-operator Sergeant with the earphones on his head. The Squadron-Leader looked up at me and frowned. "How did you get on?" he asked.

"I got one Ju 88," I said, trying to keep the pride and satisfaction out of my voice.

"Are you sure?" he asked. "Did you see it hit the ground?"

"No," I said. "But I saw the crew jump out and open their parachutes."

"OK," he said. "That sounds definite enough."

"I'm afraid there's a bullet hole in my prop," I said.

"Oh well," he said. "You'd better tell the rigger to patch it up as best he can."

That was the end of our interview. I expected more, a pat on the back or a "Jolly good show" and a smile, but as I've said before, he had many things on his mind including Pilot Officer Holman who had gone out thirty minutes before me and hadn't come back. He wasn't going to come back.

David Coke had also been flying that morning and I found him sitting on his camp-bed doing nothing. I told him about my trip.

"Never do that again," he said. "Never sit on the tails of six Ju 88s and expect to get away with it because next time you won't."

"What happened to you?" I asked him.

"I got one One-O-Nine," he said. He said it as calmly as if he were telling me he'd caught a fish in the river across the road. "It's going to be very dangerous out there from now on," he added. "The One-O-Nines and the One-One-O's are swarming like wasps. You'd better be very careful next time."

"I'll try," I said. "I'll do my best."

Roald Dahl talking

from AN INTERVIEW WITH
BRIAN SIBLEY BROADCAST BY THE BBC
WORLD SERVICE, NOVEMBER 1988

I think probably kindness is my number one attribute in a human being. I'll put it before any of the things like courage or bravery or generosity or anything else.

B.S. Or brains even?

Oh gosh, yes, brains is one of the least. You can be a lovely person without brains, absolutely lovely. Kindness – that simple word. To be kind – it covers everything, to my mind.

   If you're kind that's it.

As I grow old

A S I grow old and just a trifle frayed
It's nice to know that sometimes I have made
You children and occasionally the staff
Stop work and have instead a little laugh.